THE
QUEEN OF DARKNESS

MIGUEL CONNER

ASPECT®

WARNER BOOKS

A Time Warner Company

WARNER BOOKS EDITION

Copyright © 1998 by Miguel O. Conner
All rights reserved.

Aspect® name and logo are registered trademarks of Warner Books, Inc.

Cover design by Don Puckey
Cover illustration by Michel Bohbot

Warner Books, Inc.
1271 Avenue of the Americas
New York, NY 10020

Visit our Web site at
http://warnerbooks.com

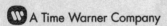 A Time Warner Company

Printed in the United States of America

First Printing: April, 1998

10 9 8 7 6 5 4 3 2 1

THE ETERNAL QUEEN

She was beautiful and ancient, wearing gowns of light, jewels of liquid energy. She was towering above me, surrounded by clouds of dusty ice, a morning star of forbidden desires, Our Mistress, The MoonQueen.

"Bravo," The MoonQueen said, regarding me through cobalt eyes. "*C'est magnifique, mon chéri.* You have done it!"

"I have done it?" I questioned. "That's all? All of this was some game? To see me betray my race and uncover the Warm Ones' plans?"

She hovered closer to me. I had to hide my eyes from the brilliance.

"I am old," she said, her voice cutting a gale. "Older than you know. A hundred times your lifespan is but a short dusk to me. When civilization was young, I was already menstruating worlds. I have been here since the beginning of time, Byron. I created you."

"You did, all right," I barked. "Thanks for the setup. I'll leave my puppet strings on the way out."

To my son Alexander,
who taught me once again how to gaze at stars

THE
QUEEN OF DARKNESS

BOOK I: STARGAZER

CHAPTER I

All I had wanted was a drink. That's it. Some nourishment and off to satisfy the mind next. A drink, and I would have left. I never knew that would be the most important drink of my existence.

I was starving after waking up. What else was new? I always thought *Moratoria* lasted too long this time of the year, with summer ebbing.

After dressing, I left my cupola and took the shaft in normal form up to The Citadel. The walkways and tunnels were already filling with Stargazers trying to get started on the nightly rigors of existence. I had my rigors, but a stop at Lilac's Bar was my first chore. I was hungry, and a certain loneliness had settled on my shoulders like old dust.

The bar had just opened. The sound of humming vacuum cleaners devouring mildew interrupted the fresh sizzle of igniting televisions and registers, all unnoticed by scurrying barbacks carrying glass-racks and clean napkins.

"Good evening," Tina, my regular bartender, said, as I nestled on a bar stool. "Hard *Moratoria*, Byron? You look wasted."

I snorted and fingered my pockets for a cigarette, a rare habit for Stargazers and usually frowned upon by The Elders.

"I keep having odd dreams," I said, while Tina slid a square ashtray in front of me. "Keep dreaming I see *Sol*. Can you believe it?"

"That is odd, Byron." She wiped the glossy amber-surface of the bar, for more Stargazers entered. "Never heard of that one. Believe me, many tell me their dreams after *Moratoria*. What did it look like?"

I kindled my smoke and blew out milky curls almost as pure white as our skins. Tina had an advantage, though, her long, obsidian locks contrasted well. I thought she was one of the few who actually looked well dressed in tight jeans and a thin muscle shirt, all black—a fashion color that hadn't left Xanadu since forever.

"That's the odd part," I said, chewing my lip, another habit The Elders also disdained—it many times caused Stargazers to puncture them with the canines. "I don't know what it looks like. How could I?"

"I don't know either," she said. "No Stargazer has ever seen and survived our only enemy. That is why we escape it at night."

"Exactly," I said in full agreement. "It doesn't make any sense."

"Maybe you saw some old archive or movie and it stayed with you."

I shook my head. "There are no images of *Sol* in our society, Tina. We've made sure of that. Even the mere image of it is said to liquefy our minds, our sanity. No, it's different. It's like I can almost remember . . ."

Tina frowned. "Remember, Byron. What are you talking about?"

I sighed and shook my head at the same time. "Nothing. Don't listen to it. You've got all night to hear people's whining. How are you?"

She smiled. "I'm fine. Would you like something to eat?"

"You know what I like."

"Type A-negative on the way." She turned and walked to the large, crystal containers lining the back of the bar. Just as I was getting to see her fine workmanship, filling the pint glass from one of the copper tubes leaving each urn, somebody tapped me on the shoulder.

I rotated my head and did some of my own frowning. "I didn't know it was last call already."

The figure encased in imitation jet leather before me growled as he usually did, letting eyes glow in enough crimson just to let me know his mood.

"Byron," Lord Crow acknowledged tersely, towered at each side by two of his Ravens. Rumors always quietly circled The Citadel on why The MoonQueen had created Crow with such short stature and stocky physique when we were a species of grace and beauty. It didn't matter, I thought, for the vicious head of the Ravens had held his post since I lost it.

"What can I do for you, Crow?" I questioned. "Care to join me for some nourishment or a video game? I hear the Scientist Guild has recently put out some amazing Virtual Reality software."

"No, no, and yes, Byron," he said. "Actually I need to have a word with you."

"No problem. Pull up a seat."

He shook his square head. "Not here. I was thinking of doing it at The Council."

Crow must have been satisfied at the faltering of my confident facade. "The Council? Why, there are more important matters transpiring there. I'm sure any of the—"

"And it's not just with me," he said, grinning. "It's with one of The Elders."

I was able to turn for a second when Tina placed the filled glass before me. She offered the trio a round, but they declined.

"I think this will be all, Tina," I said. "Upload it to my Credit Account, which I think is still healthy enough to buy a snack."

"No problem, Byron." She winked at me and gave a quick glare at the Ravens.

"I'm glad you're being so cooperative," Crow said with a mild chuckle. "It's not one of your more known qualities, Byron."

"Hey, might as well start the night on a high note," I said and slammed the cocktail. Viscous liquid gushed coldly down my throat, immediately filling my body with tingling vitality. "Whew! I needed that."

"Let's go." He grabbed me by the arm as I wiped my mouth with a moist napkin.

Before I walked out the metal doors of Lilac's, I glanced back at the containers, for a taste remained in my mouth, not of true taste but more like a dangling feeling on my lips. The source was inside the transparent urns, floating slowly in some chemical I couldn't care to remember but which kept the carcass preserved for the bars around The Citadel. The only thing keeping the body from bouncing wildly against the surface was a tube stuck to a neck, its lost face uncaring it was being drained and fed to Stargazers.

And as we walked out into the vast Mall Zone, I realized the feeling was a certain, nagging embarrassment that stayed in my mouth, similar to the certain, nagging embarrassment I felt when I couldn't remember my dreams completely. Embarrassment? At feeding? At worrying about that ball of hot gas beyond the stratosphere? Now *that's* odd, I thought, joining the traffic of perfect beings, gods in a new era, for *Sol* had never been seen and how could one feel anything concerning animals?

Maybe I should ask the leaders of our society, I thought sarcastically, since that's where I was going.

2

We sauntered over to one of the tube-shafts at the fringes of The Mall Zone, a place where shops, bars, and all other service areas flowered in The Citadel. Included there were the entertainment areas: Skating Rinks, Video Arcades, Electronic Libraries, Hunting Ranges, and such. At least a mile of this, wrapped in domes, smoky buildings, synthetic gardens. The greatest attraction of The Mall Zone was the Interactive Bars, which the Ravens exclusively attended for dining purposes. There, you didn't savor your meals from glasses or bowls, but you actually got a chance to hunt down a Warm One and shower afterward if you felt like it. The Hunting Ranges were usually long mazes or flat arenas in which feeding was entertainment or gambling in the form of armed Warm Ones or traps designed by architects. Stargazers needed some enjoyment from *Moratoria* or the menial work we did for Xanadu.

And work we did, outside The Mall Zone. Threading the fringes of this pseudocircular area rested office buildings, various plants, and small factories where the impeccable society was better lubricated, all overlooked by the various guilds. In essence, this was Xanadu: The Citadel, a city covered in nebulous domes and crowned by a gigantic one, which stops the radioactive weather outside that sometimes arrives with temperatures high enough to damage us.

This all was perhaps the less important part of Xanadu. Outside The Citadel four massive tunnels, miles long and sometimes a mile wide, flanked by villages and more factories, extended over the poisoned sand, and onto The Farms. Four Farms and four tunnels marking an X, each breeding, cultivating, and transporting Warm Ones to The Citadel in urns or alive (that's why we had to keep an atmosphere here, no matter how much economists griped about the costs). All this traffic never usually affected The Mall Zone or the other areas—underground tunnels and roads brought in the food. Those were the least of modes of transportation, primarily for animals and cargo. Xanadu was an organism of shafts, elevators, aluminum tubes, and sleek subways, all for our convenience—whether we chose to fly, walk, turn gaseous, or just take the train. It didn't matter as long as no one practiced animal changing, a gift from The MoonQueen The Elders ruled blasphemous some twenty years ago because it imitated lower forms of life.

We opted for gaseous movement and took a tube, one of hundreds on designated walls with the destination and a stop/go light over each. I didn't like this shape myself, but Crow informed me we were in a hurry.

We traveled to the most important part of Xanadu. We rose up to the top of the gigantic cupola, a place called The Tower or The Council, where The Elders schemed and found better ways for the Stargazers and the guilds to cope with our new place in the evolutionary ladder. And even they had to listen to The MoonQueen, The Queen of Darkness, Our Mistress, Mother of All Stargazers, who dwelled at the highest point of Xanadu, ruling all in her infinite compassion. Or so they told me.

We materialized in our forms right in front of a large door with a silvery rose stamped on it, access to a place few Stargazers ever went. A desk with a laborious secretary sat next to it.

"Can I help you, Lord Crow?" the secretary inquired with a patronizing expression. She could do that here.

"I have an appointment with Master Shibboleth," answered Crow.

She played with a mouse and inspected her computer screen. "Ah, yes. Nine o'clock, you and a Mister Byron, right?"

"Yes." He looked at me with distaste. I felt like lighting a cigarette.

She punched some numbers on her keyboard. The massive doors opened. "You know where his office is, Lord Crow?" He nodded. "Then please enter. Leave your guards here please."

Crow growled, but we made our way into a carpeted hallway. We took a few corners, passing scurrying Stargazers working in The Tower, stopping at an opened door with another painted rose.

"One thing, Byron," Crow said, pausing before we entered.

"Yeah," I said casually, ignoring his solid stare.

"Please don't act like yourself. Ignore the 'please.' You know where we are. I don't like this any more than—"

"This? What is this?"

"You'll see. I'm just warning you to behave."

"I'll do my best," I lied with a nod.

"Do better," he ordered and walked in.

The office was plush and elegant, but that is not what caught my attention. Most of the wall, curving upward, was of ambergris glass, giving a striking if not haunting view of the land: Clouds of purple and sparkling pink scraping golden mountains of torn rock, endless desert streaming in and out of this valley, lovely *Luna* perched above it all. The northern gusts must have been kind this night, taking away some of the dust from the sky. Furthermore, she appeared to us in full form, not in her crescent or other aspects. We could almost see her firm contours, almost notice a less potent shade of orange, not the blurry mess she had been since the nuclear winter ended after The Holocaust.

Crow and I were so awed by it, we didn't hear the other occupant rise from his desk of fake-oak and brass. He greeted us a second time.

"Uh, Master Shibboleth, greetings." Crow bowed at the handsome Stargazer with milky-hair, extremely pointed ears (more pointed than most of us), dressed in gray robes. His face reminded me of my own features—tapering, savagely noble, but with eyes that always seemed to mock everything. I owned dark hair that people said had deep red streaks in it.

"Greetings, Lord Crow," he said with a musical, yet sonorous voice. "And you, Byron. It has been a while since I saw you."

I walked to him and extended a hand, not caring to be formal. He took my hand confidently, though.

"Greetings to you, Shibboleth," I said. "When was that, last year at the Equinox Festival, Master Tsing-Tao's party?"

"Yes it was." He motioned for a decanter on the desk. "How about a refreshment? It's A-positive from a young stock, a small privilege The Elders have in our arduous duty."

Crow was already salivating and licking his fangs. Shibboleth poured us a round and told us to have a seat. We sipped the wonderful food from cordials in silence for a few seconds. Then The Elder informed his secretary through the intercom that he was not to be disturbed.

"Oh, this is tasty," I remarked. "As good as any reason to come and visit you."

"That is not the reason you come to visit me," Shibboleth said, second in rank out of seven Elders. He held his glass up, at the same time patting his lips with a handkerchief. "But it is very connected. And very important."

"What do you mean?" I asked, and Crow elbowed me, only to get a disapproving stare from The Elder.

"Please, Lord Crow," he said. "This meeting is as important as it is secret. Matters of security are at stake. Everyone in this room should feel free to express themselves and ask any questions."

I sneered at the Raven and took out a cigarette. The look on Shibboleth's face was precious.

"I agree," I said, "but why am I here? There are definitely more important power-players in Xanadu than me."

Shibboleth leaned back in his chair, touching his long nails in contemplation.

"I'm sure you're not the only one in The Tower who thinks this, Byron. But the word has been sent from the top."

"The top?" both Crow and I questioned.

"The top," he echoed calmly, although his eyes shifted murkier for an instant.

"You mean," I said, but he was already nodding. "Our Mistress?"

"Yes," he hissed and stood up, pacing by a window as if admiring the view he could see every worknight through eyes needing no illumination.

I sucked on the smoke and thought of my dreams.

"Byron," he said, hands behind him, back to us. "Most of The Elders know of your past. You were one of the greatest children of Our Mistress. We are all equal in this new age after The Holocaust when the Stargazers overthrew the Warm Ones. But you . . ." He paused, as if for the first time noticing the smoke saturating the room (Xanadu was not known for its filtering qualities). "You were the prototype of something greater perhaps. You have wondrous talents that have been, how would you put it, wasted throughout your many careers in the last hundred years."

I looked down, wondering why I didn't feel any shame. Not even embarrassment, that taste, that feeling, that topic I felt this conversation was leading to—they always did when it came to me.

Shibboleth waived at Lord Crow. "At first you served as a Raven, making sure security was impeccable in The Citadel and The Farms in the nights when we were still domesticating all the Warm Ones. You were expelled for terminating another warrior. Do you recall why?"

"Vaguely," I mumbled.

"Over what, Byron?"

"A friend," I answered flatly.

"But you weren't punished even if Stargazers are not allowed to destroy one another, the second greatest crime after transgression against Our Mistress, both punished with immediate extermination. But you were somehow forgiven and moved onto other areas. And how you excelled, Byron! You wrote the first true Stargazer classical piece, you sculpted award-winning statues, you designed great graphic interfaces that aided Xanadu. But each time, you somehow let your bravado sabotage your potential."

I felt like defending myself, but all I could do was put out my cigarette and watch smithereens of golden ash quiver to nothingness.

"And believe me, we have worried about it and pondered alternatives to your, let us say, disgraceful existence." He paused again, to make sure the words sank in to my chagrin and Crow's pleasure. "But we are civilized; and The Elders and The MoonQueen only wish the best for our civilization."

Enough was enough. My legendary short attention was already kicking in, which was usually followed by my legendary boredom.

"That's really great, Shib. But what am I doing here? Most of my disciplining has been carried out by the Ravens or other guilds. Not a superior of your stature."

He grinned, but his eyes turned putrid orange. I heard Crow gasp, but my sight would not falter. "It's simple, Byron. We wish to offer you another chance. The MoonQueen wants your aid, to prove her infinite wisdom is just that. You were birthed the perfect Stargazer, Byron, now prove it. Or else."

"Or else." I took out another cigarette.

"Or else." He sat back down, this time offering me a light. Another privilege of The Elders.

"Since you put it that way, Shib," I said, leaning over to catch his illumination. "I guess I'll be at your service. What's going on?"

"Lord Crow," he said, slowly swinging his chair left and right.

"We believe there are certain, potential instigations in Xanadu," he explained after clearing his throat.

I frowned. "Instigations? From whom? Stargazers?"

"No, of course not," Crow spat, eyeing The Elder's decanter. "From the Warm Ones, in one of The Farms."

"Don't those happen all the time?" I asked, remembering my nights in those dreary places.

"Yes and no," Shibboleth said. "They do, but they are of little concern. Many times we allow them to give the Ravens and scientists a chance to sharpen their fangs, pardon the expression, or to prune the volatile parts."

"But this one is different?"

"We believe so," said Crow, "especially since one of our own was found . . ."

He glanced at Shibboleth for help at the lodged word.

"Fallen," The Elder said calmly. "Destroyed."

"Destroyed?" I said. "And you think it was a Warm One?"

They watched the shaking of my head. That had never happened in this city, as far as I knew. Not when I was the head of the Ravens, not even with Crow.

"If our intelligence is correct," Crow said. "It might be more than just a very isolated event, perhaps a collective insurrection."

"What exactly happened?" I asked, still unbelieving.

"You will be detailed once you get there and then you must act quickly."

"I still don't understand," I said. "Why me? Why not eliminate a few hundred of any potential troublemakers and be done with it?"

Again, he looked to Shibboleth for words. The Elder was glancing to his side, lost in his own churning thoughts.

"As Shibboleth informed my Ravens," Crow said, "The MoonQueen doesn't just want a massive squashing of the rebellious element. One, our food crop has lessened in the last ten years—spilled juice is not desirable. Two, the Warm Ones are covering up very well. Our Mistress wants somebody with a good eye." He glared at me. "Someone with a very good eye."

"Not just that," Shibboleth added, "but someone who understands the ways of places away from The Citadel, someone who is sensitive, who can perhaps look at the Warm Ones and read them better than most."

"Sounds like me," I said acidly in a low tone.

The Elder stood up again, as if not getting enough of the scenery. "It is you, Byron. You will be an example and you will be redeemed. Small feat for someone like you."

"An example?"

The Elder sighed. "Yes, an example, Byron. The Moon-Queen told me personally that she believes that we, as a species, are growing soft. Not exactly soft, but perhaps complacent, lacking in dynamics. It's been almost a century and a half since The Holocaust. When the nuclear winds settled and the endless ash blotted out hateful *Sol* for decades, we rose from the rubble of what we caused as the supreme species. The new offsprings of Our Mistress, who gives birth to all of us from her black womb, almost starved but were able to find the Warm Ones, those who survived."

I felt a speech coming but this one struck me with a certain melancholy.

He turned his head and regarded us both. "And thus came the city-states, wondrous metropolises in the wastes where the Stargazers could thrive with new technology. Of the five built, how many are left, Byron?"

"Let me see," I said slowly. "Two failed, disappeared; we believe a massive radioactive surge or an earthquake on the west coast obliterated Rice City and New Tenochtitlan. Hard to tell, long-distance travel and communication is so hard. Then there was Utopia, New Atlantis, and Xanadu . . ."

"We know what happened to Utopia." He leaned on the desk to make sure I heard him loud and clear. "The first of the city-states, our cradle."

"At least we know the rumors," I commented.

"You blasphemous idiot!" Crow exclaimed. "The Moon-Queen, who originally dwelt there, told us what happened. It *was* the Warm Ones only who revolted and sabotaged our facilities. I ought to—"

He was silenced by Shibboleth's risen hand.

"Please, Lord Crow. We are not here to prove Mr. Byron's character. That will be proven very soon. And then it will be judged."

"By whom?" I asked, for the first time feeling like a prisoner of some didactic ploy. "Our Mistress? The Elders?"

"You will be judged," he said firmly. "Our civilization, new as it may be, even though Stargazers roamed the earth since the beginning of time, must evolve unhindered. We have lost much, Byron, we have much to gain. You must understand that once, some of us wiser ones hunted in the open, underneath the stars and a naked *Luna*. That is why we baptized our kind with a name that makes sure they always remember, hope for, and seek that time when they can hunt under stars and a naked *Luna*. One of these nights the atmosphere will cleanse itself and the land might grow. It's taken *much* longer than we had theorized, but when that happens, when we can see the stars again, it is our intention to have as many city-states, separate yet united, ready to converge in the greatest empire this planet has ever witnessed. And morale and example are good ways to begin. We do not want to grow lax, for nature is still harsh and ingenuity is scarce. We will *not* become soft as the Warm Ones did in the end. We will move forward! That is my duty as an Elder." He pointed to the silver rose pin that all The Elders wore. "We are like roses—beautiful, enigmatic, but ready to prick anyone if their growth is disturbed. Do I make myself clear?"

But I wasn't looking at him. My gaze was fixed on *Luna*, a bloated tangerine dangling between veils of sickly clouds, always watching the land, always filling our kind with hope, with hunger.

"Perfectly clear." I matched his sight, and raised him infinity simply to show him that his speech hadn't worked *that* well on me.

3

I didn't do much else that night. I dropped off some work to an engineer leader I did freelance work for once in a while. Archimedes took my drafts with a satisfied nod. "Good work, Byron. Why don't you come work full time for me?"

"No thanks. Work ages me."

He didn't get my humor, inspecting my work a second time.

"That's nice. Come here, I want to show you something."

I followed the guildmaster through laborious cubicles all the way to his office. Few of the Stargazers dared a glance at me, drowned in their work behind computers or drafting boards. After locking his office, he pointed at massive plans strewn across his desk. I was more interested in the chemical plants on the other side of the window, refining plastics and testing new synthetic fuels, a small part of a society mostly dependent on electricity coming from minute nuclear plants a few blocks away, underneath another dome.

"It looks like," I said and paused, catching the vast size of the plan's intentions. "A plumbing system?"

The barrel-shaped Stargazer with the large chops at each cheek grinned proudly. "Got a copy from some connections in The Tower. It's going to be wonderful, you know."

Archimedes explained it was nothing less than a new, over-hauling construction that would change the face of Xanadu. Within the year, nourishment could be transported through high-tech plumbing all the way from The Farms instead of in live or dead cargo. This would eventually save a lot of funds in transportation and tunnel wear and tear; it would also give Stargazers a chance to wake up at night and simply help them-selves to nourishment from the tap instead of having to keep it bottled in fridges or have to go to a bar. The idea came from New Atlantis, our modern sister.

"What will they think of next?" I mused.

Archimedes slapped my back. "Isn't it amazing? Thought you'd enjoy this, oh pessimistic one."

"Maybe I won't have to leave my cupola ever again."

"Goddess help me, Byron. Always so sour."

"Sorry, Arch. They are impressive, I'll admit. Anyway, I have to go. The night is short."

"Tell me about it. Well, get some *Moratoria*, will you? You look less than perfect."

"So I've heard. I'm fine, really, just been hobnobbing with the powerful of Xanadu," I said, and he chuckled.

I left his offices, somehow glad I'd interacted with him. Archimedes, unlike the more important of the city (no one was important, we're all equal, The Elders always said), treated me rather well. Not coolly, like the rest. The fact I'd destroyed another Stargazer was enough to make most of my peers cringe, but I'd hurt others, just as I'd created so much.

I decided to hobnob with the rest down at The Mall Zone. I strolled through the shops and boutiques, crossed fluorescent parks where Stargazers practiced their powers or meditated, stood in elevators witnessing the countless levels of glass and reinforced steel. Hands in pockets, whistling a tune, I suddenly felt very lost here.

The nagging, embarrassing feeling was still lingering in me. Shibboleth's impassioned speech hadn't galvanized me as much as I'd wanted. I knew I had an opportunity to start over, perhaps redeem myself, as he'd stated. Somehow, I didn't care that much about that, about anything, no matter how many times I told myself that this was the only world I knew and we were at the summit of creation. I could either exist with it or be judged by it.

I moved on to thinking about stupid, inane things as I brushed shoulders with other pallid creatures. Why did we all look different in our embodiments of perfection? Some of us had slanted eyes, others had red hair, some of our skin was almost a brownish tint. There were tall ones, ones who walked with bow legs. Obviously, just like Crow, some of us were smarter than others. Why?

I could hear The Elders talking through computer monitors, like they did every night on Channel 6 or at The Fusing: The MoonQueen creates us in variety to create oneness. You do not question the motives of Goddess. Our traits are shared by the Warm Ones, for we coexisted together long ago, but we are the natural step in evolution.

We will move forward!

Somebody shouted at me. I shuddered, obviously way too wrapped up in my mind.

I was in the middle of a narrow walkway lined with quartz-halogen lamps of verdant tint. Ahead of me, a Raven waved at me with one hand, the other dragging a large cage. In it, through the glass-covering metal bars, I could see a herd of Warm Ones cowering in the center.

"Move it," the Raven yelled.

"This isn't an unloading zone," I said, taking a step to one side.

"Damned Railway B-8 broke down," he said angrily, "got to take this cargo and more all the way to *Munchies* on Mall Level 25. There's a Century-Birthnight."

"A Century-Birthnight," I whistled, the cage passing me. "I never had one."

The frustrated soldier gurgled some more complaints, but I wasn't paying attention.

Even though the tightly sealed glass covered most of the cage, I could smell them through small air holes. I could smell their rich juice, pumping, flowing, gorging their cases. I realized how hungry I was, how hungry I always was, and how it always bothered me. Were all the rest like me? I could easily feel my eyes ripple to another color, fangs pulse inside gums, nails sprout from flexing fingers.

Then I actually noticed the animals. All of them were

adults, except for one, the meal of honor, for sure. All shared the same terrified look, pulled here in the middle of the beautiful and pale, in the den of hunters. Even in their state, tattered and mildly fed, impounded like they had been since birth, they still held a certain frail determination, as if this couldn't be happening, as if there was an escape. It was fragile, slight, but I caught it.

I saw a tear sprout from the pup at the same time his cheeks flushed in color. How curious that water came from its eyes, how delicious was the fact juices coagulated in certain parts.

"How pathetic," I said, not knowing why.

I walked away, because I could already see groups of Stargazers surrounding the cage in mist or physical shape to see the specimens.

Strolling away, I noticed I was famished and had to do something about it. At four at night, I reached Lilac's. The place was emptying—The Fusing was tomorrow and everybody had to be at their best. I grabbed a seat on Tina's section. The music was too loud, the tingling of mildew returned.

"Back again, Stargazer?" She grinned, looking as fresh as when she started the night. Part of her strap was down to her arm, revealing an upper view of her right breast.

"Need some nourishment, Tina," I said, inspecting an empty pack of cigarettes. When had I smoked them all?

"You sure do, Byron," she said, already filling a glass. "Shouldn't go all night with just what you had, if I'm not mistaken. You look like you just saw nuclear fallout."

"No, just working hard at not working hard." I crumpled the pack and threw it on the floor.

She handed the snack to me, still grinning, still showing part of her bosom.

"I hear the radiation count is way up outside," she said, watching me guzzle the stuff and quiver in delight. "Maybe that's why you're feeling depressed. Many from the Scientist Guild say it can affect our moods."

"I'm not feeling depressed, Tina, it's against the law," I said, handing her back the empty cup. She concocted me another one. I tried not to look at the container. I tried not to listen to some petty conversation on the results of the arena scores by two jerks sitting on a bench outside, fifty feet away.

"Whatever, Byron." She leaned over the bar, and the sight doubled. "This one's on me."

"Thanks, Tina. You're great, you know." I took only a couple of sips, watching how the maroon liquid stained the glass.

She leaned her head on a dainty hand. "And you're an odd fellow, Byron. I've heard so much about you, much of which I can't believe, but I can't seem to dislike you like the others."

"Well, do you like me?"

She reached under the bar and pulled out two cigarettes. I took one.

"I'll take it as a yes," I said, and lit hers.

"I don't know why I do it," she mused, a cascade of smoke drizzling from her nostrils. "But who we are and why we act in such ways, why we even appear on this world at all is all because of The MoonQueen, uh? She is the reason for everything, and there's no point in questioning her."

I shrugged, taking another gulp. "I guess. The reason you hear so much about me is because I've always done things for my own reasons, even if I don't know them."

She waved the cigarette at me. "Which brings us back to what I said."

"You're right," I said. She giggled. "You're damn right."

"Oh, Byron, you're an interesting character, and—"

"—and you see your share, Miss Bartender."

"Yes, I do."

There was an odd silence between us, so I broke it.

"How about it?"

"How about what?"

"A date?"

"A date? What is that?"

I smiled. "I don't know. Let's find out."

She stood up. "Byron, you're not talking about one of those primitive habits Warm Ones and other animals have?"

"No, not at all. I'm just talking about companionship, Tina. Let's do something tomorrow after the ceremony."

Tina pursed her lips, but they wrestled themselves to a smile. "Okay, that's fine. I'm not working, and most of my friends will be at Gilder Arena for an art-gallery opening."

I smiled again, adding a wink. "Good. And then we can do one of those primitive habits Warm Ones and other animals have."

"Silly," she scoffed and dissolved to mist, vanishing to take care of some Stargazer on the other side of the bar who needed service. "Meet you here at nightfall," she added when turning to her natural shape before dealing with the customer.

"It's a date," I whispered, and also took off on foot before she changed her mind.

I strolled around for a while, stopping to see some news bulletin from The Tower. A spokesmen from The Elders proudly informed about how scientists had discovered a vaccination for an odd malady in the Southeast Farm that had reduced our supply. What followed was the usual good news: positive economic forecasts, new advances in computer processing, and the start of a major plumbing system in Xanadu. A first ever, an attractive Stargazer said, pretending to read off papers in her painted fingers.

I was about to say something snotty to the television, when the first alarm went off, booming across miles of steel and concrete, turning every light to murky red. Two more, and *Sol* would send its first shards of hate to Xanadu. It was time for all to reach their elevators or shafts and return to their cupolae. At the second ring, in another half hour, Ravens would sweep The Citadel and make sure no one was piddling. At the third one, you were on your own. As *Sol* rose, our bodies would be immediately forced into a necessary slumber, regardless of our location.

Thus, while the angry star swept this part of the world, nothing stirred on the surface of this city, nothing happened as an entire civilization entered into this brief, shielding hibernation called *Moratoria*. Our god-soul, the source of power and perfection granted by Our Mistress, the real reason why we were more than just animals, survived and was revitalized during this. Many of the scientists spoke of times when robots would take over while we went to *Moratoria*, but we'd have to see. They hadn't done it yet in New Atlantis.

I took my specific shaft to my cupola, flying as quickly as I could, along with thousands more. They weren't exactly cupolae, but more like large chambers with rooms, furniture, and electronic entertainment, a couple hundred feet beneath the earth. Only The Elders were allowed to *Moratoria* above the ground in The Citadel. This all worked for protection, our protection. When a Stargazer sealed his chamber, he or she was safe from anything: An atomic bomb, a Warm One revolt, or a natural cataclysm. Well, one was almost safe, I thought, recalling the other two city-states.

I punched the codes in, and the door neatly shut. A mainframe somewhere would keep it locked, until *Sol* vanished again to another part of the world. I was safe and alone here. I took off my clothes and inspected myself in the mirror. Besides being safe and alone, I was still handsome, I told the reflection. The reflection didn't cheer up.

I checked my computer, no messages, no new news, nothing. Damn, and I didn't want to *Moratoria*. But I was who I was.

Feeling black pulling me down in a haze of tiredness, I dreaded two things instead of one. *Sol* was coming, somewhere outside, and the Stargazers must dream; but I only dreamt of *Sol*. That was one thing, I groggily mused, lids feeling heavy, body not making it to my bed but staying on the couch. The other thing was that in less than a week I would spend healthy time in The Farms with Ravens, scientists, and the animals.

I wondered if that pup still cried, and was gone.

CHAPTER 2

I woke up that night and didn't leave immediately even though I was famished. I checked the news on the computer, searched some archives on Warm Ones and The Holocaust, and played some violent video games. The latter out of frustration, because I swore the history of the Stargazers changed every time I researched it; very little could be found on pre-Holocaust nights, besides how we were persecuted and almost ultimately destroyed by some secret weapon.

Thinking of secret weapons, I totally forgot about Tina. I dressed in a hurry and sped to Lilac's. She was pacing the entrance before throwing a few insults at me for being late. I apologized five times and treated her to a quick meal before we attended The Fusing.

The Fusing was held in a stadium in the center of The Citadel. All Stargazers were required to attend our holiest event, held every two weeks. There, filling ten thousand seats, maybe more, we watched gigantic screens with the images of an Elder impart their wisdom and recent news. We were always reminded that our god-soul, the Dark Instinct, was nothing more than a fragment, a spark of The MoonQueen's eternal cold fire, that our divine part was made in her image because of her grace only. We were always reminded that the stars would shine one night and we would rule the earth just as *Luna* presided over the constellations. We were always reminded of many things.

Eventually, the more popular part of the event started. Liquid music boomed. Stargazers tore off their clothes and began touching, wriggling, holding one another for hours under strobing light. It was a ceremony of oneness, a carnival of true adoration, thousands of us feeling, grappling one another with exposed fangs, lost to the beat and heavy light, praying in savagery to The MoonQueen. Sometimes people bit one another in rapture, sometimes the ceremony took to the air in primordial dances. It was the ultimate achievement of our species, and even outside The Citadel in the villages and The Farms, Stargazers performed this ritual in smaller scales.

Once in a while, rarely, the image of The MoonQueen appeared, glorious, breathtaking, telling us with her mind-voice that a new Stargazer was to be born, perhaps because of the accidental demise of a prior one or for her own reasons. In awe and supplication, we watched as her being detonated in chromatic fury and another being fused from the ghastly illumination. It was quite a sight. All of us were born this way, from her, The Queen of Darkness.

No one was born that night, but Tina told me she felt disturbed, almost too excited after the event. I agreed and told her to give her senses a rest at a park. She leaned on me as we shouldered our way out of the stadium, along with a content population.

"Whew!" she said, sitting on a bench by a river of mercury. "Haven't felt so filled after a Fusing since I can remember, Byron."

I didn't say anything at first, admiring her short dress of

cardinal, after I'd just admired and rubbed her lithe body for a long while. This felt different. I wanted this to feel different.

"Maybe you're not filled, Tina," I said, standing right in front of her.

She looked up at me.

"What do you mean?"

I placed a hand on her cheek, then followed the contours of her bright-red lips with my fingers.

"Maybe you're not filled, maybe you wanted to be, but you are still empty."

I stared into her and found a path.

"I don't understand," she said shakily. "What are you doing to me?"

"What did you feel in there, Tina?"

"I . . ."

I kneeled. "Tell me. I'm your friend."

She looked away. "I felt somehow lost, somehow very lonely, even though I was sharing with the others. It felt so . . . anticlimactic yet secure at the same time.

I moved her face so she would regard me.

"You see how I feel, Tina? How Stargazers really feel."

"Is this bad?" she questioned in a hushed tone. She looked so ghostly. So beautiful.

"It just is, Tina." A tear of red rippled on the corner of my left eye. She took it in one finger and licked it.

"Maybe it is, Byron," she said, as if noticing for the first time. "But it's more. It's you. This had to do with you."

I smiled warmly. "You and me. Part of that lonely, anticlimactic feeling . . . what we did."

She swallowed hard before speaking. "Then how do we truly fill ourselves?"

I kissed her and held her and squeezed her, not as part of a species or a ceremony, but as her and me. She tensed at first but came into my cold grasp. Her fangs accidentally ripped into my lips. I groaned, she giggled. I told her to lick what came out. She did, and I groaned more. I slid my hands up her snowy legs. She caressed my hair.

"Byron," she whispered, "this is forbidden, we are not . . ."

But she continued. And suddenly we were mist, suddenly we were one, swirling away from the shouts of disgust of other Stargazers, sucked by tubes until we reached her cupola.

There, we shed our clothes and caressed each other.

Under olive sheets, her hand closed around a penis that shouldn't have been solid, that should be just a useless appendage of evolution's laboratories. I kissed hard breasts, bit swarthy nipples. We both gasped in something akin to delight, converging into a cacophony of growls. Eyes bleeding light, mouths salivating, we rose into the air and sparks danced around us. Suddenly, unconsciously, we mutated to gas, twirling like a small cyclone with a flaming texture. We still felt the same sensation, the fire, the heat, our only voice. We didn't question, we let the wave of forbidden intuition guide us to a tunnel, to a light.

In the air, we became one again in our true shapes, amidst howls of anger and claws ripping skin open. I'd never felt anything like it, a surge of sadness and excitement truly fused in pleasure. Over and over, I thrust and bucked, over and over, she held me tightly and shivered.

"Outside of me," she purred, "outside, Byron."

I didn't know what she meant, what her lips implored.

"I want to see," she kept on saying, "outside."

And as something rose and exploded inside me, I knew.

Yelling with a voice I didn't know, I pulled out from her moistness, also wanting to see what happened.

It wasn't like the old videos of mating Warm Ones or other creatures kept in laserdisk libraries. It wasn't seed, it wasn't creation, not for me. Not for me.

For only red spurted from the tip, bathing her in stickiness, also the same hue. Juice came out from me, pulpy rivulets of red, or as the Warm Ones called it.

Blood.

I shrieked in terror for some reason, but Tina laughed, bringing it to her mouth, lapping away.

Blood.

I collapsed on the bed. I felt exhausted. She lay on top of me, shaking at what we'd done, what we'd tried.

"Again," she begged coyly, reaching for the dial on her stereo.

"Shit," I said tiredly, and we went at it again. Blood.

So the next night went.

Actually, that's how the next few nights went. Tina called in Lilac's, making some excuse. I avoided all the work I should have been doing.

"We'll get into a lot of trouble if we're caught," she would always say in between pants after we finished, hair teased wildly, body spotted in my redness.

"They don't have to find out about everything," I would answer. Then we'd get some food out of her small fridge, talk about something, and mock creation one more time. Knowing we might get in trouble was just half the fun.

That was the whole reason I'd done it, I rationalized over and over through the ritual. I almost felt bad for manipulating Tina, but maybe she had done it for the same naughty reasons. The Elders had forbidden us to imitate lower forms of life. It was embarrassing. Yet, as I'd realized that night walking around in The Mall Zone, we *did* imitate a lower form of life, from our habits to our domain. How could we have not when we coexisted for hundreds of thousands of years before The Holocaust? I'd seen enough footage from scant files. We couldn't transform into animals but there we were acting like our most important stock once did. There we were, borrowing from their past. There was nothing wrong with it, was there? We were a curious species, a free and curious species. Why were they so many damn rules?

Maybe it was just disobedience that truly drove me, the chance to rebel because they were trying one more time to control Byron, push him in the right direction.

We will move forward!

During the raging of *Sol*, while we rested in each other's arms, my dreams shifted. I didn't dream of things I couldn't see, but of things I didn't want to see. In the haze of *Moratoria*, I could see me running out of wreckage through sheets of fire, carrying wounded people to safer havens. The image changed, the wreckage was larger, me in the center, alone with shadows slowly surrounding me. Someone tugged at my legs. Somebody told me to run for shelter.

When I awoke, I jumped out of the bed and scanned Tina's computer. Xanadu was still here. No fire ripping civilization.

"What's wrong?" she asked, floating to my side.

"Nothing," I said.

"Dreams again, uh?"

She leaned her head on my shoulder.

I nodded. "They're different. I think maybe I'm just feeling guilty about something. Not what we've done, but the work I should be doing."

"Me too." She put an arm around me.

"We should get out of here and return to reality."

"We should."

"We . . ." But I was already kissing her.

After the third night, I finally left her to research. She hugged me, but something akin to sadness was lodged on the corner of her eye. I told her we'd soon be sharing each other, filling each other again after the trip. She only nodded, draped in a blanket, and saw me leave through the shaft.

I didn't have time to ponder the hollowness inside me. I rushed to The Council and argued with the secretary for about five minutes. Finally, she got Shibboleth on the line, and I went to his office.

"What can I do for you?" he inquired, holding several faxes in his hand.

I told him I needed to use his databases—The Citadel's were rather limited.

He regarded me seriously for a few seconds.

"We said you will be debriefed when you get to The Farm. What exactly do you need to find, Byron? Maybe I can help you."

I shrugged lightly, knowing exactly what to say next.

"If you want. I can always use your help. I just need to find out more about The Farms. It's been a while since I was in one. You know, how the farming system has progressed, grazing and irrigation dynamics, advanced zoological theories, and other matters. Where do you want to start?"

He gave his faxes a quick look.

"Tell you what," he said. "I am quite busy at the moment. Why don't you use Balkros's computer. He's with Our Mistress on an important trip to New Atlantis trying to find out more about the new plumbing system. He won't be back for nights."

I thanked him and was led by one of his assistants to another office, past the news studios and data archives, which made Shib's look like a Warm One hovel. Good advice, Shib, I thought. A slovenly and eccentric Stargazer, Balkros was the mastermind wizard that had set up most of the computer systems in Xanadu and one of the main architects of The Holocaust. When we didn't talk about an equal society, Balkros was at the top of the hierarchy. When we didn't talk about lower emotions, Balkros commanded the most fear.

His computer had about five trillion codes and passwords, making it very hard to surf his databases. I figured some of them out, but learned less than I'd wanted.

My primary search was to learn about The Farms and Warm Ones. Despite the fact I'd worked there for years in the early nights, much of it was blocked out that evening a dark rage took me and a Raven was destroyed by my hand.

I printed out the findings and then went deeper. Something about my visions in *Moratoria*, perhaps in Shibboleth's passionate speech or my own guilt had sparked a raging curiosity, a curiosity I sensed I'd denied for a long time. I wanted to find out more about Utopia. What had happened? How could it be avoided here . . . how could my dream not come true?

Why would it come true?

2

The next evening, I was on my way toward my mission.

I'd forgotten how civilization eroded away from The Citadel. The farther we rode on the subway, the less tended scenery became. Broken stone and rusted metal broke flashes of passing lights, those which worked. We passed rustic villages and towns, zoomed by other trains and flying Stargazers. We'd left The Citadel about an hour ago, making a few stops to load and unload cargo. Less than five miles, and the Northwest Farm would be nigh.

I stood quietly, gripping a handle, rocking against the torrid rhythm of the subway. Our compartment swelled with fresh Ravens and members of the Scientist Guild, who oversaw the breeding and living habits of Warm Ones. A few feet away, Crow and some assistant spoke during most of the trip about ways to tighten security.

"Maybe we should lower the ozone levels around the villages," the assistant said. "The higher radiation might keep the cattle even more docile."

"Wouldn't be prudent," said Crow. "Even though they've been studying this for years, it was tried in New Atlantis a while ago. The Warm Ones started producing diluted juice. Believe me, they are as docile as they can be."

"Too bad we can't take their brains away," said the assistant.

"Then they'd be hired as Ravens," I muttered under my breath.

"What did you say, Byron?" Crow asked with a snarl, both hearing what I'd said and probably most of the compartment. Chuckles echoed.

"I said, why can't we just create our own retarded Warm Ones with all the genetical research we have from pre-Holocaust times? I hear they're already trying it in New Atlantis. Imagine, dumb, mute Warm Ones that can be used for menial tasks and then be happy to have us eat them."

Crow's voice was steel. "Byron. Your insolence knows no bounds. It will, though."

"Come on, Lord Raven," I said musically. "They used the technology once. We just hate having to borrow more than we have already. Why not admit we have imitated them?"

The chuckling stopped. Crow, his assistant, and the other soldiers stared at me in shocked revulsion, scientists looked at one another as if just discovering this new approach. What was wrong with everyone?

I wasn't going to bother wondering about that anymore. Instead, I thought about all the data I gathered the night before in Balkros's office.

Utopia: A massive city-state south of the flatlands of a place once called Oakhoma or just Oke-home. It was large, primitive, and bulky compared to Xanadu, with a population of almost sixty thousand Stargazers, twice ours. It was a fascinating place, grown from some metropolis of pre-Holocaust times instead of from scratch like the rest. It thrived and expanded incredibly for the first forty years, and there The MoonQueen and Elders oversaw the other city-states, communicating and connecting with other Stargazers surviving in the fatal wilderness. A hard task, but they did it. It was a great feat.

So what happened?

Blood . . .

It seemed, the archives said and proved Crow and the rumors wrong, their mistake was that some of the population somehow grew, let us say, fond of the Warm Ones. Conflict arose within the ranks, breaking seams in the society to allow certain mutinous acts. It wasn't known how it truly happened, but some explosion occurred, destroying half of the city and permitting Stargazers there to die under *Sol* and the radiation, so much stronger a century and change ago. The MoonQueen and four surviving Elders escaped to Xanadu, making it their home base. She obviously held a stronger reign after what happened. I'm sure the Cataclysm of Tears, sixty years ago, which took away two more cities, didn't make her any more relaxed. Even though these databases hadn't been shaven of information about the real fate of Rice City and New Tenochtitlan, there still wasn't any conclusive evidence on what had happened to the city-states. Perhaps she knew, as Our Mistress was the only being that could easily travel the world without worry. But, like many things, she communicated only when her will decided it, if it ever did.

There was no information on what occurred to the remnants of Utopia. Everyone, Stargazer and Warm One, had probably perished in the tragedy. You would never hear one of The Elders who survived talk about it. Ever.

"All right, we're almost there."

I turned, shaking from my trance to see Crow's ugly face leering at me, my little quips long leaving his mood.

"Ready to go into a slaughterhouse, Byron?" he said, right next to me. I hadn't heard him move. The train was slowing down. "Let's hope it's not your own."

His assistant chuckled behind him. I rolled my eyes.

"Don't worry about me, Crow. I've got the situation under control."

His face closed inches from mine, even though he had to crane his neck.

"That's not the only thing you've got under your control from what I hear," he whispered with loathing.

"What do you mean?"

He shrugged lightly. "Oh, nothing, but getting a meal at Lilac's has been kind of hard lately."

I didn't say anything, turning hands to fists.

"One way or another, Byron," he hissed, "You're finally going to face the consequences."

"Can't wait," I said, but he was already walking off, cackling all the way to one of the doors.

I stood there for a minute, a crick in the flow of Ravens and others getting off to The Farm.

"Shit," I then said and grabbed my bags.

CHAPTER 3

The Farms are as fascinating as The Citadel. And as necessary.

Too enamored by my thoughts on rebellion and Utopia, I never noticed the train tracks engage an upward angle, rising hundreds of feet. We stopped at Commodore Station, renamed after one of The Elders left behind in the fall of Utopia. The station was basically where all the subways stopped, directly at a large and steep canyon. At the bottom of the hill, after a small strip of bare terrain, The Farm spread before us, dozens of little villages and towns separated by stone walls. All of this was surrounded by Ozone Fields, nothing more than encircling poles that trapped electricity and oxygen in a dome of magnetic waves. Besides detaining enough of the radiation to to give the Warm Ones a functioning health, it corralled the animals and filtered *Sol*'s nutrient rays, allowing them to grow the feeble crops needed to survive. To leave the fields was assured death for the animals, to reach Commodore Station was climbing dangerous heights to a hive of terraces and gargantuan cranes. For us, the radiation was less of a concern, and we could fly, carrying at least ten times our weight without too much effort.

From one of the many balconies carved out of the sedentary stone, I admired the rustic view of Northwest Farm, the oldest but smallest of the four. It was a flat vision of adobe houses broken by brick walls, dank fields where they grew their nourishment, and other quaint things I'd forgotten about. Below the ground, canals connected to irrigation systems and wells, the source underground lakes that had to be relatively close to any area where animals were raised. Precipitation was very rare, only transpiring high in the mountains this time of the era.

The field pulsed invisibly over me, its humming always heard, haunting and judging at the same time.

If that wasn't enough reminder, the Slaughterhouses to my right should have been, marked by the chimneys smoking much of the night. Each night Warm Ones were led to them through cranes into large hangars. From there it was a spectacle of simmering fumes and winding lines, steel pens, chemical vats, a labyrinth of walkways to destinations that served only to deliver the most important ritual of their existences. In the end, the animals either became an item to be perused from table tents in some bar or sport for the recreation-seeker.

I remembered that part of my downfall as a Raven, besides the impious deed, was creating a black market of jewelry that became very popular in Xanadu. Instead of wasting some of the corpses, I had some workers debone them so I could carve out earrings, bracelets, and other baubles. When I fell from grace, my little stint outside the Artisan Guild's jurisdiction came into full view.

I leaned over the railing, vision capturing so much for thousands of feet. Even though the Warm Ones chose *Luna*'s presence to rest, I could see forms moving behind tattered curtains—families, clans, huddling together as the Ravens were never too far away, skulking around their neighborhoods to make sure their property behaved. Occasionally, as I knew, some hungry soldier or even scientist might snatch an animal from their home or alley and hide the remains. It really didn't matter, for all ended up as food sooner or later. No Warm One survived after thirty. Many were chosen way before that during holy nights or for special orderings.

I straightened, taking a generous gulp of smell. Nostrils flaring, I could almost taste a thousand forms of juice. They were all out there for the taking . . .

"Hard to stand sometimes," a voice said behind me. "That's why we issue nose-plugs to most who go down there."

I turned to see two figures coagulating from vapor, recently expunged from one of the tubes by the door. One was Crow, as I now understood, my chaperone in this quest. The other, an old friend of mine, was to be my quick guide before I headed out on my investigation. Seeing both of them standing together didn't make me any happier than I already wasn't.

"Never was," I said. "That's why discipline has to be the first virtue in the farmlands."

"Good to see you," Mephisto said, putting a hand on my shoulder. "It's been a while, Byron."

I nodded, eyeing his white robes. He chuckled lightly, also nodding.

"Yes. My nights as a Raven ended . . ." He paused and glanced at Crow. "That evening, Byron. My services are better utilized as an anthropologist for the Scientist Guild."

"Better than being a Heretic," I said with a harsh smile, and they both shuddered.

Crow might have wanted to growl, but Mephisto had regained his easygoing composure, something he'd always done well. All too well.

"Byron, you never change, do you, old friend? Always so humorously morbid, always the shadow on somebody's outline?"

"But you have changed," I said, turning to The Farm. "And I don't know what you're doing here. Last I heard you were in the Southeast Farm doing menial work for some expansion of farmland."

He chuckled again and asked Crow if we could have a word alone. The Raven snorted and disappeared. Mephisto stood next to me, perhaps to catch my focus on the primitive borough.

"Things always have a way of coming full circle, Byron," he said in a low tone.

"I guess."

"Master Shibboleth wanted me to give you the first tutoring when you got here."

"So an old comrade of mine might curve my volcanic attitude, uh?"

"Byron, I'm being honest with you. Believe me. This is uncomfortable, too, old friend, if I can still regard you as that."

I scrutinized him then, Mephisto, the old trickster with flames in his eyes, long, cropped hair complementing a long nose and lofty cheekbones, thin, almost gaunt, but full of haughty passion whenever things went his way.

"I don't know," I said. "When dust rose after my crime, you took off like a nuclear wind. I'm sure your chameleon loyalty went to good use."

"You haven't done so badly yourself," he said, but wouldn't look at me.

"I'm still me, and you study animals."

"We'll see about that," he said with a wink.

"What do you mean by that?" I was getting tired of that sentence.

"They're fascinating creatures, Byron, you'll understand. And I don't have to fall any more than I have, and you might."

"That's why you're here."

He shrugged. "I still think of you as my friend. It's a way of maybe helping you. I'm actually considered one of the top five zoologists on Warm One habits this side of The Citadel."

"Wonderful," I said, "I'm sure you'll impart all your wisdom to my yearning ears."

"That's all up to you," Mephisto said, going for the door, knowing at least that one would open. "Even if one of our own hadn't been destroyed, many here believe they have something dangerous down there, for no reason other than the way they suddenly look at us with expressions of pure, confident defiance. You're the master of confidence and defiance, of finding the heat in ice, Byron. This will be your greatest challenge."

I heard him stop at the door, as if waiting for an answer. His only answer was to watch me take out a cigarette.

"One of my helpers will get you to a proper cupola. I will meet you at the first level by the Slaughterhouse an hour after dusk. Good night."

I lit the cigarette over the silence and the sultry aromas.

2

The next night, after more vivid dreams of a city in ruins, I met Mephisto where he'd asked. I was able to avoid some of Crow's lackeys by flowing into a rusty crack on the floor of my chamber, which unlike The Citadel was located above-ground and was not very guarded. When I met him, he didn't seem bothered I walked alone.

The first level was still about seventy feet above the ground; alone, we flew down the outskirts of The Farm. There, amid traffic of Stargazers escorting hordes of Warm Ones to cages and teetering cranes that would transport them to the Slaughterhouses, he spoke out constantly about the sections of city. Quite a lot had changed with the Warm Ones in the shape of aqueducts, irrigations systems, and healthy modern technology.

"We're not too worried about them getting too good for our own good," Mephisto said, checking notes from a laptop. "As you know, we have always believed that letting them own and thrive in their own societies prevents desperate uprising—"

"Yeah, yeah, I know," I interrupted, strolling ahead of him to a wide, empty street. "If they have an illusion of normalcy, they feel less threatened by us and our intentions."

"Has worked very well," he continued, "but it's so hard to fully understand them in their primitiveness no matter how similar to us they look. We've tried it all; even video cameras are less than effective because of the radiation levels—"

"That's not the problem, Meph," I said, scanning the area.

It was his turn. "What do you mean?"

"The fact we rest during *Sol* and they during *Luna* makes it hard for both species to fully interact, therefore we basically can't get under their skin unless we're eating them."

"Good point, Byron, but—"

"And they have the advantage because they can survive under *Sol*'s rays, while we cease to exist. Makes you wonder, eh, Meph?"

I enjoyed watching his expression of disbelief. Once, we'd both spouted such statements in the old nights for no other reason than amusement at getting a reaction.

"No, The Elders have told us that it is because of our superiority that this occurs. Stargazers and their god-souls must store incredible reserves of power for their own use—"

"Has any scientist proven this?"

"No," he stuttered. "You know that it is forbidden to practice science on Stargazers—"

"Relax, Meph." I raised a hand. "I'm not disagreeing with you. I'm just saying it's going to be a chore to figure them out. I'm sure you and your associates have some ideas. What are they?"

He appeared more comfortable accessing information, away from my mouth. As he did this, I wondered if I should slide on the nose-plugs like he'd done. Back in my nights, it was only you and your will keeping you from going on a mad reaping every evening. A Stargazer could devour the juice of an entire Warm One if he felt like, but actually only needed about three pints a night to survive. I could almost remember the old 'Don't Waste What Can Wait' ad campaigns from The Elders.

"Well," he started, spewing out paper from a pocket-printer latched to his belt. "We have a few leads. One, as I mentioned, is their recent grasp on technology, which we monitor very well. Unless they have stored weapons somewhere—"

"That's not it," I said. "We still have the Ozone Fields and a population of hunters. It would have to be more if you're bothered by their expressions."

"Then perhaps it is their new religion," Mephisto said.

"Their new religion?"

"Yes. Since you left, they have all on this farm embraced some dogma in which they worship clay idols."

"Interesting." In the distance, I could see Warm Ones getting out of our way, turning corners, grabbing offspring, locking doors, whispering to one another. I was sure the next few blocks would be empty by the time we took a few more steps.

"We believe it is some imitation of Stargazer worship of Our Mistress, or perhaps some regeneration of their old cult of a singular, supreme being."

"Who really helped them during The Holocaust," I commented. "What kind of idols do they worship?"

"Most of the idols are vaguely of a male figure. They try to hide them from us. Most Stargazers really don't put much matter in them because it's really no threat."

"Unless it unites them in some religious crusade against us."

Mephisto shrugged. "I suppose. What can they do, Byron? They still don't have the power to challenge us, they still aren't suicidal enough."

"Maybe, but that's the key."

"I know." He handed me the papers. "That's what you have to find out. I would start there, Byron."

"Who leads them?"

"What? No one leads the Warm Ones."

"Right. Do they have some religious leaders, as should be natural. Their type of Elders?"

Once again, he seemed out of balance at my colorful remark. "Actually, they do. The epicenter of this new religion is someone called the Shaman. That's what's perplexing. The Shaman is always some extremely sickly individual who never lasts more than ten years, never even reaches close to thirty. At the end of its tenure, before wasting away, the Shaman chooses another one. It is usually of the opposite gender, much younger in age, and the changing is done by some public copulation."

Mephisto stuck out his tongue in disgust. I thought of a bartender.

"Have you ever brought a Shaman in? Maybe to see why their lives are so short."

"Our policy has always been to leave this Shaman alone, for his presence allows them that 'illusion of normalcy' you talked about, making them tamer. The Scientist Guild wanted to make an exception and bring him in recently, but Shibboleth informed us to stay our hand because of the rioting that might ensue. The low reserves of food, you know." He winked at me again. "He offered us you instead."

"Great. Let's talk about the fallen Stargazer. Who was he?"

"His name was Leztant," Mephisto said, "a Scientist. He had been analyzing water pollution levels in one of the wells on quadrant eighteen. It seems he wandered down one of the underground tributaries and . . . well . . . he floated back to the well, Byron. We sent a troop of Ravens down there, but they found nothing. Master Shibboleth, who oversees the evolution of The Farms, was then informed."

"I see." I nodded. "I'll need to examine his remains, and any reports on what caused his 'floating back'?"

He didn't say anything, pretending to inspect his screen.

"Mephisto?"

He sighed. "Byron, I just told you it is forbidden to practice—"

"Even one who's been destroyed?"

His shrug made me even more annoyed.

"Well," I said. "Can I even take a look at his body?"

"The Elders confiscated it," he said in a low timbre. "The Raven who found Leztant was immediately transferred to another farm. I'm sorry, Byron, but you know this is a sensitive occurrence that should never reach The Citadel's ears. Most of the population here doesn't know about it. But I did hear a rumor that it was as if he'd been severely burned."

I shook my head. "That's wonderful, Meph. How am I supposed to uncover a possible rebellion when I don't even know what their weapons might be? You give me rumors, religions, and Warm Ones looking at us ugly as a debriefing, but I don't have any hard facts."

His eyes widened when I crumpled up the papers and threw them to the side of the street.

"What's wrong, Byron?"

"Nothing," I said. "I'm just so happy that you and The Elders have already aided me so much. Now, if you'll excuse me, I obviously have a lot of work to do."

"Uh, don't you want company?"

"No thanks," I said, before pivoting on a heel. "You've already done enough, Meph. Working alone, I might be able to get this over so our blessed leaders can leave me alone for a while. By the way, I'm impressed on how well your new arm grew after I saved you."

I could feel him churn in silence as I left him. I paced down the street in my usual gray slacks, turtleneck, thick-soled boots, and long, black coat, hands in my pockets, whistling some song I composed but would never put down on paper.

It felt good to anger him. Somehow, it also felt good to cross a border to another civilization.

3

I spent the next few nights as nothing more than a shadow. I didn't do anything direct, going from corner to corner of The Farm in different modes. The Warm Ones avoided my path, as much as they did with Stargazers flying above them or Ravens in patrols. A few times, Crow or one of his lackeys found me and insisted they be present. I usually ditched them or just annoyed them enough to leave me alone.

Everything seemed as docile as it should be. They lived in fear. We ruled them. But I did notice the certain confidence in their sullen eyes and even in their aroma, especially the ones residing around the religious hub. Something was going on, and I was heading right into the middle of it. The thought that I might be bait of sorts from The Elders had already crossed my mind a few times. After all, if I ran into a dangerous rebellion and was destroyed, I'd be erased and that was fine for our society; if I uncovered a great scheme and redeemed myself, then that was also fine for our society. For those reasons I was going to avoid the wells and underground springs for now, start with this Shaman.

Deep in all of our passion and hunger, no Stargazer was too

worried about the Warm Ones. We had enslaved them after The Holocaust, we had broken their spirits many times since at large costs. Evolution continued and some night nature would return to us as it was intended.

And we might once again gaze at stars.

One evening, after the dreams had settled too real on my temples, I wandered to the area where the Shaman resided. He inhabited one of the many courtyards in the center of The Farm, where the Warm Ones held their little festivals or gatherings.

I skulked around in a side alley, witnessing a party of sorts. Dozens of animals sat at stone tables next to a primitive fountain sharing a scarce meal. In the center, their young played various games under round lamps threading the tops of the roofs or on poles. Odd music blasted from one of the many opened windows. I was surprised they had learned to install electrical systems so proficiently.

I almost had the urge to put on the nose-plugs, such was the scent brimming from the happy meeting, but I suppressed it. I tried to concentrate on their faces, on their small joys, on the talking coming from their thin lips. Nothing. No secrets. No hidden innuendos. But their expressions . . . it was there . . . as if even *they* didn't know why they felt confident.

A ball rolled directly to my feet at the lip of the alley. For some reason, I picked it up. A herd of pups followed its path.

Most of them stopped in midtrack when they saw me, eyes full of curiosity. One didn't stop, a male who was almost old enough to be tattooed. As he walked toward me, gasps and shuffling echoed throughout the alley.

"Can I have my ball?" the pup said.

I eyed him for a second or two before saying, "Can I have my ball, *please*."

The pup gave out a small snort. "Can I have my ball, *please*."

I extended my arm. He did the same.

"No!" A scream caused both of our heads to rotate. From the terrified crowd that had swarmed around us, a Warm One female rushed us. She snatched the pup and put him down a few feet away.

"Do not speak or interact with that, Clannad," the girl spoke sternly to the pup, who was for the first time afraid. "You know that is not allowed—"

"Hey, relax," I said. "I wasn't going to do anything."

The animal stood up from her crouching stance with a look of anger. I was surprised. It was the first time a Warm One had looked at me that way. It was more, though, it was her features. Despite the drab clothing, the shaven hair required after the twenty-fifth year, the sickly countenance, fire burned within her, within a youthful face, within rag-wash eyes of brown with long, strong eyelashes. For a moment, I was paralyzed by the creature before me, even though I could extinguish her life with the flick of a wrist, with the lash of my jaws.

"Do not involve yourself in our matters, *please*," she said with a mocking snap.

I raised a warning eyebrow. "I heard you refer to me as a 'that.' "

She extended her arm and pointed at me. Her sleeve rose then, revealing the tattoo all members of her species received after ten, painted numbers that the Stargazers inspected every week in massive, random roll calls to see who was to visit the Slaughterhouses. It was a simple method: They lined them all up in the courtyards or streets and used a glowing scanner on each tattoo. The codes were fed a computer at the station. Then amid screams and fighting, they dragged the Warm Ones to their end. Those stupid enough to try to save the chosen were more than often chosen themselves. I couldn't even start counting the numbers I'd tossed into cages or brought to the Slaughterhouses, the looks of despairs and pleading, the number of credits I'd won after wagering bets to see how long a Warm One lived while being drained.

"And who do you think you are?" she questioned rapidly.

I shuddered. The question caught me off guard. All of a

sudden, I saw the crowd encroaching where I stood, their expressions mirroring hers.

I couldn't answer, so I asked. "And who do *you* think you are?"

I tossed the ball at her. She gave me an answer as she caught it.

"I am Medea, Shaman Appointed, from the clan of Sith, daughter of Durgo."

"What—"

She threw the ball back at me. "And who are you? I asked again."

I caught it. "I am Byron, uh, Stargazer, Offspring of The MoonQueen."

"You lie," she said with a narrow smile. I could hear Ravens converging on this area, their sharp ears noticing the disturbance blocks away.

"I lie? I told you—" I got ready to throw the sphere at her again, but her mouth was faster.

"You cannot be anyone's son," she said, "because we created you."

My arms froze, body tensed. We created you? I'd never heard such a comment from an animal. The audacity of those words not only pierced me but stunned me. I found myself blinking rapidly, knowing I had no remark to counter her absurdity. All of sudden, I felt every stare from the crowd, felt closed in, almost trapped.

I opened my mouth, but all I wanted to do was take a step backward. And then another.

A troop of Ravens appeared from all over, yelling at the Warm Ones to get back into their homes. The crowd rapidly dispersed in segments, rushing away from the snarling Stargazers with raised fists. Tables knocking over, children crying, dust rising, doors slamming, I stood in the middle of the fracas holding the stupid ball. The Warm One called Medea slowly walked away with the pup in one hand.

One of the Ravens, following his instructions of aiding me, came to my side. "Want to make an example out of her?"

I blinked a few times more. "No. Not necessary. Just doing a little research."

The Raven laughed. "Well, let's hope you don't start too much more trouble in your research, Byron, even though we'd like to wet our fangs once in a while."

"Don't worry," I said. "It didn't go exactly as planned. Won't happen again."

"At least you got a nice toy out of this," he said, still laughing, leaving me to make sure the area was settled. When it was all done, splintered furniture, spilled food, and shut doors were all that was left of a party my species quickly dashed. Somebody had turned down the music.

Her name was Medea.

I carried my 'toy' back to the station, deciding to start fresh tomorrow, more prepared. Mephisto wanted to inspect it, and Crow wanted to make sure no bombs were planted in it, but I told them I'd play them a game of kickball for ownership. They declined.

We created you.

CHAPTER 4

What's happening? What do you mean?
The dream, it's burning everything away. I'm running

through walls of heat, past shattered mortar. Above me, a sky swirls in chromatic hate. I'm sweating. I'm carrying somebody. She's so heavy. I reach a street. Bodies and body parts litter injured sidewalks. The ground shakes, and my nose smells something other than juice. Flames cover me . . . and . . .

I'm standing before a stadium of Stargazers, a stadium I hadn't seen before. They look angry at me. They look hungry for me.

Why, I haven't done anything yet. I'm trying! Don't leave your seats, don't cross the air with salivating fangs. I'm not enough. I'm a citizen of this city I'm . . .

I hear the laughter of a lady, but it's not a lady . . . it's a goddess.

She laughs, and I'm covered. My skin tears, bones pop from sockets, my skull implodes. They won't stop. I won't go away. More flames. More juice.

2

I shuddered into wakefulness. The sheets were drenched from the juice I'd just sweated.

But that's not what bothered me just then, laying in my cupola. That's not what caused me to go into whimpering convulsions and fall off my bed.

"No," I croaked, seized by acute aching from toe to fang. I converged into spasms, more juice left me.

Sol!

I was awake. It was outside, fuming, a searing abyss, heating up the land with its enormous hatred. It was outside. I was awake.

Even through steel and rock, even though I knew it was already falling off the horizon, it pierced me. I felt its anger assaulting my mind, making it self-sabotage completely. The punishment on my body felt a thousand times worse.

I shut my eyes, hoping I could return to my darkness, but suddenly realized I couldn't go back there. I was too scared. My dreams sent me to it prematurely.

Flopping on the ground, my body coiled erratically in place, for the first time truly understanding primordial agony, so much more than physical. I grabbed one of the legs of the bed and squeezed, howling in pain. The metal twisted in my grasp, and I would howl all the way to the night.

3

"This is very unusual," Mephisto said in his infinite wisdom.

Crow kicked something on the other side of the room. I sat slumped in my chair, holding a large bottle of food, sucking it slowly through a straw.

"Unusual?" Crow echoed angrily. "We have a Stargazer who woke up way before *Moratoria* ended, and that's all you have to say?"

"Look," Mephisto said, still pacing the chamber. "You know we can't touch Byron. I know that a Stargazer perspiring very rarely happens, only in times of great stress, but it does happen."

"I know," Crow said, "it's happened to me before, but I've never woken up before *Luna*'s rise. Has anyone?"

"Not to my knowledge," Mephisto said. "But the point I'm trying to say is that this might have occurred because of some psychosomatic symptom, just as the perspiration."

Crow crossed his arms, I noticed, for the first time raising my head. The room was blurry, something I'd also never experienced.

"I'd rather play it safe," he said, "and assume it might have been something the Warm Ones did. This could be very serious, like a form of nerve gas. Maybe that is what destroyed Leztant. Byron, do you still have that ball?"

"No," I said, licking my lips, not bothering to tell him that chemical gases only worked on lower forms of life. "I gave it to the scientists."

"It's clean," Mephisto said. "Nothing unusual as far as we can discern."

"That's comforting," Crow said sarcastically, "but I must take severe precautions, like eliminating any Warm Ones in contact with Byron that night. Plus, The Elders must be contacted imm—"

"That is a little drastic, Crow," Mephisto cut in. "Like I said, it might have been just Byron himself. He's a notable Stargazer."

"Notable?" barked Crow. "Did you rise before dusk as well? I'm in charge of all security here, and that's what I need to—"

"No," I said in such a tone they both gave me their attention. "Whether this is some new weapon or just me going insane, I'll deal with this."

"No way," Crow said.

"Yes way," I said, standing up wobbly. "You know what Shib wants. One way or another, I need to get closer to them and see what happens. If I get completely changed or disintegrated, then it won't be much of a loss to you, Crow."

He pursed his lips and eyed Mephisto. The tall Stargazer shrugged.

"Fine," Crow said. "Continue with your work. But I still need to inform The Elders."

"If that will make you happy," I said, heading for the exit.

"And don't expect any more Ravens to help you out, either. I'm keeping the area cleared until I'm sure."

"I can take care of myself, Crow. Kindly clear yourself out of my area from now on."

He started hurtling obscenities at me. I heard Tina's name a few times down the corridor. I didn't care. What were they

going to do, turn me into a *Heretic*, the worst punishment decreed by The Elders in Xanadu, which simply meant banishment in less romantic terms. Considering what I'd
experienced recently, that would be a great favor.

4

This time no gathering filled the courtyard. I met an empty silence the following evening. The Ravens weren't the only
ones avoiding this place. It was time to use yet another capa-
bility enhanced by the god-soul.

I stood in the center and closed my eyes, ignoring the
humming of the fields in the distance. I concentrated on listening to everything transpiring for blocks away. Hundreds of
voices gorged my ears from inside the various buildings, each
one separated in my mind.

*Look, it's that monster who almost ate little Clannad. He's
coming back for more.*

Hide the children, Brunna. I'll bar the door.

*I hear they took Osros to the Slaughterhouse. He was
twenty-eight . . .*

Yes, they're getting desperate.

*Getting desperate? They don't even know . . . they just
guess most of the time.*

Why is he just standing there?

They'll kill us all in the end.

*He's dressed different from the others, though, still in all
black . . .*

Eat your dinner . . .

Master, I'm worried—

I opened my eyes. Her voice. I zoned in on it and walked
toward its direction. I made sure to curse myself for not having listened for clues the first night I was here. But, like my
brethren, we had grown accustomed to simply taking what we

wanted from the animals without acknowledging their minds or customs with any seriousness.

I reached a house about a street down. It looked like all the rest, except for a painted circle of dried juice on the door. I sniffed and grimaced. It wasn't Warm One juice, but that of the large rodents they ate, one of the other few animals that survived The Holocaust, a *Ruka*, usually hunted in the vast sewers of The Farm.

I had to chuckle internally. Another obvious sign Crow and his idiots had missed. They could have found the living quarters of this Shaman long ago. I didn't go in then, hearing some more . . .

. . . ceremony soon, Master. You are weaker every week. You can barely walk, much less—

I am fine, Medea. I can still raise the old pole if necessary.

But, Master, you cannot give your wisdom with full mobility. We are losing more and more people to the monsters. You . . .

Her words stopped at a sore, reluctant groan.

Fine, fine, Medea, my dearest. If it's any consolation, I had already planned my abdication. Are you ready?

Yes, Master.

You better be, my dearest. You are the chosen one.

Maybe we should not choose just one Shaman, Master. We are too many here, and your word only spreads so far. Envision many Shamans throughout the villages until the Revolution can be fully completed. The Blood of Circles all around!

That will be your choice when you are Shaman, Medea. Now, please fetch me some berries from the fields. I am hungry. I like the red ones, the blue ones are too acidic.

Your will, Master.

I heard her coming toward the door. I should have hidden to further snoop on her. Instead, I took a few steps back and lit a cigarette by the time she opened the door.

Her features didn't change much when she saw me, except for their harshness. She wore long, baggy robes with the same circle painted on her chest.

"You?" she questioned, quickly closing the door behind her and then hiding her hands inside the folds of her clothing. "What do you want?"

"I want some answers," I said plainly. "You will give them to me."

She laughed once. "Why should I?"

"Because I need to know some things."

"Your kind never needs anything from us," she said, standing right in front of me. "Except our blood."

"Existence is tough," I said, making sure not to lower myself to her absurdity again. "And I'm not here to discuss irrelevant things."

"Then what are you here for?"

"Information," I responded, amazed the animal still showed not an ounce of fear or respect without the rest of the herd.

She smiled without humor. "Information? I thought you Stargazers, as you call yourselves, knew everything there was to know?"

"Almost everything," I said slowly, stamping my cigarette and putting on my nose-plugs. Something about her, perhaps just her resonant juice, was keeping me off balance. "You're not afraid of anything, are you?"

"Why should I be? We live in the shadow of death, Star—"

"You may call me Byron."

"Okay, *Byron*," she said with distaste, pointing to the east. "Right down the street in that hill you live in, our kind are butchered constantly. My mother and father went one evening when I was young and never came back, and so it goes. We've heard stories about the butchery there—the lines, the draining, the little games you play like pretending you're going to allow some escape and then kill them for sport. I don't even want to fathom what your civilization might look like away from our homes. Even here we exist enslaved, always afraid, never too far away from one of your kind who might get brave in the middle of the night. I do feel fear, Byron, because that is all we truly have, but I can also use it."

"To create hope," I said, having not heard the first part of her speech. The nose-plugs were not working very well.

She half smiled and looked away.

"Yes. To create hope."

"And then you can have your revolution."

The girl stared at me, her firmness slightly wavering. "Yes, we will have our revolution."

"And what makes you think that? We are superior to you."

"That was not always the way. That is not natural."

"Why not?" I questioned. "Because you created us, right? Why did you say that last night?"

She crossed her arms. "Why would you care what I said?"

I recalled *Sol* greeting me when it shouldn't have. Stress, Mephisto had deducted. I wondered if it was more . . .

"It doesn't matter," I told her. "Like I said, I'm not here to debate but to find answers. One of ours was destroyed by your kind, and it won't go unpunished."

"Are you sure it was our kind?" she asked with a sneer.

"A Stargazer would never . . ." I started, also recalling an old friend and a mortal battle here in this farm a hundred and five years ago.

"You have doubt," she whispered with joy. "Though I wouldn't trust you with a *Ruka*, but you do."

"And you are sure open, Shaman Appointed. Too open for your own well-being. I could call the Ravens and have you and your little religion wiped out from memory. I could destroy everything you knew before you ever saw *Sol* again."

She appeared unfazed by the comment. "I have nothing to hide, Monster, and even less to lose. Your kind has granted us endless harm and suffering. It doesn't matter. The time is coming, the signs are obvious."

"What signs?" I inquired with mock interest. "Tell me about them. I can't do anything about them, can I?"

"No," she said, inspecting the expression on my face.

"Then tell me . . . Medea, right?"

"Medea," she said, not happy at all she had given her name to me before.

"Well? Tell me."

She pondered for a moment and then grinned at me. "Okay, Byron. Meet me in two nights by the temple, you know, the big building across the courtyard. At midnight."

"And then I will have my answers?"

She nodded. "Then you will have your answers."

She turned and left me.

5

I returned to Commodore Station soon after. I was still very weak from the past night, and it could happen again.

Before flying up to one of the busy balconies or openings, I made another visit to one of the voices I'd heard. In gaseous form, I slithered through cracks and under doorways until reaching a small bedroom of a hut. Three pups slept in it. I condensed and walked to one of them.

I smiled at him, resting peacefully under a waterfall of moonlight coming in through tattered curtains. At the same time, I was glad for the nose-plugs—his exposed skin from a craned neck looked tasty. I didn't feed, though. I simply took out an object from my coat and left it by his side, immediately jumping out the window without a sound.

When the one called Clannad woke up he would have his ball back and hopefully I would be in *Moratoria*. Even animals had feelings and things of worth to them. More than that, the pup had shown no fear toward me, not because of focused hatred as with the one called Medea, but because he didn't know any better. His personality hadn't been tainted by experience yet. I admired that.

Walking toward my cupola, I passed Crow and several of his henchmen in one of the loading docks. He was barking instructions about magnifying defenses or some crap like that.

"You never know what those creatures do during the raging of *Sol*," he shouted. "I even hear they burn effigies of us while we are in *Moratoria*."

I sneered quietly and, without notice, went to my chambers, avoiding a hundred people who'd want to know where I'd been. My little escapade was keeping people very wary.

I surfed my computer the rest of the night, a little machine that couldn't even reach 400 megahertz. News was beautiful at The Citadel: The glorious return of The MoonQueen with great tidings on the plumbing system; within a year, Xanadu would have the same luxury our smaller cousin, New Atlantis, enjoyed. Not bad for a species of immortals. Radiation count had dropped after steadily rising the last year, perhaps due to some pacific low-pressure system sweeping the land. Rumors kept circulating about the thought of a new city-state to be built to the south in the next five hundred years because of an incoming ice age, but most guilds said it was still in the alpha stages.

I ate a small snack before going to bed, thinking about how this Medea somehow intrigued me with her insolence and bravery. The animal reminded me of someone.

I dialed Tina's number through the modem, but only got her answering machine. Things must be busy at Lilac's.

I finally went to rest, more excited than I'd been in a long time. I dreaded the dreams of *Sol* and fire in the sky and my people angry at me, but I rested unperturbed through most of *Moratoria*, comfortable like an identity. There was much to discover.

6

The crowd disappears before and above me. I'm not a mess of shredded skin and bitten bones. I'm whole. I'm me.

The Goddess stops laughing, standing right before me. She is blue and beautiful and ancient, wearing gowns of light, jewels of liquid energy.

She extends a perfect hand to me, skin like the lightest glacier, deep cherry nails on long fingers.

Glory unto the highest, she says, and her voice is the night.

I look into her and I see twin Lunas in a dim sky. I almost reach for her, but I can see a dark fire behind them as strong as Sol's oven.

No, I say.

Glory unto the highest, she repeats, and I go to her.

CHAPTER 5

When the Shaman Appointed had left me that evening with her offer, I had thought of one thing while staring at her small back.

She's the one.

Being simultaneously insolent and brave more than likely meant she was close to the reason why I was here. She had shown no visible fear toward me at any juncture, the crowd had converged at her heel when I first met the Warm One. This Medea wasn't the formal leader of their religion, but there was a poise about her that disclosed she was their moral leader. In time, as I'd heard, she would be their spiritual one. It was almost more than luck how I had encountered her and that she had offered to show me part of her world.

When I met the animal at the designated spot, her visage remained stony toward me, flavored only with more confidence in her eyes. Yet there was an aching light behind them, a physical pain she was trying very hard to conceal. Medea wasted no time with the first direct comment.

"Are you ready? Do you still wish to see what the inevitable is about?"

I noticed that her right hand was in her robe pocket again. Warm Ones watched us from across the street, peering through curtains. A lonely Raven was standing on a guard tower a block down, also watching us.

None of this bothered me, I informed all their curious eyes with a smile.

"It's a date," I said. Both the Raven and Medea winced.

I followed her into the temple, mostly empty except for a few throbbing candles by a bucolic altar. She led me down into the basement, where they stored all their ceremonial artifacts and more. She told me they were only brought up for ceremonies, held during *Sol*'s raging except for extraordinary reasons.

"I see," I said tersely.

And Medea showed me everything in the cellar, a chain of dank, moldy rooms that stretched beyond the borders of the temple. There was a lot of dust and scum, cobwebs and crude tunnels with fist-size insects scuttling across our path. This place was more hallowed than the temple itself. For generations, they had chipped away underground, linked and isolated certain parts of the sewers, creating a place where they could seclude all that was sacred from us, if we'd ever care.

Following her meek lamplight, which I didn't need, she showed me sealed pantries containing hidden caches of food in case we destroyed their supplies as punishment, which had happened before. Others housed rows of clay pots holding liquid from fermented fruits mixed with certain herbs. "They help us in our trances and meditations by temporarily erasing our identities and our reality," Medea explained. "Help us touch the spirits of our ancestors who linger in the Endless Cycle and teach us our creed."

Whatever, I thought, as she took me to makeshift workshops where the Warm Ones had once tried uselessly to devise weapons strong enough to battle us. Medea told me quickly that this had been outlawed, since only the power of the Blessed Circle was destined to break our hold on them.

"What are you talking about?" I asked, not hiding my boredom.

"Come this way," Medea said. She took me back to where the stairs were. I knew what she was going to show me next.

And you know why, my thoughts told the animal. Because I've already seen all of this gloomy place. Did you think I was going to walk into a potential trap? Make you and The Elders happy by fumbling into destruction like the other fool?

The night before, I'd arrived late in the twilight. Using darkness as my disguise, I entered the temple. To the Warm Ones it was their largest building, their place where they gathered for emotional succor; to me it was a decrepit structure of dried mud with no rooms and a high-beamed ceiling. Strangely, Medea had been in there, still awake. Actually, almost awake. She sat in the middle of the floor of the temple, squatting nude before large bowls filled with liquid clay. Now I understood that her wild expression hadn't been because of some trance, but because of the effects of that liquid from fermented fruit, apparent from the empty containers next to the female. Perhaps that was the reason she appeared to me in uncomfortable pain during the tour. Eyes glazed in pink, she had chanted vague words while her fingers prodded at the clay. Her sacred sculpting was taking a bit of time, I could tell, by the unfinished globs she'd tossed to the side. She had yet to get one right. She continued and would probably continue into dawn.

I passed her and entered the stairwell, down into the darkness and the tangy aromas. I inspected every nook, every crevice for something interesting, something threatening. I found nothing of that sort.

Medea evaded a section of the cellar with me, but I had already inspected it. It was a locked chamber filled with rune-etched stone blocks amid sheets of spiderwebs and mounds of grime. Seeping in mist form into the cracks of the nearest one, I had found the robed skeleton of a Warm One, a nest of spiders inside its skull. The rest probably held the same items. This was likely a sacred burial place, a catacomb for the Shamans before. Nothing threatening.

I did find the secret entrance to an underground stream. After capturing the sound of water, it had been easy to pry off a slab of stones in one of the hallways connecting the main parlor. Very cautiously, I had followed it to its source. It led to a well in quadrant eighteen. The only things that had caught my interest were a few streaks of where something had burned the sedentary rock by a narrow bank. It had come as no surprise that the Ravens had missed it, their duty only to enforce, while the Scientists here only cared about analyzing data. The burns were for me to find, for I was the first Stargazer in Xanadu to have to investigate such a matter.

The rumors Mephisto heard were right. Leztant had been burned by something powerful enough to scorch stone. The source was in this cellar but, again, there was nothing of that sort here. After replacing the stone, I had decided to exit through the well, frustrated that the temple and its hive held a clue but no source.

I knew Medea was going to present to me odd icons and figurines lining the high shelves. I'd already scrutinized them.

New idols dried in the corner underneath a cloth canvass, presumably the ones she had crafted yesternight. I'm sure they were exactly the same as the ones she now showed me. Nothing threatening.

I pretended to behold the idols for the first time. I still needed to know more, perhaps find out some other hidden cellar in this farm. At the same time, I couldn't deny that Medea's feisty attitude was intriguing and perhaps even necessary to solve my quest. She had already made it apparent in front of the Shaman's abode that threats or violence weren't going to change her attitudes. She was the one I needed to watch.

"Do you feel afraid of them?" she asked suddenly, holding out one toward me while teetering on a high stool.

"Terrified," I said. "Why do they all have eights when your clothes and some doors have circles?"

"Those are signs of infinity," she said, descending, looking almost disappointed. "We are all eternal in a sort of way. Everything is done in cycles, everything happens not once but many times. You have learned to believe that time travels forward, we believe time travels through us, every dusk and every dawn are the same."

"I can understand why," I said with a smirk. "So what is the difference in symbols?"

"We are circles, but the Liberator is an eight, the true breaker. To him, eternity is undulating and transposing, but still very much the same. He has been everything and nothing, has been everywhere and is always with us."

"And he will come to save your species from us?" I asked, this time with a larger smirk.

This Medea, so small, so secure here with a hunter of her species, hidden from everyone, frowned at me.

"In every time and place, a liberator comes to save the oppressed, the downtrodden, and to righten the balance. It is a universal law, Byron. Our faith will bring him here, our hope will bring him here, our fear will bring him here."

"And when is this time?"

"He will come soon, for the Shaman and I have seen the signs in our meditations. When he is here, our faith will be our shields and our weapons, just as they defeated your kind long ago. Perhaps I will be gone, but it doesn't matter. It doesn't matter what I say." She grabbed for the lantern on the floor. "We are cattle to you, are we not?"

She never saw my hand moving. I held her arm before she could seize her necessary illumination.

"We need to survive."

"Do you need to kill us?" she asked sharply, glaring at my ivory fingers on her forearm.

I opened my mouth. No words shielded me, just a disconcerting hanging of my jaw. I wasn't amazed this time that the animal was speaking to me that way, but I was amazed that I had felt compelled to respond. Again! Enough was enough.

"Did you kill the Stargazer?" I asked plainly, trying to pierce those fierce eyes with a fiercer gaze.

"What do you think, Byron?" Her shock dissipated, replaced by a dull fire. "Do I look like someone who could kill a god, as you think of yourselves? How could a small Warm One female accomplish such a feat? Tell me."

I released her. She allowed momentum to take her back against the shelves.

"I think you did it," I said. "By your little speeches I definitely know why you would. But I still don't know how, Medea. I'd like to know."

She exposed her teeth to me while speaking. "What does it matter? Like you said, you have the power to make me vanish from memory. Why not do it, Byron? Why worry about evidence and simply delete me and my religion. Animals don't deserve justice!"

"That would be unfair at the moment," I said. "I'm not like that."

"Then how are you, Byron?"

"I'm different," was all I could say. Something about her words unbalanced my thoughts, made me taste that nagging embarrassment, recaptured those dreams that had been my tormentors even before I was sent to find the reason of a murder, the ember of rebellion.

Animals don't deserve justice . . . justice . . . me surrounded by angry Stargazers . . . justice . . . rebellion . . . me running in a city of flames . . . Sol coming to get me . . . judge me . . . justice . . .

Do you need to kill us?

Her expression softened, just a bit, as mine had faltered. I was relieved there was silence lynched between us instead of innuendos and angry words. I knew she wouldn't allow it for long. I just knew it.

"Why did you bring the ball back to Clannad?"

Even animals have feelings and things of worth to them.

"Your offspring needed it more than I did," I said flatly.

"Offspring? He is not of me, although I take care of him and his siblings. His parents were sent to the Slaughterhouses two years ago. Why did you do it?"

"Because I'm different," I said with a lopsided smile, suddenly smelling her intoxicating nectar. I'd gorged myself before arriving in order to interact with a clearer mind than when I found her the last time, but that wasn't working anymore. It was stronger than the usual scent, different, as if more than my senses desired her all of a sudden.

Oh, I was hungry.

"Perhaps you are different," her voice said, almost as loud as the thunder of her living heart in my eardrums, the rivers that were her veins. "Perhaps you do have a sense of fairness, Byron. But fairness is a quality of goodness, of civility, and that is not of your kind. Don't you understand that nothing you try can truly work? You are not creators, but only steal creation. You are destroyers by definition."

When I spoke, I felt that my lips, my face, my body no longer belonged to me. The Dark Instinct was rising, usurping, informing me it was time to feed. It was as if the god-soul didn't want this conversation, this creature to even stand before me.

"Give me a break."

I followed her gaze, which settled on the holy statues of her eight-religion.

"Maybe I just have," she said.

I made my way to the stairs. "And maybe I have, too."

Outside, more comfortable in the breeze and the darkness, I sensed my hunger abating just slightly. Without further thought, I flew toward Commodore Station, heading for the nearest feeding area. I silently thanked the Dark Instinct for rinsing away the thoughts and memories, for giving me a certain purpose, a certain knowable direction.

Yes, she was the one. She had now answered the why, though maybe not the how. No matter what the animal said about justice or goodness, she would never understand that the pulse of nature is perfection but it does not know justice or goodness; the elements only understood to fulfill their purpose, and that went the same with Stargazers. We were perfect and we were destroyers.

2

Lightning shuddered a hundred miles away in a stew of chemical clouds crowning the mountains. As majestic as it was, volatile ignitions of somber white, struggling through phosphorous gray and blue to outline the ancient peaks, it was also soothing, almost hypnotic, here in the quiet of the twilight.

And, of course, Mephisto had to ruin it.

"It won't get to us," Mephisto said, leaning over the metal railing. "A storm of that magnitude never lasts. The Warm Ones used to think it was their primitive deities coming to rescue them a long time ago, before they became monotheistic. Remember?"

"Vaguely," I lied, putting out my cigarette on the floor of the balcony.

"We're fortunate none of those storms or nature itself ever did anything too bad to Xanadu. Not like its cousins during The Cataclysm of Tears."

My ears caught the rumble of that rarity called thunder. It was faint, almost absorbed by the radioactive gases and the crackle of neutrons—junk that was part of its constitution these nights.

I lit another cigarette, my only movement in a chair by the doorway. More lightning. Mephisto wouldn't shut up.

"It's the only good thing about the northern Farms, besides the important work we perform for Our Mistress and our society. In the winter, if you look hard, you can see the phenomena of—"

"When were you given existence?" I asked, staring at the lightning and its distance.

He pivoted to rest on an elbow. "Uh, I don't know. Shortly after you were, I believe. We met when they decided to split The Farms into four. You were already a sterling leader, Byron."

"Do you remember being birthed?"

He shrugged, and then shrugged a second time, more for himself.

"Slightly. Do you?"

I didn't answer, pretending to be busy blowing smoke rings.

"Why are you asking this, Byron? It's The MoonQueen's will. We exist, genesis and ending irrelevant to our immortal essences."

The most important canon of the Stargazer, gleaned through endless Fusings, flashed in my head: Warm Ones and other beings live; we *exist*. Life ends, existence eternally *is*. The Dark Instinct will outlast time, the cosmos, consuming everything until it completely *Is*. When the flash ended, Mephisto was ending his dissertation.

". . . know belief isn't in your vocabulary, Byron, and you can be a pain sometimes, but acceptance is a noble pursuit."

"I did accept Dante's ending, didn't I?"

"I guess," he said, pursing his lips.

"Did you?"

"Byron," was all he said.

"Did you?"

He spoke slowly, "You did save my existence, and maybe it was my fault because I provoked his infamous temper. I mean, I didn't think we had to pillage the whole farm section even with the high food reserves. I still stand by that. It didn't matter what we thought because you were our superior." He shook his head sadly. "But you and Dante always had a way of taking matters to the extreme. Yet, to this night, I wonder why you had to destroy him. To this night, though, I can't help wonder if you two would have ever done it otherwise."

"You're very good, Meph," I said. "But you still haven't answered the question."

He watched the scenery instead of answering me. I thanked him silently and fingered another cigarette.

The night wasn't evolving with any more velocity, it seemed. I'd risen without dreams, thankfully, but whispers echoed from the obscure din that was *Moratoria*. Voices I thought I knew, perhaps hers, glory unto the highest.

My first action had been to jot down a few bytes on my computer, putting them in the form of a field study. My inter-action with Medea, her inane religion, what I'd seen in the an-imal's eyes, it was all in there. I stressed many times that action wouldn't be prudent until the source of Leztant's end-

ing was unearthed. Part of me could already predict Shib and
The Elders' pride at my assiduous work when I zapped it to
them. With a quick movement, disobeying any rational objec-
tion, my finger deleted two hours of work. It was all gone. I
leaned back in my chair and felt partly relieved.

What was wrong with me?

Thinking maybe I just needed company, my kind, I went to
Mephisto's office on the other side of the station. He seemed
glad to see my form at his doorstep, almost a little surprised.
He invited me for a meal. Like any Stargazer at anytime, I
couldn't deny it.

The population curiously eyed us as we entered the feeding
area, two companions they still remembered from early
nights. Mephisto seemed in very good spirits, and I was sure
he'd tell The Elders how well he was keeping me under his
eye. Perhaps to show his appreciation or just to loosen my
tongue, he had the fresh carcass of a Warm One brought to our
table.

"An accident in my laboratory," Mephisto explained, raising a steel straw in a toast. "It was supposed to last a few more
weeks, but my assistant keeps forgetting her strength. Her
punishment is to watch us from the other table, ha ha. Enjoy,
old friend."

I glanced at the animal's features, tepid and rubbery and
permanently devoid of ardor, not like another Warm One I
knew, looking at naught from an odd angle caused by a splintered neck. I toasted back at the Scientist and jammed my own
straw into the plumpest vein I could smell. Before long, the
straws lay on the floor, the Stargazers in the other tables eyed
us with envy, while we suckled juice through puckered
mouths and flicking tongues.

Unusually sated, we wandered through rocky tunnels to his
quarters, after he'd delivered a few orders to his offices.

In one of his wardrobes, he showed me his collection of
memorabilia from Raven nights. There were carved skulls

and antiquated whips, framed proposals and essays on animal control, uniforms grafted with medals and rank patches. Mephisto showed me everything with detailed care. I nodded politely most of the time, showing emotion only when he got to the pictures, old pictures of simpler times.

My image graced much of the glossy surfaces. There I was, in one, standing proudly with fists nudged to my sides. Mephisto squatted to my left with folded arms, while my other friend, my closest friend, Dante, grinned to my right, all three of the great Raven mavericks posing before a row of Warm Ones hung by their feet after a hunting match. There I was, dressed in black trousers and a long-sleeve shirt, with the rose-stitched armband marking my leadership status, looking fierce and confident and smiling a lot, like the world was ours. There I was, marching, performing flying drills, giving orders. There I was, before I started breaking down a decade or so later. We lampooned and laughed and took the vestal Raven regime with so much passion to new heights. And, yes, we believed that it was going to be a better world, that nature would come to its senses by our little prank, that The Moon-Queen would deliver us all the way to the hidden stars. We believed.

And there I was.

"By the way," Mephisto said after a dialogue drought, kicking his feet over the ledge. "I like what you've been doing."

"What's that?"

"By"—he paused to stress his distaste—"interacting amicably with this animal, this leader of cattle, you will learn much without fuss. If anything, at least you've got a pet for the time being. Everyone here thinks it's hilarious."

"It's getting funnier by the night, Meph. I might even decide to keep her."

He chuckled loudly. "You're a sly one. So when do you think you'll have concrete information?"

I smirked at his back. He didn't feel it. Good old Mephisto.

For the first time in hours, I stood up. Jumping on the railing, I kept my balance without my gifts. He stared at me oddly.

I wanted to be closer to that thunder and lightning out in the mountaintops, in the wilderness, but that wouldn't happen. It had distance. And there I was, with my own distance, realizing I was as far away here with my kind in my land as I was to Medea and her kind. Like the storm clouds that struggled with their intended purpose, I was caught between two worlds, it seemed, each tugging at me for reasons I didn't understand. Maybe the whole struggle was just my way of making situations harder for myself and those surrounding me. Just like when I lost my Raven rank and took the profession of a rogue, it was all by my own doing.

"I'll have what I want," I said, my response tinged with its own storm. "Tomorrow."

"You're a sly one, Byron."

3

A ceremony was being held. From what I heard from the Warm Ones entering the temple and the hundreds left outside because of space, this was just one of many before the new Shaman took on the Blood of Circles. And that was Medea. My Warm One pet.

Hiding over the rafters of the temple, I harmonized in the shadows without a sound. I knew my eyes burned with reddish tints, a reaction at being in the company of so many prey, but none saw me in the candlelit shrine. Most of the time heads were bowed in prayer, as the Shaman spoke loud supplications to The Blood of Circles and its Liberator.

"Infinite Eight, Blessed Circle, we ask you to lead us to The House of Tomorrow," the Shaman bleated at his congregation. "We know that evil is good tortured by its own hunger and thirst, we know good comes from being one with the self. But The Den of Thieves, The Womb of Hell, does not understand this, separated from time and the gardens of innocence. It only knows to drink from dead waters, to steal in the night . . ."

Medea was always by his side, dressed in the same beige, circle-painted garments, praying with the rest, assisting the gnarly man who seemed too ill to finish his didactic tirade.

"We ask that you arrive, Liberator, and lead us to the House of Tomorrow. We know that death is but to stand in the wind and melt with *Sol*; we know we have turned our back from good as much as The Den of Thieves. We ask your forgiveness, your return, your eternal blessing!"

I listened to it all, to every dripping word. I heard the prayer of each Warm One. Any other Stargazer would have laughed, scoffed at this. I just listened and, after a while, enjoyed its poetry, its foolish meaning, savoring a little peace at the same time, the first since being woken to *Sol*'s raging javelins.

I took time to grin when I saw Clannad, bored at the ceremony, elbowing another pup at his side. How peculiar, these Warm Ones, that they should breed from themselves, grow and grow old. They had no real power, obeying physics. What they ate many times was expunged in waste. Eventually, they wasted to dust, all but worthless if we weren't around to consume them. How odd.

I slapped my forehead, forcing my legendary short attention span to concentrate on any clues from his speech or the crowd.

Byron, you're worse than Clannad and the other pup! Listen well, but don't worry about their words. They don't mean anything as much as The Elders' words really don't mean anything to you. They're just words from animals. They're just words.

We created you.

When it ended, the Warm Ones left quietly with satisfied expressions. They would go to their rest with hope, while a few would be snagged before reaching their homes. Crow had ordered the area cleared, but we had to feed civilization.

While workers hid the benches and some of the artifacts downstairs, I listened to Medea order a Warm One to escort the Shaman to his abode, saying that she needed to prepare for the passing of the Blood of Circles. It was tomorrow.

As soon as she was alone, getting prepared for her nightly duty of maintaining the basements, I descended and landed with a small bow.

"Byron!" she exclaimed with outrage, rapidly moving away from me. "You heard it? You were here!"

"I'm sure any Stargazer in the vicinity heard this, Medea."

"But you are not part of this!"

"Yes, I am. You've showed me. Like you said, you've got nothing to hide from a monster like me."

Her eyes widened and collapsed to that glare. I felt that few comments ever halted her pugnacious anger, and none could ever temper her edge.

"What are you doing here?" she asked, one arm sliding inside her robe. "Have you decided that it is time for judgment?"

I snorted. "Not yet, if I decide there is to be one. There are still a few things I need to know."

Medea dodged my gaze. "All the answers that you need I have given them to you. And now you come with the same questions."

I paused, admiring the eight sculpture over the altar.

"Not exactly. I'm giving you the option to learn more about us, Shaman to be."

Her brow crinkled. "What do you mean?"

I shrugged.

"A tour. The place you wouldn't even fathom, remember? Commodore Station."

"Commodore Station? You mean The Den of Thieves? Hell?"

I shrugged a second time, this one chaperoned by a chuckle. "Sure, anywhere you want."

"I don't know," she said. "Perhaps you have been . . . civil, Byron. But your kind . . . in there?"

"No one will harm you, Medea. I promise you that. I'm doing this out of fairness. Let me return the favor. What do you have to lose that you really don't have?"

She thought about it, her gaze slowly descending to her bleak clothing.

"Fine," she said. "But this isn't about fairness, Byron, no matter what you think."

"Then what's it about?"

Her defiant look had arrived again. "Strength, perhaps?"

I laughed. "Oh, you are entertaining, Warm One. Let's go."

"Wait for me outside," she told me. "I must arrange a few things and lock this place. Make sure you are not seen. I cannot be seen consorting with—"

"I'll wait outside," I said, going to the exit.

It took her less that half an hour to join me. A good amount of it, I heard distantly, was spent performing the act of prayer. She didn't use the fermented fruit this time. Once outside, Medea scanned the area, until I detached from the darkness.

"One thing I don't understand," I said casually, "is that you don't seem to have the Shaman's flair for gab. I think he would have told me the same lines about houses and dens if I had encountered him."

"You are right." She half smiled, taking a step toward me to show me where she stood in her fear. "I know all the holy words of The Circle, Byron, but I was chosen not for my eloquence but—"

"Because of your demure attitude, your pacifistic persona."

Her smile became full. "Yes, Stargazer. And why were you chosen?"

I held out a hand to the Warm One.

"It has something to do with a sensitivity and a good eye."

She held out her hand to me.

4

Everyone takes things for granted, even gods, I suppose. Medea had not truly wanted to enter my arms when I told her how we'd get there and she groaned when my feet divorced the ground. Soaring high above The Farm, I couldn't help but enjoy her expression of pure joy. Her face cringed in delight at the raking wind, at the world left underneath us.

"Blood of Circles!" I heard her say through the bawling air. "We're fly—"

Her sentence was terminated by her own scream, as I swooped in a loop, wanting to see her myriad of expressions deepen. Yes, we were flying, in my arms, two different creatures in, you got it, two different worlds.

I sailed around The Farm twice, ignoring several Ravens chasing me until they saw who I was. For a fleeting instant, I climbed over the cliff, edging close to the Ozone Field. Medea's eyes absorbed more wonder, clasping a quick flash of The Citadel many miles away.

Rice City had been carved from a massive cliff overlooking a wild ocean, New Tenochtitlan once thrived in a savage desert in the form of pyramids, New Atlantis existed in the form of a steel carapace in the ground, while Utopia was built from the skeleton of a Warm One city. Xanadu wasn't like any of them—it was The City of Domes, an emerald gem in a caustic valley. Medea saw this, and I felt a certain pride at showing it to her, just briefly.

Then I took off for Commodore Station. I asked Medea what she wanted to see first.

"Take me to your leader," she shouted, holding me tighter. "Take me to confront your evil queen."

"I don't think so." I laughed. "Something closer."

Her determined expression remained. "Take me to the Slaughterhouses."

"Are you sure?"

She didn't answer. Her grip tightened. I changed course, heading for the massive cranes on the north side of the canyon.

And tried my best to ignore my rising hunger for her being.

I knew of certain defects in the station, old tunnels and cracks I'd used decades ago in my black market ploy. Most were still there. I zoomed into a large crevasse above the rocks and descended through narrow shafts. I almost forgot that some needed access in mist form, changing direction several times. When a Stargazer melted to gas, anything touching skin joined him or her in that state. I wondered if Medea would transform with me, but I didn't want to put her through the shock. She had her own when we arrived at a high ledge overlooking the Slaughterhouses.

She left my grasp immediately, leaning over the edge, trying to peer over the smoke of the furnaces and machinery. The floor of this place was always well lit, lamps tended throughout the maze of walkways in the middle, for the guests of honor were none other than her species, here in but one of the three massive hangars comprising the Slaughterhouse.

The other two were used to package the food for businesses and private galas, nothing more than a process of immediately drowning their bodies in chemicals. This one, the main one, served to make distribution more economical for the population.

Standing by her, I chased her vision, followed every twitch of her face. Medea sweated, shook with vigor, but her sight would not falter. I felt she was hot in here, perhaps in danger due to the unclean air that swirled in oily tendrils.

Down there, she saw something so common to us, so necessary. The cranes appeared at large openings, tossing Warm Ones into metallic corrals. In each, a Raven with an electrical prod commanded them to strip and continue in single file through slim walkways. Those who did anything silly, such as beg, fight, or try to return to their cages, were swiftly shocked into submission. A few passed out, and the Raven threw the bodies in the corner. When the soldier had a break, he'd strangle them, dragging the bodies directly to their destination at the end of the shift. Leftovers, we used to call them.

Nude males and females and some pups walked, silent with bowed heads, turning several corners, where hygienic sprays doused them in case they were needed for a more festive purpose. If that was the case, a Raven would open certain doors at a specific interval and take the Warm One to holding barns next to the Slaughterhouse. The flow and choosing was regulated by scanners set at every ten feet, counting heads and the tattooed numbers for inventory. Again, if some Warm One faltered in terror, a Raven would be notified from control rooms and depart the many terraces on the high walls. The soldier would land over the iron mesh encasing the walkways. They could keep walking or suffer the same fate as the disobedient ones at the entrance.

Then came the end, which Medea witnessed many times, as a cargo had just been unloaded.

In my times, the glory nights of Xanadu, the Slaughterhouse was open all night. Out of laziness and the fact I thought we Ravens were below this, I'd even used Warm Ones to aid in the process, a calming effect for the chosen. Their reward, I lied, for working as guides was to be absolved from the end. The Elders banned this after a few years. These nights, Ravens were lucky to get a six-hour night load.

The walkway forked to three different portals. As soon as three Warm Ones entered, a red light flashed and a door slid shut. The next ones waited for the door to open, their spirits and hopes going up with the silky smoke. After a minute or more, perhaps only hearing a faint groan from the other side, red shifted to green, the door opened, and three more went in.

They probably knew what came next. Medea had heard. In a small, circular chamber of stainless steel, seemingly without features except for a few speckles of juice here and there, they

stood with heavy breathing. Sometimes they had to wait minutes, as the machinery was old, a century old. Then they might
hear a humming noise, followed by a clicking sound. Before
they could react, steel clamps disjoined the walls and pinned
their necks, waist and arms down. Fear replaced desperation,
one last time. Metallic straws half an inch in diameter, much like
the ones Meph and I used, but much longer, thrust from the
walls from invisible openings at a blinding speed. Some engineer in a booth overlooking the maze had quickly set the right
coordinates for the tubes, or Gutting Syringes. Two plunged into
each side of the neck, one in the chest, one in the stomach, two
in the thighs. Many times a tube would miss the specific location, but it didn't matter for the others would take care of the job.
The animal twitched in what must have been incredible agony
at first, skin and flesh ripping slightly in different areas during
the struggle. Then their juice was drained. They couldn't even
scream for the tubes crisscrossed to block their air pipes. Probably feeling dizzy, perhaps tired, all so rapidly, pain and light
dissolved before them. Then it was over. The tubes and clamps
regressed, their juice poured to large vats beyond the high walls
to be treated and cataloged.

The carcass had little time to fall, a trapdoor opening at its
feet. Medea, tears seasoning her perspiration, would not see the
empty husk fall on a cart a story down in small tunnels that led
to the furnaces. When the cart was full of broken corpses, a
worker would drag it to be emptied. The workers were called
Lickers, I recalled, and they were Stargazers that had committed
minor infractions such as theft or lying. Their punishment, besides the debased work, was to survive by supping the remains
of juice left in the receptacle. I was threatened with this discipline a few times, but someone at the top always had mercy.

Then it was off to the fires, destroyed, forgotten in the
fumes meeting the indifferent sky.

Although I was thoroughly fascinated by her interaction
with her grimmest nightmare, I couldn't help admire my pet.

She watched without a flinch, taking the view of something so ghastly to her species, so wrong . . . so evil? Medea was stronger in will than any animal I'd ever seen, any Stargazer. Yes, this was about strength, and she had shown mounds of it.

At the same time, I wondered about Medea's comment about having to end them for nourishment. Did we really have to slay them? Couldn't we simply drain their juice in proportions? They would live, making more juice for us, reproducing, perhaps creating a labor force for our needs. It made more sense. I felt this debate had happened before, that somehow I'd been in the middle of it.

Flames . . . smoke . . . judging me . . . running away from her . . . her justice?

Utopia.

My feet shuffled away from her, for the sound of the Shaman's words returned from the expanse of my memory.

We know that evil is good tortured by its own hunger and thirst, we know good comes from being one with the self. But The Den of Thieves, The Womb of Hell, does not understand this, separated from time and the gardens of innocence. It only knows to drink from dead waters, to steal in the night.

Medea suddenly started to shriek, raising her fists at the Slaughterhouse. I'd heard Warm Ones shriek through the years, but not like this. It was curled in hate and defiance, so pure yet so pain-filled. Her hands fumbled inside her robes.

"CRAWL YOU!" I heard when her voice took on words. "CRAWL ALL OF YOU, IN THE LIGHT OF THE LIBERATOR AND THE HOUSE OF TOMORROW. YOU BASTARDS, YOU PATHETIC, EVIL THINGS. CRAWL!"

Admiration turned to envy for an instant, a very small instant, and I placed my hand over her mouth, pinning her body with my other arm.

She struggled without success. I could hear Stargazers flutter toward us, knowing something was amiss in this place, this most important place of our civilization but which few Stargazers gave much thought to.

Fanged monsters with swiping talons surrounded us in the air. My people. They recognized me and growled in warning. I growled back with such vigor the walls shook. They paused in their flight. They saw my own warning flaring in my eyes, so bright the whole chamber lit in sulky red. I fell with the animal over the ledge until smoke engulfed us. Then I darted toward the entrance. At my heels, they followed cautiously.

I increased my speed, bolting out off the canyon. My people stopped at the entrance, knowing their territory was secure, perhaps understanding that it was just Byron and his little pet.

I felt Medea quivering erratically, suddenly recalling that Warm Ones needed that thing called oxygen. My hand abandoned her face. She gasped, still full of anger.

"I want to see more," she rasped. "Take me back, Byron, damn you! I want to see more!"

I didn't changed my direction. I flew back to The Farm. She kept on repeating the same line. She hit and elbowed and kicked me, but I felt nothing.

I took her back to the temple. When we landed, still screaming, she tried to run back. I grabbed her again, taking her down to the basement. Tossing her on the floor, I stood guard at the stairs. As Medea fell, a small statue of the eight-painted male, which she had hidden in her robes, popped out and shattered on the ground. She started weeping, legs folded under her, covering a face I realized was almost precious to me. The hunger, tamed by my sly plan, returned, fortified by the vast juice I'd smelled so recently.

"Maybe this wasn't such a good thing," I offered, rolling my eyes in admittance. "Not a good trade-off, Medea."

She shook her head, lips twisting in aching. The aching was also reflected in her gaze, scanning the fragments of the statue. Then she swallowed hard. Then she wiped the odd moisture off her eyes.

"Yes, it was," she said between sobs. "I . . . I . . . had to see it . . . Byron . . . I was—"

"No," I said. "Maybe I haven't been entirely fair with you."

She hinged her stare to mine, slight fear echoing behind defeated features. Two different worlds with so much distance. And there I was . . .

"I knew you would want to go there," I said with tightness in my voice. "You're so full of hate, and you wanted it to consume you. I understand. At the same time, I wanted to see you with the rest of the animals and their fate, show you our world and the reality you won't accept." I shrugged. "Maybe I just wanted to punish you for your comments that might have slightly bothered me . . . break you down a little." I laughed. "That's all."

Medea lowered her head. Her lips quivered. Yes, I had broken her down. She had seen reality. But was that fair of me?

"I . . ." My words stopped briefly, for I realized I was about to do something no Stargazer had ever done. I closed my eyes. "I apologize, Medea."

I heard the rustle of her clothing, gentle footsteps toward me. My eyes opened, surprised to see that her expression had cleared up. Medea tilted her head, breathing leveling, pinkish eyes looking at me with a certain newfound interest.

"It wasn't just that," she whispered, "why I wanted to be there. But it doesn't matter now, does it? Maybe you are right. The world is the way it is, and perhaps I cannot change it. Only one person can. But know one thing: I have said things not to 'bother' you but to show you the truth. I have concealed and I have been indirect, but I have never lied to you, Byron, for your kind has shown me that lying is worse than death."

"Did you kill the Stargazer?"

"Yes," she hissed. "Yes, I did."

"Thank you," I said, but her answer didn't make me feel any better. I wish she hadn't. I wish I'd never known.

Before I could ask any more questions, she suddenly placed

a hand on my face. I was too astounded to flinch, absorbed in the warm curiosity from her large eyes.

Her fingers traced the terrain of my face. I felt at first she was just inspecting an object, a piece of art of sorts like the idols behind her. Fingers prodded at the lips, at the chin and the nose of a god, a being far away from her.

"You're so cold." Her tone reflected a certain pity I didn't like. "Cold and solid like a statue, but so full of life, fake life."

I flinched to escape her pulsing skin. Her hand lowered to rest on my chest.

"What are you saying?"

"Your heart, Byron. It does not beat, it never will, but you opened some of it to me, nonetheless. I'm trying to understand. Perhaps all we'll ever share is some understanding."

"There is nothing to share," I whispered. I still wouldn't move against her impudence. It was almost as if I enjoyed her curiosity, her tender stroking. Her touch.

The hunger surged. The Dark Instinct. Two worlds tugging at me.

"Is it horrible to exist like your kind?" she asked, hands now reaching to unpluck the buttons on her robes. "Horrible to always hunger, to always starve, to be so full of icy passion, no matter how hard you try to act civilized?"

"It's not so bad," I stammered, watching the dress open. "The existence of a god, you know."

"Yes," she said, grabbing my right hand and bringing it to her chest. My palm pressed against her spongy breast. I could feel her juice vibrating, her heart nurturing her body, her warm, pink body. She was so pink. So warm. "Gods suffer, but you are no god."

"Your species suffers, too. I hear many times by your own hands."

I couldn't look at her. I turned my head, craving in more ways than I could fathom.

Hunger . . .

"Can you lust without killing, Stargazer?" her voice asked. "Can you know friendship without black desire?"

"I . . ." I closed my eyes again, feeling my nails grow into claws, every inch of my body wanting to assault her.

Medea, what are you doing?

"Are you so different, Byron? You weren't always this way. Is there only the possibility of our warfare as it has been since the dawn of time?"

Utopia . . .

I didn't answer. Something unspoken surged from the base of my spine. My feet felt hollow.

"Medea," I warned.

"I'm trying to understand."

Blood.

The Dark Instinct.

When I opened my eyes, they were gorged in crimson. I spoke with the voice of the god-soul, the hunter, the destroyer.

"The only thing you need to understand, animal, is that your second-best destiny is obedience. Your first is being consumed by me!"

"You bastard!" she snapped, slapping me across the face and immediately springing backward.

All I saw then was a veil of deep red stamped over my eyes, guiding me to prey, to my real destiny, the fate of the hunter. This is what it's all about, the Dark Instinct informed from deep within my being—hunt, slaughter those with warmth, break them in your grasp until their warmth is yours for even a little time . . . hunt . . . it is your destiny, your identity.

I swiped at the Warm One once. Her spine would have shattered, her breath would have been stolen by the force. Yet I missed. I missed because I wanted some enjoyment, some challenge. That is why I missed.

Thinking she had really dodged my assault, she stumbled on the dirty ground. Medea dared a glance and witnessed me cackle with pulsing fangs. Thinking she had a chance, she crawled madly toward the idols, the ones in the corner still covered by the canvass. I allowed her a little distance and moved right behind her with blinding speed. I growled. She screamed, twisting in place.

Hunt, slaughter. That is your destiny. Don't think of anything else, for it is *Sol* and insecurity that bring doubt, which will hand you your destruction, Byron.

Medea kicked upward, catching me in between my legs. The force propelled her backward into the covered idols. I simply stood without any effects and gave her a few seconds of more false hope.

She madly pulled at the canvass, a glint of relief in her features. Her time was over, I decided, and it was time for me to face who I was and what I was doing here.

Hunt, slaughter . . .

The Warm One grabbed one of the idols, the ones she herself had created that night in her trance. She lifted it above her head. I took a step forward and prepared to slice her throat open and begin feeding.

She shrieked. But not at me.

Surprised, I held back my weapons. It was different from the one at the Slaughterhouse. Her shriek was tinged in rage, deep strain. She shrieked for a while until her sound collapsed into pitiful choking. She crumpled on the floor, once again defeated, hugging the idol. I blinked, wondering what had happened to this scenario. I couldn't deny the disappointment that something else had caused her more dread than that of the hunter.

"No," Medea whimpered. "No . . . no, no . . . it can't be . . . no . . ."

"Medea?" I said, glancing at the idols. The features on their faces. They were familiar . . . similar.

"No . . . it can't be . . . mistake . . . Blessed Circle . . . no!"

"Medea?" I said with a glint of fear. The faces on the idols. They weren't just familiar. They weren't just similar.

"No . . . it can't be!"

They were mine.

"Medea," I repeated, recalling she had touched my face like a sculpture. "What is going on here? Stop this nonsense, I say."

"No," she kept on saying, rolling into a ball like she'd just heard a terrible, tragic story.

My hunger, my intentions, they were all swept away by the images. I didn't like what I saw.

"There is no Blessed Circle or Circle of Bloods. It is all a farce. You were just thinking of me when you created them. Medea . . ."

She wasn't listening, and I was feeling incredibly uncomfortable. The god-soul was silent, the strange feelings had returned. I didn't want to see them, I didn't want to understand them. They were all wrong, she was wrong.

Mercifully, something broke the moment.

"Someone is coming into the temple," I mentioned, cocking my head, still frozen in my spot.

Medea unfolded herself and sat up. Her face, dirt-caked and teary, regained some semblance of composure.

"It's the Shaman!" she said, turning almost to my same pallor. "He's coming! There is another service tonight for the holy eve of the ceremony."

"What?" I asked. "You mean you're going—"

"Yes," she said in terror, shifting eyesight from idol to stairwell. "But not if he finds me here with you. I will lose my position and be punished."

"Punished?" I felt like I wasn't here.

"To death." She looked around, as if to find a hiding place for me or her.

"They'll slay you because they find you with me? Not if I decide otherwise."

She handed me a polluted look. "You cannot stop that, Byron, just as much as you cannot stop the ceremony."

I took a step back. "I must think matters overs. I won't stop you from copulating with that mummy."

"It must be done!" she snapped. "The blood must be passed. The line must be continued."

"What blood?" I could hear a group of people heading for the stairs. In a few seconds, she would be able to hear them walking down.

"The Blood Circles," she spat, starting to hyperventilate, holding the idol to her chest. "Blessed Circle, what have I done?"

"What have *we* done?" I said, not knowing why.

Any fear or concern vanished from her features when she saw it happen, saw something that should never happen with our species. Flesh compressed, size faltered, molecules struggled to other forms, and a *Ruka* darted under her legs to the back of the room.

When the door opened and light sifted in, Medea stood alone with the idols and I was burrowing my way out of the temple.

CHAPTER 6

I tried again to avoid anyone on the way to my cupola, but Crow appeared from nowhere with the usual goons at his side.

"Byron," he commanded. "Master Shibboleth wants you to call him as soon as possible."

"I'll do it later," I said tiredly, mixed feelings splashing inside me. I should have ended things, but somehow what I'd seen, what she'd told me hadn't given me any concrete answers on anything. I needed some time to ponder things, bring rationalization to events that made no sense.

That's why you spared her, I told myself. That's the only reason.

I felt like cringing.

"Do it now," he said, moving in front of me when I tried a little sidestepping. "Don't think your little stint at the Slaughterhouse hasn't reached The Elders' ears. He said it's important."

"And I said I'll do it later. Is everyone here deaf as well as blind?"

He grabbed me by the lapels of my jacket. "I don't think you understand what—"

"And I don't think you understood what I said," I said in a low, firm rumble.

Red foam pasted the corners of his mouth. "Listen, you disobedient—"

My hands sprung outwardly and struck each of his arms. He must have been very surprised—he never moved when I clutched his neck and raised him from the ground. I felt arms snaking around me, unable to stop me from slamming Crow into the wall.

The Raven shuddered; cracking veins spread where his body was imbedded. It takes a lot for a Stargazer to realize dangerous pain, but in any case only horror came from his bulging eyes.

"I think we're having a communication problem, Crow," I said, hands still attempting to pry me off him. Ignored. Voices drummed my senses. Ignored. "Get out of my way." I pushed harder, and he clenched his teeth when wires and tubes broke behind him. Mortar began falling from the ceiling.

"Damn you, Byron," he was barely able to say.

I dropped him then. He collapsed on the floor amid ruin. The two goons tried to fasten me down, but I shoved them away. Each skidded on the ground for about ten feet.

"That's the only thing I like about you, Crow," I told him, as he uselessly tried to get to his feet. I'd done some damage that would probably heal overnight. "You're blindly loyal to things and ideas."

"And you're not, fiend!" he gasped, eyes trickling mild crimson.

"You're right." I sighed and continued my path. Not ignored.

2

I didn't call Shib later. Or the next night. I stayed in my room with my dreams of *Sol* and burning cities and my species angry at me. I stayed in my room thinking of Medea performing her ceremony, more than likely close to an idol that had those features.

The following night, I simply stood in the middle of my chamber, trying to gain vitality from silence, hoping the silence would scrub all the thoughts and memories away. I didn't move at all. My voice didn't speak. I tried not to think. I wanted the silence, the inaction. My computer remained unanswered. Often I heard banging on my door, which I ignored. It was as if I wanted to turn back, start over. Clean slate, I craved.

But as soon as I felt crystalline in my identity, close to serenity, some thought would rush at me from the void like a predator. It was always a quote from a dream or Medea, Medea or a dream. By the end of the night, one sentence hung in my thought, blazing so clearly it almost gave me the sensation of my body warming.

You weren't always this way.

3

I saw her a few times the following weeks, but I wondered if she saw me. She looked older perhaps, as if carrying a burden, an acceptance that didn't allow too much pride. I spied on the parades and carnivals held for her all the way to the late-night hours. I wasn't exactly trying to hide, but I wasn't exactly trying to be a participator.

I knew, too, that the rest of the population wondered what had happened. They could see it in her serious demure, in the reason my presence was never too far away. Rumors fluttered to my ears, dark looks came across my path from both species.

She will be the end of us all. I hear she wants to befriend the monsters.

Never. Medea's soul is like a steel spike. She will take us farther than we've ever been.

But the monster, the one who follows us. I hear he is an avenging demon who will cut us down before the Revolution.

Don't be a fool! She destroyed the other, didn't she? She will destroy this one.

Clannad, eat your dinner, please!

She had performed the ceremony. With the aid of acolytes, they rolled around inside each other, under pretty lighting and droll music, crowd clapping, parts of their bodies painted and carved in holy symbols. Juices spilled that night, and Mephisto gave me an earful on the ritual.

"Fascinating if not repulsive, Byron," he told me. "But it keeps them content and docile. By the way, you really do need to call Shib. He's known as one of the more patient Elders, but I wouldn't tempt it. I hear he's under a lot of pressure to solve this situation. Our Mistress's tolerance isn't what it used to be."

I ignored him, and the Ravens ignored me. Most Stargazers ignored me, and to the Warm Ones I was a grim specter, following the new Shaman around The Farm. They made me angry. They were in my way. I wanted to send them all to Slaughterhouses, into the piercing machines that took away their hotness, and gamble in their faces and show them they were animals. I wanted everything gone. They were in my way. Everybody was in my way, telling me things, pointing me in different directions. I was a god . . . I was Byron . . . I . . .

I wanted answers that made sense. That would make me secure again.

Medea.

She was mine. She belonged to me. It made no sense, this attraction, for it was her words that more than bothered me, that made me insecure, unsure of myself.

I have never lied to you, Byron.

One night, as she sat on a straw throne, overlooking thousands of her subjects dance in a large square, I caught her gaze. She had been looking for me. She knew I was there.

Tortured gazes locking, we both forgot about the merriment and its buzzing noise, the viscous warmth never too far away.

Her jaw dropped, her lips formed words. I heard every one, as heavy as resignation, as solid as true light.

"I've been thinking about you," she mouthed, and only I would hear her.

I nodded, perched on top of the building right across from her, a hundred feet away.

"I've been thinking about you a lot."

I nodded again, because that's all I could do.

"I hate you."

I smiled and wondered if she could see it.

"I hate you because I realize who you might be. I hate you because I feel something for you."

I shrugged immensely.

"We have become contradictions, Byron—a fair, doubtful monster who is our savior, a Warm One who feels for all she despised. But it does not matter, for the revolution must begin, Byron. I have my duties, and so do you, but you haven't faced them yet."

I started laughing. In time, Medea, but they're not the duties you're thinking. In time, which is something I have an eternity of.

Heads turned, shouts blocked her voice.

Before I could do any more damage, I disappeared into the twilight, realizing that there was a larger chasm between us than ever before. She was the Shaman now, ensconced in her world, her side with her species, and my teetering was only causing me to lose myself. Her reality wasn't true, for I had shown her true reality of the Slaughterhouses, the voice of the hunter. She was so wrong, but I still couldn't help being drawn to her words that clouded my already stormy mind.

I decided that perhaps only one person could clear that stormy mind of mine.

4

Shibboleth's face crackled on the screen. Most Stargazers used modems and speakers to communicate. One of his stature could afford enough credits to show his holy face on the computer.

We spoke for a while. Mostly, I talked. His princely features absorbed my words with occasional nods or lip curls.

"The Blood of Circles," he said. "Very interesting. It all makes perfect sense now. I'm glad you finally decided to call. I thought I was going to have to bring you in shackles, Byron."

"What do you mean by very interesting?" I asked, not liking the knowledge swelling behind his ancient eyes.

He didn't answer immediately, as if contemplating what

exactly I should know. He seemed to look from side to side of his office, until the right answers came to him.

"Byron. This has to do with pre-Holocaust nights, with something most Stargazers don't know about and, Goddess help us, shouldn't."

"Well," I said. "You might as well tell me if I'm going to do something about it."

He laughed like a Stargazer did, full of snarling and sensuality. "Oh, you will, Byron. Don't worry about that."

"Will you stop this shit and tell me?" I asked angrily.

He stopped laughing and stared at me, eyes now full of cryptic humor. "Do you know why The Holocaust really came about?"

"If I did I wouldn't be here banging my head against your secrecy, Shib."

"Well, you know that once we were the minority, Byron, that we were hidden stalkers in a world swarmed, littered with Warm Ones and their artifacts."

"I've heard. Sounds scary."

He thought for another moment, reminiscing perhaps. A cigarette appeared in his hand. "It wasn't that bad. It was almost natural, I recall. Since the dawn of time, we reaped from the massive supply, hunting them out with tact and skill. The stupid ones got caught and sometimes destroyed. The smart ones became fodder for their overabundant imagination. That's the way it was, and I can actually say I miss it."

"So why The Holocaust, Shib?" I asked with more frustration than I wanted to show, than he wanted to see. "Why did Balkros infiltrate their military computers and pit different Warm One clan against the other until the land blazed?"

"Because we had to. Evolution changes things."

"Specifics, Shib. Keep to specifics."

He sighed and then spoke like a Warm One parent to his pup. "Byron, don't get too cocky with me, please. I actually have a fondness for you."

"I feel like I have nothing to lose," I said with a lopsided grin. "Specifics."

He shook his head slowly. "The world was changing back then. The land overflowed with pollution, the skies churned in black, the world's resources were strangled. In other words, the Warm Ones had pretty much abused their leadership of the world. They corrupted, they poisoned, they overran."

"And what does that have to do with us? What did we care? According to you, we still had plenty of food, and their little destruction couldn't affect us too much. We are gods, after all, right?"

"But they did."

"They did?"

"The Blood of Circles, Byron, or as we called it The Killer of Giants. That's what I'm getting at: Before The Holocaust, the Warm Ones had somehow tainted much of their juice with a strange malady. A disease that killed them, that wasted them to putrid husks."

I gulped, thinking of the Shaman, the new Shaman.

"And you know what? It was also lethal to us. Although we are unaffected by most of their material ailments, somehow the malady did the same to us as it did to them. Worse, Byron! It also drove us mad, sapped us of our power, like a curse to our god-soul. It was poison, akin to tiny shards of *Sol*, and this poison was in our food supplies. Perhaps some mad god had decided to punish them as well as us. It had happened before. We knew that soon, because of their ineptitude and arrogance, it would spread all over their population, and it was very hard to detect even with our senses."

"And you wouldn't allow it," I commented with certain awe.

"Oh, but we did," he said with humorless smile. "We have been known for our own hubris. In the continent once called Africa, over the swirling, boiling ocean, is where the malady came from. Our kind perished there in the masses. In the other continent, Asia, we were wiped out completely except for a few like Tsing-Tao. All the hunters really left were here, on this land."

I shuddered, trying to get the image of the circle, of the eight, of the Shaman out of my thoughts. To drink from dead waters . . .

"Thus, a group of us guided by The MoonQueen devised a plan, these nights called The Holocaust. You've heard the tales on how Balkros and the others did it. As they cultivated the seeds of destruction, the rest of us thought of new havens, new metropolises in a storm of destruction, where we might sprout supreme once and for all. It was the only way, Byron. We have paid dearly, the earth and *Luna* have paid dearly, but we will succeed because that is the path we were destined to take. It's our turn now, and one of these nights we will show creation that the harm we did was actually necessary for a harmonious world."

I was barely listening to his last sentences, trying to swallow his revelation, trying to come to grips with any answers in our future.

"The Shaman . . ."

"Yes, the Shaman, Byron," he said with concern. "Obviously, the animals in that Farm have kept the secret of The Killer of Giants from us, still passing the disease from generation to generation, waiting for the right time to hand it to us as a deadly morsel. It's partly our fault we didn't catch it, for most Stargazers should not know about this."

"Is that what killed Leztant?"

"No, Byron." I thought I heard a drop of fear in his voice. "I have a feeling I know now by what you've told me, but that's not something you should know. You have uncovered all that we need, Byron. Good work."

"Thanks," I said without much emotion. "Can I be dismissed?"

"One more thing," he said, and I screamed internally.

"What?"

"Kill them."

"What?"

"You heard me," he said. "Kill any possessor of the venomous juice. Don't cut flesh, but get creative. Throw them in the furnaces, break their bones. Go ahead and kill any immediate family or friends. Have Crow help you. Destroy their little square, their temple and leave nothing. Make sure you get rid of all of their little religious symbols."

I wasn't looking at the screen when he spoke. When I glanced up, he was grinning at me, knowing the little prank I was caught in.

"Kill them, Shib?" I stammered. "Isn't it too early to—"

"No, it isn't," he countered. "Those are my orders. I don't want to see any evidence of this disease. I want this wiped out from memory. It's crucial for security reasons."

"But—"

"What's the matter, Byron?" he asked with a sardonic tone. "Did you think that just because we spared you when you destroyed a Stargazer we would spare your pet for the same act? Are you getting a soft spot for the animal? Just like you had for Mephisto a long time ago."

By the top of his head, a little window appeared. I wanted to close my eyes, but the image held me. There I was, on fuzzy video, coming to the aid of Mephisto, both of us dressed in the stark Raven attire. At the time, Mephisto had his arm torn completely off, groaning in the dirt of some Warm One village. Before him, Dante, a mighty Stargazer, held his appendage in gleeful victory. Until I jumped him.

I don't really remember the reason . . . it was Mephisto, who back then was the one with the soft spot for the Warm Ones, who wanted to halt his superior's decision to exterminate a whole section for pure entertainment, back when the supplies were abundant.

Out of honor, I defended Meph, who was being made an

example by Dante, the closest friend I had back when the Ravens were much more regimented. I could have simply given an order. I could have simply stopped it all. But no, I let fury take me to flight and took the Stargazer in hand combat.

I was able to shut my eyes when we rolled in the air, smashing into huts and walls. I recalled the ghastly howling, the ripping of our bodies, the rising dust and debris.

I recalled a devastated block, groups of Ravens standing in a semicircle when things got too quiet underneath the rubble. And then me, coming out, alone, victorious, grunting like a territorial predator.

I placed a hand over my face, but Shib wasn't done.

"And that's not the only soft spot you have, I hear," he said, and I heard the image shift. I tensed when I beheld the figure of Tina being led out of Lilac's by a squadron of Ravens, fearful, perhaps ashamed. "You seem to break laws and traditions every time you get those 'soft spots.' We don't like them, Byron, we want a strong and loyal species. We don't want to make any more mistakes."

"Fuck you," I whispered.

He snorted drolly. "Kill the 'soft spot.' She's only a domesticated beast, Byron. I know, I know it's hard to terminate a sickly pet. I once owned thousands of Warm One slaves long before The Holocaust, and I actually grew an affection for a few. But the reality is that you've already hurt enough people, our civilization, the only one we have. There's still a chance to fully redeem yourself and those around you. Do it, and we will embrace you fully as one of our own. Don't, and the pain you cause you'll never even know because you won't be around to witness it."

"Fuck you," I repeated, but no sound came out from twitching lips.

"You have two nights and that's it," he said, and his face exploded in a rainbow of static.

I reached for my cigarette, but only a stump of filter remained, dead, burned out, with not much else to do.

CHAPTER 7

Dark wings bear me invisibly past the aroma of blood and stinking earth. None see me, none notice the shadow of destruction snaking through alleys and streets and fractured houses. I have a mission, a mission of cleansing, a mission to break the circle. I am a god, a hunter, and my killer awaits in its womb somewhere in a desolate temple.

Little animal with the large eyes of confident brown, can you see me, can you understand the dreams of those who might gaze at stars one of these nights, those driven by instincts too high to be understood? I have been caught between two worlds but I must choose one only, and that is the one I know.

All I must hear is your juice palpitating, your breath swelling body to life. That is all. That is enough. Then it will be over, and perhaps I can begin again with a cleared mind, leave this well of murky questions. Then I can be myself again, not what you see in me, not what everyone, even the stars see in me. I must touch you one final time. I must realize that Sol was never for me.

Little animal, don't hate me for what I must do . . .

2

Three figures were in the temple. Three figures never saw me come in. One was a pup of perhaps ten years with bright red hair and verdant eyes, watching the contents of some stew in a fireplace by the corner. One was a man in a bed surrounded by candles and icons, thin under thin sheets; he appeared so sickly he barely moved except for the myriad liquids gurgling from orifices. His skin was breaking like wet paper, orifices expunged liquid that was black like the thing called oil.

The third one was Medea, and that was enough description.

I thought about not making myself present, striking without further good-bye. Yet, that felt sort of unfair, not very honorable. Farewell was a rarity of Stargazers.

Besides that, the stench threw me way off guard. Now that I knew it was there, I could smell the killer, so alive and lethal in the Shaman's body, bubbling evilly, sapping his being to nothing more than a depleted scarecrow of sorts. It made me afraid. I'd truly learned that feeling right then.

I sniffed again. Medea smelled as supple as ever. No traces in her, although I knew it could be there. The Killer of Giants. A curse from some mad god who decided to pit one species against the other.

Medea tensed and Clannad turned, both sensing an intruder in this holy place.

"Byron," she said in surprise. My name felt so good on her breath. "What are you doing here?"

The Shaman lifted his head for a moment, yellow lips twitching in some mild curse. His head collapsed, chest heaved in wet sounds.

The pup stood up and ran to me. "Mr. Byron," he said quickly, as Medea left her master and also came to me. "Thank you for giving back my ball, I really think—"

"Clannad," she said, putting an arm on his shoulder and pushing him behind her. She didn't like what she saw in my expression.

"You're welcome," I said, thinking about the Slaughter-houses. *It's the least I could do.*

"Byron," she repeated, tilting her head. It struck me then that this had been the first time that we'd met that she didn't reach in to her pockets for the security of her religious icons.

"Medea," I said and added, "the new Shaman."

She nodded. "Yes, the new Shaman. Why are you here? This is a time of passing. I must attend to the last rites."

"Medea," I said, pointing to the former Shaman. "This disease, it is the Stargazer's bane. I cannot let it grow again in this time or we'll just go back to the beginning."

"It is a necessary thing," she said sharply, a sad, self-realization settling on her features. "All must come to pass. That which brings waste must also leave something born. Such is the way of the Circle."

"Yes, I know," I said mechanically, catching Clannad peering curiously from her side.

"I told you," she said, a lonely tear making a guest appearance, "that you cannot change that, Byron. It is destiny, and it is the way things are. And you are part of—"

"Medea," I said, almost patronizingly. "You can't believe in your heart that I can allow this thing to go on or that I could ever be part of this. I must protect my species. Don't you understand?"

Her tone veered to angrier crevices. "Understand what? That we are doomed to horrible deaths? That we are enslaved like food. At least *Rukas* have freedom, Byron."

"It's the way it is," I told the bald little thing with an empty tone.

"Why?" she questioned furiously. "It wasn't always that way."

"Yes, yes," I said, anger now challenging hers. I felt my

fangs surging from wet gums, my body tensing in anticipation. "Because we weren't always that way. Because you created us, right?"

"Right." She smiled in rebellious contempt. The tears still came. "And you do not have freedom, either, I see. I feel pity for you."

"Don't say that!" I screamed, and they both backed away. "I'm tired of your little games, Warm One. Just because we are dependent on your juice does not mean you created us, by definition—"

"NO!" she shouted back, still backing away from my twisting form. "It's not that, Byron. Why are you so blind when you see so much? Don't you understand?"

"Obviously not," I groaned, my body clutching like a spring ready to detonate upon them in one last encounter. It's time, the Dark Instinct ordered.

"Fine!" she hissed, ripping open her robe to give me a naked target. "Maybe I am wrong about you and our religion and destiny, maybe I am living a lie as well! Do it then, Byron! Do it so that you can continue as dead as I will be for the rest of eternity."

"What?" I halted my progress for a second. Something in her voice froze me. "Is this another little argument, Medea? I cannot die because I am not alive. I exist. I am more than life or death. I exist!"

She shook her head. "You don't understand—"

"I don't want to understand anymore."

"Exactly," Medea said with gritted teeth. "Because you can't face the truth, because you were once alive, Byron. *You were alive because you were once a Warm One!*"

I felt laughter somewhere. I felt mocking somewhere. I stood paralyzed, wondering if it came from me.

You weren't always this way.

"I was a Warm One?" My voice came out too thin for my own taste. Clannad kept backing away, but Medea stood like a pillar of trembling, boldness, and exposed breasts. "Is this some kind of joke—"

"Yes it is, Byron," she said quickly. "A joke we keep from your kind, a joke we only whisper about when you sleep in your graves. You were once a Warm One."

"I was not!" I said, gripped by an alien frustration.

"You and all the rest of the Stargazers," she said. "We were never separated. Don't you see the similarities? Haven't you ever wondered why your personality is such, why alien memories crawl to you from strange places like a half-remembered dream, forming your speech patterns, your mannerisms? The only difference is that you were cursed with eternal death. You are not real, you are husks of longing, walking corpses in the twilight."

"That's impossible," I said, placing a hand over my face. But in the dream, fire hurt me and I could barely carry people and other Stargazers were angry at me. Why? Why? It was just a dream! A corruption of profane *Sol*.

"It's been that way forever, Byron," Medea explained. "Somehow, your goddess created you from our blood. Somehow she made you undying in the shadows of life. You are no different, Byron. You're just one of us who died at her hand and was brought to eternal servitude." She broke into a deluge of sobbing, as if she didn't want to believe this about me, as if this untold truth had rested in denial's wings for far too long in both species.

"That's a lie," I said, glancing at my body. It was my body. A Stargazer body, with powers and passions no mortal being could attain.

Bloodshot eyes once again held me in thrall. Trembling lips made words, steady, sultry, so full . . . of life.

"I have never lied to you, Byron," Medea said. "I told you that once. I will never lie to you. I . . . also never wanted to hurt you—"

"You can't hurt me! Your words can't hurt me! Nothing you do can hurt me, animal!"

She cringed slightly, but continued with a trembling voice. "Don't say that. I feel, and so do you. You made me feel, Byron, not because of my religion and the idol, but because maybe I saw something . . . something good in you . . . something human."

"You lie," I said, trying to convince myself. "It's all lies. I was never a Warm One. I am a Stargazer, Medea. A Stargazer!"

She dropped her head. The Shaman coughed loudly in his little cot by the altar.

"Yes," she said sadly. "Yes, you are."

"I am a Stargazer. We are not alike."

She glanced away without much energy. "Yes, you are. That's why you were born fully grown and with that witty personality. You don't even recall being brought to this world."

I shrugged. "Neither do you."

We locked gazes. The argument was over.

"Clannad, leave the room," I said. "Please."

The boy stared at Medea, who only nodded and whispered a few words in his ears. He tried to clutch her skirt, but she shoved him toward the door. On the way out, he gave me a yearning look. I avoided it.

"Go ahead, Byron," she said softly. "I thought it would come to this. It was never my destiny to destroy you before you destroyed—"

"I am a Stargazer," I said and started walking.

She closed her eyes, chest heaving, hands clutching the sides of her robes.

I smelled her juices, her vitality, her warmth, which was mine, mine to fill my cold, my void . . .

But she didn't hear me strike. She didn't feel me strike. No, all she heard was the clean snapping of a spine, echoing with finality. Then she heard silence.

3

Once again, I returned to Commodore Station. The Den of Thieves.

I entered one of the cafeterias. Nobody dared my gaze. Mephisto stared at a bowl of juice, sounds settled to nothingness.

I sat by myself in a corner after ordering some food. I didn't want to eat, but my being shrieked in hunger.

Somebody shuffled toward me. I didn't lift my head until he stood by my table for almost a minute. It was Crow.

I ignored him, sipping the juice, the blood, slowly.

"Have . . ." He started and gulped. "Have you followed in your mission, Byron? I have to know, you know. Shibboleth."

I eyed him, and he seemed even more nervous. Yet he didn't see my usual look of arrogance this time. Lord Crow must have seen a certain comradeship in my expression, a certain admiration for him. If he only knew it was because I felt so close to one who was but a puppet of something, not even a mad god and his concoctions.

"I burned their holy place and destroyed Warm One being," I said. "I will carry out the rest in the next three nights. When it's done, it will all seem like . . ."

He didn't wait for an end to my faltering voice. "Good, because we just found out The MoonQueen desires her monthly feast, and she has chosen one from this farm."

"Memory," I finished after Crow had dissipated to smoke, getting everything ready for the important ordeal of feeding Our Mistress.

"Great," I said with a huge sigh. "She's hungry. I know what I'd like to feed her."

I sat alone for the remainder of the evening and then wandered to my chamber to prepare for *Moratoria*.

My computer off, doors locked, I sat in my own darkness

and trembled in a new rage. More answers led to more questions, more discovery led to more self-deprecation, more light showed more shadows, and I was stuck somewhere in the middle with my stormy mind. As usual.

I have never lied to you.

She was an animal, and that was it. I was a Stargazer and that was more than it. I existed. I existed to fulfill my purpose. I was atop of evolution. Our lust, our passion was higher than physical or emotional, it was tethered to joys unheard of, to passions that could only be held in the context of a god. No lies or desperate stories could change the reality Shib spoke of. Her species had simply diluted itself, once again. Not my people. Not my species.

You weren't always this way.

"Yes, I was," I said over and over again, crossing my arms with such force ribs cracked like hollow wood. But those wounds would heal easily in the context of a god. But the other wounds she seemed to have caused wouldn't that night, I knew.

4

She is blue and beautiful and ancient, wearing gowns of light, jewels of liquid energy.

Glory unto the highest, she says.

I try to reach for her in apology for the "what I'd like to feed her" remark, but I'm bound by chains of gold. I'm naked. I'm warm. I hear jeering from an invisible ocean of people.

Good job, Byron, she says, her voice the song of dusk, but you're cutting corners again, dearest of dearests.

I try to speak, but I never see her hand move, her steely nails slash my chest open so easily. It's not the pain that bothers me, that causes me to shriek. It's the juice flowing from my chest, from my warm, hairy chest!

She giggles and a mountaintop somewhere freezes forever. She licks part of me from her fingertips.

You did not finish your mission completely, Byron. Why?

I open my mouth, and this time she cuts my forehead. Blood blinds me, stinging makes me dizzy.

You killed the Shaman first and burned his place and his body, didn't you?

I don't answer this time, but she wounds my thighs anyway. Exposed tendons sweat more juice. Collapsing on the floor, I think I see something behind the goddess.

She voices something else, but an aching heat clogs my ears. More heat bayonets tender eyes.

Is that Sol behind her, ready to crush her, ready to burn away her icecaps of might?

No, you fool, that is the end of the dream. Remember, I will always find you because you are my favorite. Get the job done.

And suddenly a hundred Stargazers converge on me in a frenzy and once again I'm screaming until all that's left of my remains is my screaming, which will never end in the winter of her thoughts.

5

I shuddered into wakefulness. I had been floating in midair. I hit the ground with a heavy thump. What had woken me up? *Sol* again? Ready to punish me, teach me a lesson?

You weren't always this way.

It was a sound. A sound coming from my computer screen, a red pulsing in frequencies only a Stargazer could hear.

It was an alarm.

There was trouble in Commodore Station, The Farms, or both. The alarm never sounded unless it was of grave importance.

"Shit," I said, reaching for my clothes. "Just what I needed."

There wasn't any information on what was going on, except it was near the Slaughterhouses by one of the many balconies overlooking the cranes.

"Shit," I said again.

I dressed quickly and headed in that direction in mist form, ignoring my messy chamber and the juice I'd left behind on my bed and on the floor, dreading the fact I was probably crossing another forsaken threshold in my destiny.

But that was the existence of a Stargazer, and I was one, right?

Wasn't I?

Glory unto the highest.

CHAPTER 8

Silky, dark smoke marked the origin of the problem. It was no accident. Stepping onto one of the large, concrete verandas, I noticed the shattered skeleton of one of the cranes. It had obviously been transporting a cage of cargo upward to the Slaughterhouse when something damaged the engine.

"What is going on here?" I asked Mephisto through a flow of nervous Stargazers.

He looked up from his laptop, trying to concentrate through the flurry of communication coming from a headset perched on his thin head.

"Byron, that's what I'd like to ask you," he said. "Yes, yes, make sure all exits are sealed . . . including B-4. Crow will be descending in exactly three minutes."

"I don't know what is going on here," I said, observing through the smoke a crowd of Warm Ones awaiting at the bottom of the canyon. Not just a crowd but hundreds of them, possibly more. "I just woke up."

"Late start, uh?" He nervously punched in messages to his computer. "Seems you didn't uncover all of their weapons."

"Weapons? Shibboleth told me—"

"I don't know, Byron," he said, turning to the ledge. "No, don't pursue any action until all areas are secured, especially the laboratories."

"Damn it, Meph!" I exclaimed, grabbing him by the shirt. "Talk to me."

For the first time, he really looked at me, not enjoying the slight sense of fear he must have been experiencing. "I said I don't know. Somehow, as we were transporting the chosen one for Our Mistress, something nailed the crane just as it was rising."

I released him. "The chosen one? I thought that was in a few nights."

"It got advanced; I don't question Her motives, Byron. Anyway, I think right now it's more important to find out what did it and if this is a full-blown rebellion."

"Shit," I said, leaning over the railing. "I guess they decided one more life was just too much."

"I guess," Mephisto said, waving at some people hovering in the air. "You would think they would act with a little more judiciousness over one of their pups, but they're just animals."

The smoke was diluting, granting a better view a thousand yards outward. The crowd swelled over a semicircle at the rocky base. Separating the cage from the masses was also a semicircle of Ravens carrying flamethrowers, only used in dire need. Curiously, the only things the crowd had were their fists and the little idols of The Circle.

"Wait," I whispered. "Didn't I destroy the temple?"

"That's what I heard. No, I'm not talking to you. Do not—"

"Then, how . . . ?"

The cellar, you fool. The cellar. The icons. All things must come to pass.

"Hold on!" This time I grabbed Mephisto by the sleeve as he walked away. Visions swarmed me of Medea with her hand inside her robes, burned stone in a tunnel, the lack of fear in their eyes. "The idols! That's it! I can't believe it!"

"What are you talking about?"

"Their faith, somehow it gave them powers," I said in awe, recalling what Medea had told me.

He shook his head. "Did you just hear what you said? Are you saying those are their weapons? They don't have the technology. We don't have it!"

"You idiot," I snapped. "Their religion . . . the whole time . . . amazing . . . but why now? Why do they bring it out now?"

My voice evaporated when I noticed a red flash in the cage. The chosen one. He was a young one, a pup that would be fed to Our Mistress.

"Clannad?" I released Mephisto a second time, and a vision of the Mall and the dragged caged pounded my temples. "Jesus Christ!"

"Byron," Mephisto asked with new fear. "What did you just say?"

A city burns. I run. I wasn't always this way.

I furiously scanned the mob. Warm One after Warm One, each shouting, scoffing at the Ravens, some holding the idols, the idols, all so defiant.

Until my gaze stopped at the center of the semicircle, at the apex of who had led this crowd to a stand against their masters.

And then I recalled my last dream so vividly, most of all the words Our Mistress had imparted to me when pain and *Sol* were unbearable.

You let the slut live, didn't you?

My fingers traced my body, expecting wounds to appear from her ethereal talons. They weren't visible.

Sure, sure, Byron. After slaying the Shaman, you couldn't bring yourself to terminate her. You gave your pet the choice to leave forever or die that evening, to risk herself in the wilderness of poisoned atmosphere. How honorable of you. Did you think that act would satisfy me? Get me out of your heart, Byron? Get her out of your heart?

"Medea," I said and shut my eyes but the vision remained. There she was, solemnly holding her ground, face shut in determination. I should have known Medea wouldn't have chosen either of my options. I had never waited for an answer that night, busy razing the building while she ran outside weeping.

Why had The MoonQueen chosen Clannad? Part of her joke. Part of the joke.

Get the job done.

"Byron? Are you okay?" Mephisto's voice echoed in the distance of a thunder exploding inside me. All I noticed were the two species in the wilderness ready for conflict. Two species with similar traits and customs, who could communicate with the other when fear and hatred were ignored for a while. Two species divided by time and circumstance. Two species? The thunder increased. The answers that had always been there flashed before me like spiny lightning. The answers had been in my dreams, in my reality that wasn't reality. The MoonQueen herself had given me the clues, showing me as I was before I was baptized with the Dark Instinct. Everything had been so obvious.

I wasn't always this way.

And the only person who had never lied to me from the

start, who had actually cared for me and reached out to me was Medea. She wasn't an animal, she wasn't my pet.

She was my friend.

The storm broke, the tide shattered, and I found a large smile spreading across my dead features. You got it, Byron, dead features.

"I won't be part of the joke anymore." I turned to Mephisto, who gasped at the searing light from my eyes. The light of the hunter. But this light was full of relief.

"Byron, for Goddess's sakes, what—"

"Time to get serious," I said and took the laptop from his grasp.

I gave it back to him, but not like he'd wanted it. He barely saw the computer smash into his face, shattering in sparks and slicing shrapnel. Mephisto screamed, his tool lodged against his head in burning sizzles, and fell to his knees.

I heard shouts of dismay around me, but I was already flying down to the little melee about to happen.

2

At the same time I left the security of the station, Crow and several of his men also skated through the dirty air toward the semicircle. They had to, for I was wrong. There were more Warm Ones than a few hundred. The streets leading to town were saturated with them, coming out of their houses, leaving their sickly crop-fields. By the time I reached the ground, at least five thousand bloated the jagged area between the canyon and where The Farm commenced.

I couldn't see all of this, a veil of clean rage marring my senses. My head felt so lightheaded for I had not eaten, but there were things to do. I was Byron, The Stargazer, once a Warm One, and it was time to truly do the fair thing.

I landed between the two encroaching lines, between threats and ugly stares, between two species that were one and the same, each at a frontier of life's territory. More of my kind fell behind me, more of her kind filled the zone until they couldn't even move.

"STOP!" I shouted with such fervor that the noise levels dropped and hands were stayed. I raised my clawed arms to each side. "STOP NOW!"

"Byron," Medea shouted at me. "What are you doing here?"

I don't know, I thought, cringing at her sight.

Shouts boomed to my back. Ravens warned me to get out of the way. The wave of Warm Ones took a step forward.

"Get out of the way," Medea hissed, less than ten feet away. "For whatever we have shared, get out of the way."

I could still sense the pain in her eyes for what I'd done to her master and place of worship, I could sense the hatred from her people, and I could definitely feel the disdain from those of my species. The only logical thing to do was to get out of the way.

"NO!" I yelled. "THIS MADNESS ENDS NOW, I TELL YOU! WE CANNOT LET THIS HAPPEN!"

A brief silence suffocated the tension, but I could hear the gurgling of the flamethrowers, the rasping of shuffling feet.

"You're right, Byron," Medea said and others nodded. "We cannot let this happen. That is why we are here."

"Medea," I said in exasperation. "Please, you must—"

Another voice broke the discourse. A thousand gazes released me and wandered toward the cage, toward a floating figure holding a smaller one.

"It does end, tonight," Crow roared firmly, holding the squirming Clannad with one hand. His other one rested under the youngster's neck, nails ready to split open the soft skin. "But not how you want it."

The crowd gasped. Medea paled at the sight of Crow and his victim landing to my side.

"You want the pup?" he questioned harshly. "Then begin to retreat, or you will lose him."

"Crow . . ." I started, impressed at his tactical prowess. My arms dropped to my sides.

He winked at me with an odd look of fondness. "Do what you have to do, Byron. I'll do what I have to do. It's okay."

"Crow—"

"No," Medea said through gritted teeth, holding up her crude icon. Around her, the crowd started humming in prayer. I thought the sky shifted for a second to a lighter color.

"No, what?" Crow snarled, holding the weeping boy tighter, nails digging teasingly into the Adam's apple. "You heard me, animals. He'll perish, and we will leave you here to regret your foolish actions."

"We will not go, monster," she pressed. "You have no power over us. It ends now!"

"I won't barter with cattle," Crow spat, somehow less sure of himself. "I command you to retreat."

"No," she repeated sternly. Sparks started blushing the rough texture of the figurine. "You will let him go, or feel the wrath of The Blood of Circles, the Endless Cycle."

The veil collapsed. The god-soul warned me from the depths of my soul. "Crow, you don't understand, let go—"

"Never!" he said, taking a step toward her in the challenge, trying to speak over the rising communing that made Stargazers glance at one another in wonder. "I'm not going to say it again, bitch, go back or—"

His eyes, my eyes, everyone's eyes widened when the idol burst in wicked light. I was able to cover my face from the spectral illumination, from the acute heat, just after catching what happened to Crow.

Clannad acted as if he didn't see the energy, struggling in the Raven's arms until released. Crow, though, almost had a chance to scream when a pearly beam struck him in the face with scalding impunity.

The boy ran to Medea. Crow spasmed on his feet when more bolts cuffed him from other directions and collapsed on the ground in several pieces. Suddenly, all flamethrower spouts pointed at the female.

"No!" I shouted, a massive current of dreaded realization swelling within me like a cold explosion. For a second, Medea took her satisfied sight off Crow and touched me with her gaze. I wished then she could have understood my glare, my blazing thoughts. There was so much I wanted to say now, and we had just run out of time for dialogue.

The Blood of Circles had more than one weapon, didn't it? That night, when you invited me to the cellar, you had wanted to test your hidden power a second time, didn't you, concealed away by generations of fearful, beaten-down Shamans, and start the revolution because that's the kind of person you are. If Leztant's destruction didn't make your people believe, then mine would. It would bring the whole Farm to your cause. You wanted to destroy me, but couldn't do it, couldn't bring yourself to do it. You unconsciously recognized my face on the idol and part of you recognized my goodness. Then I took you to my world and you wanted to destroy it with one of the idols, show the world your power, become a martyr if need be, but I stopped you, Medea. Isn't that true? Isn't it?

The Warm One barrage abruptly destroyed the semicircle, as Stargazers in the sky settled on the crowd, rivers of flames bit the masses. At the same time, more beams from different directions, not as intense as Medea's, bit back.

I was able to strike a Raven who had his weapon pointed at Medea and Clannad. My fist sent him smacking against the cage several feet away. Bodies and sounds bouncing off me, I saw a Warm One pick up the flamethrower and begin dousing the sky and its hunters. Several of my people burst like midnight torches.

I turned to look for her, through the storm of fire and rays of faith striking random Stargazers.

"Medea!" I shouted, pushing frail Warm Ones to my side, many already singed or wearing broken bones from the assaulting Ravens who wanted to do things the old-fashioned way.

She ignored me, Clannad hiding between her legs. As she finished her prayer, another shard exploded from the icon, reaching upward until demolishing one of the balconies, right next to the one where Mephisto was probably still holding his face together. Stone and Stargazers blasted from a mushroom of dust and flame. It was all complete pandemonium, more smoke dirtying the already polluted air, the smell of boiling juice, the surprised last shouts of mutilated Stargazers.

"Medea!" I shouted again, and she heard me. No anger exuded from sooted features, only a certain gladness. I went for her.

"Byron," she shrieked pointing to my left, "watch out!"

I leaped to one side, just as a torrent of heat brushed my back. Clothes blazing, skin bubbling to wet pops, I rolled on the ground along with the agonized, fuming bodies of Warm Ones not so lucky.

Rising to my feet, I saw an angry Raven pointing his flamethrower at me for a second try. His foaming mouth spat curses of betrayal, his face was a mask of disgust.

"I don't think so," I said and flew in an arc toward him, barely missing another stream of bright gold, which this time melted my boots and more.

The Stargazer tried to recharge the bulky machine set on his back for a final strike, but I was quicker than any of them, than all of them.

One blow turned his head so severely his neck almost broke, not lethal to a Stargazer. The other sunk into the metal sphere holding the fuel, puncturing it immediately. I fell on my hands behind him and pushed with enough force to land on my feet several paces away. I tried to get farther, hobbling without some of my toes, which were burned off in the second attack.

My tactic worked. Dazed, the moron pointed the tube to his back hoping to hit me, but the baby blue flame caught on the leaking liquid with detonating effect.

The blast catapulted me backward, and once again I rolled with fighting Stargazer and Warm Ones. I heard bodies breaking against me, more shouts of resentment.

In this little pocket many in the area, the surviving Warm Ones from the explosion, and me scuttled away.

But Ravens jumped me while I admired the ground spin.

Punches, clawing, bites slashed me at all points. I wanted to call to Medea, but used all my ebbing strength to fight them off. You should have eaten, a thought informed from somewhere.

Somebody called me names. Somebody caved in my rib cage. Somebody got his eyes gouged out by my fingers. But every time our bodies shifted in the battling stew I lost ground, barely noticing the angry heat and cries of agony all around us.

Was that more praying to my right?

Another veil came before me, but this one of pitch nothingness. I was going down. They were taking me out. For some reason, my head escaped a wrapped arm that slid from my bloody sweat. I bit it hard, ripping muscle from bone, and something caught my eye. It was another damn semicircle, small in a haze of blackness where I was going. In the front, she stood with the idol.

I wanted to warn her about more Ravens collapsing on them from above, but a light of chaste white palpitated against us. Limbs released me, hatred turned to horror, and I fell completely into the unforgiving light.

3

There were no dreams this time, no voyages to possible pasts, only the aching realization I rested among other unmoving forms. A sea sounded somewhere. It wasn't a sea but the slow rhythm of flames. My swollen nostrils barely smelled vast juices in various temperatures. I opened one eye; the other was in the process of re-creating itself because someone had jammed a fang in it. His other one must have given everyone a nice view of my cranium, since the breeze hurt an exposed skull. Yellows and blacks coalesced in my senses, forming not much more than blurry yellows and blacks.

I sat up, shoving limbs and torsos away. Whoever had assaulted me had made a good shield from The Circle's power—I had survived and they surrounded me in sections.

I didn't have time to cope with my battered body, even now healing itself at a pace slowed because of my hunger. The view took all my attention.

Stretching to each side of the canyon, a massacre greeted me. Countless Warm Ones and Stargazers littered the whole land in pieces and in burned mounds. Ghastly bonfires lit the battle areas marking where dual powers had been used instead of physical methods. But the physical methods were there. Ravens had left a debauchery of disemboweled or shattered men and women in their wake. Dried blood spread against the walls of the canyons, the broken cage, the moist ground. It didn't matter, I could see, for Stargazer had befallen tragedy, injured by the Warm One magic or their flamethrowers brought against them. I could see paths in the carpet of death going toward the station, as those with enough energy had dragged themselves out of the fray, many times leaving appendages or innards behind.

In front of me, part of Commodore Station smoked silently in fractured portions. Several of the cranes, balconies, and metal doors leading to the Slaughterhouses or trains were all but molten shambles. Their faith had worked well. Even though the Warm Ones could not climb in masses to our haven, they had destroyed the gateways, crippling our operation for a long while; I could already see the price of juice rising. I noted no movement from the station. My kind had probably retreated to inner sections, waiting for aid or orders since much of our soldier corp had been exterminated.

Getting on my feet, I glanced back. The Warm One farm looked equally barren. Part of the fringes, some houses and vegetation, were singed, but that was about it. I could tell by the light of *Luna* my collapse had been about seven hours ago, maybe more.

"Sir," a meek voice said to my left side. I started and strained an eyeball. My damaged nose had not smelled him, my eye had missed the small figure skulking toward me.

"Clannad," I said, spitting out juice and parts of my stomach, feeling all too dizzy. "What . . . what are you doing here? What happened?"

"It all ended," he said full of sorrow, wobbly on his feet. "They retreated back to the canyon . . . we went back to our homes."

"Good," I said, starting to recollect. "Then it is all over."

"No," he sobbed, "they took her, sir."

"What!" I exclaimed.

Medea.

He placed his hands over his face. "They took her."

"Oh no." I felt gravity inviting me back. I collapsed on my knees. "Where? Why?"

"They took her, sir," was all he said.

I grabbed him by the arms, fingers barely able to flex. "Clannad, listen to me. I can help, but you have to tell me what happened. I know it was horrible, but you have to tell me."

He clamped his eyes briefly, stifling crying. He shook his head. I shook him.

"You must tell me," I said, "if I am to help."

"You will help us?" His timid eyes changed to growing awareness, to reality. "You will save the Shaman? She is all we really have."

"You have your faith," I said.

But I don't. I need her.

"Yes, sir," he said, suffocating any crying, handsome features brightening slightly. "That is why I'm not afraid. She is our Shaman. We must have her back or the circle might break for a long time."

"I know, Clannad. I know. Tell me what happened."

He spoke slowly, as if something else was bothering him. "When we were trying to save you . . . they came for us . . . a group of them. We got to you, but they attacked us . . . somebody knocked me down . . . somebody said . . ."

"Said what?" I asked with restrained impatience, trying to get to my feet, but finding it improbable.

"They said something," he stuttered. "They said, 'that's the one for her' and grabbed her . . . and took her up into the sky."

"The MoonQueen's feast," I groaned weakly.

Medea.

"You must help her, sir," he said. "Please. She is all I have, all we have."

"I can't make it," I confessed, shutting my eyes so as not to let more juice abandon me. "I'm too weak."

"You need . . ." Clannad paused, looking into the sky, perhaps just understanding it and what bothered him. "You need to feed."

"Yes, yes," I spat and allowed my ass to kiss the ground. "I'm too wasted. Shit!"

He sighed with the bravery of innocence. "Then you must eat in order to save our Shaman."

He looked into my eyes. I understood something. I wanted to scream.

"No!" I gasped. "Clannad. I can't . . ."

"You must, sir," he said. "Save her. I am not afraid. It's worth it for our kind."

"Don't say that," I whimpered. "I can't do it. It's just not right!"

"They will destroy her," he pressed, starting to weep again. "It will all be lost. You must do it, sir."

"No! I won't let it happen to you . . . it's just not right!"

"It is right," he whispered.

His gaze would not release me. He knew it. I knew it.

"I can't. Stop saying that. Stop talking."

Medea.

"You must, sir. The Shaman must return to us, so that the Liberator will come."

"Damn it," I said, trying to look away. "Why? Jesus Christ."

"Please, sir," he said plainly, "you must . . ."

I quickly placed a hand over his eyes. I let dark instinct try to take me to my true state.

"I can't," I said. *It's just not right.*

"Sir," Clannad mouthed. "I won't hate you for this."

Medea.

"Don't call me sir," I croaked, and went for his small throat.

Feed, hunter.

I tried to do it as quickly as I could. His small body struggled for a while. I made sure my hand kept his lids closed and the other went over his mouth.

Energy filled me, once such delicious vitality. Now it seemed putrid, unholy, like a necessary narcotic lower forms of life fell into. As my body healed, the god-soul churned with power. I needed more. I found myself ripping his body open, gulping the last drops of tepid juice I could find in any pulpy crevice. I lost myself in the feeding.

You weren't always this way.

When it was done, I walked away from the remains of Clannad and folded into a ball on an empty spot in the carnage. I sobbed uncontrollably. Sorrow shifted to other shades. A pure anger replaced it.

On my feet once again, I glared at the station, at what lay beyond it, and screamed over and over again.

"Damn you, damn you, damn you!"

And as I flew high above the ground, into the venomous air and the lying light of *Luna*, the same phrase pulsed on my curled lips. At full speed, a bird of doom, I flew toward my birthplace, toward the cradle of my quest, arms outreaching to the uncaring heavens.

"Damn you, damn you, damn you!"

And I didn't know who I was screaming to, who I despised so much then. All I knew is that Xanadu came to view in the misty distance, and that was my destination.

Damn you, damn you, damn you!

CHAPTER 9

If my old superior was surprised, he didn't show an ounce of it. The smashing of his expensive glass, the eerie creature standing on his desk, skin of effulgent pink from radiation, mangled body only received a droll look from his angelic countenance.

"Shib," I said, crouching.

"Byron," he said, brushing off shards of glass, many embedded on his shoulder. "Did you really fly all the way here?"

"What do you think?" I grabbed him by the robe and lifted him up. His head hammered against the chitinous roof, slightly cracking it.

He laughed seminervously in my grasp. "We expected you later."

I pulled him closer to my face. An alarm sounded somewhere in the distance. "You did? So the whole thing was a setup, a little game?"

Shibboleth's oval eyes narrowed. "Nothing has changed since the beginning of the mission, Byron, only you."

"Where's Medea?"

"You know where the thing is, little traitor," he said with a thin smile.

"Fucker," I said, throwing him in the corner into a glass table. He got on his feet quickly, the silver rose and robe slashed even more.

"Byron," he said angrily, pointing a finger at me. "I don't think you know who I am and how much trouble you are in for just doing this to me."

"I'm in enough trouble as it is, thank you very much," I said, trying to think where The MoonQueen's cupola rested. All the way to the top, a few more hundred feet, where no Stargazer treaded.

"You fool," he said, "do you know the power an Elder has? I haven't battled in centuries, but I haven't lost my might."

"I'm really scared." I leered at him, wishing I had time to challenge his boasts. He probably did have more than the average brawn of a Stargazer, but I was in the mood for some quick retribution. "Maybe another time, Shib. I have to go."

Footsteps thundered down the hall.

"Do you know what you're doing, Byron?" he asked, as much care as he could muster in his tone.

I looked down at my bedraggled body, lacerated, toe stumps already growing, so full of bogus life.

"Do you know that you're dead, Shib? That your existence is stolen and fake, just like all of this?"

He opened his mouth, as if surprised. Maybe he was. Maybe he was just surprised I knew or just believed.

"I thought you did," I said and took to the air just as the door shattered and Ravens swarmed in.

Once again, I rose into the pollution, into the thick atmosphere, this time to the tip of the gigantic cupolae of emerald, marked in frosty white, where I was to meet Our Lady in the flesh for the first time since given existence as a Stargazer.

2

I scanned the blurry glass for a random strike of entry before the hot toxins beating my hide took me down for good. I shouldn't have been surprised to see an open window. Either The MoonQueen enjoyed a little radiation before *Moratoria*, or I was right about the whole thing being an elaborate trap. What else could it have been?

I also shouldn't have been too surprised to see Tina's severed head hanging from a thread on the doorway as a grim welcome amid melting icicles. Her expression held no contempt for me, my heart did enough of that.

"Shit," I said, snapping the line and letting the head roll down the arched slope. "DAMN YOU!"

I walked in. The window mechanically slid shut. It appeared I was alone in a desolate kingdom of ice—all ice, shaven on the ground, in intricate statuettes marking narrow paths, in large blocks and detailed bridges over frozen streams creating a sort of maze under bluish lighting. I shivered, not because of the low temperatures in her abode. There was a sadness here, trapped in the artwork, screaming from the frigid water, in the creamy air. This was her domain, all cold-ness except for a few sealed computers and consoles and cameras perched at the top of the small dome.

I didn't want to fly. I didn't want to look like an easy target. Instead, also not to appear as too much of an intruder, I took one of the paths and followed its slender contours. More statues of people and animals I'd never seen before, creatures from pre-Holocaust nights, Warm Ones Our Mistress might have prowled in simpler times. More shaven ice. A tinkling music played from unknown sources. This was her domain.

Clouds must have shifted outside, for *Luna*'s streaks entered the glass and clipped the ice, gorging the whole area in a magical, almost callow texture. I was awed at the pale azures and dreamy whites glowing from everywhere, at the true glittering expertise of the craft here, at the pure, beautiful loneliness of this place, only shared by *Luna* and her, Our Mistress.

At the same time, I heard a breathing, a Warm One breathing. Very faint. Too faint.

"Medea," I said, and my voice echoed in the distance. No answer. The breathing was failing.

"Medea!" I shouted and ran, slipping here and there, almost falling a couple times in one of the static fountains. I didn't care. I had to get there.

About twenty feet away, I came to my senses and turned to mist. I fluttered toward the right direction, but found it hard to move in these conditions. The Queen of Darkness had made sure that in her home even gaseous form would be an easy target.

Passing statue and block, I saw my friend lying on a bed of the pruned substance The Elders called snow in another age. But this snow wasn't white, it wasn't clean. Part of it was stained in red, in juice, in blood. Medea's blood.

"Medea," I shouted and materialized to hold her that one last time.

She quivered in my arms, opening eyes devoid of most vision. Medea tilted her head toward me, making me wail at the sight of the two punctures on her neck, the traditional Stargazer method of feeding.

"Byron," she said without energy, managing a small smile. "You came."

"You knew I would," I said softly, stroking her cheek, kissing her hairless head.

"She . . ." Medea started, a flicker of fear in her large eyes. "I think I'm dying."

I swallowed hard, trying not to shake too hard in anger so as not to harm her.

"I can't believe they did this to you," was all I could muster.

"Yes, you can." I wanted to turn my head to not see her skin slowly turning the color of the winter around us, to not smell her dwindling reserves.

"Oh, Medea," I said through a clenched jaw. "I'm so sorry."

She shook her head feebly. "Don't, because you taught me to hate you so much."

I smiled. "I can't let you go."

Her expression grew serious, and another dying wisdom was about to rock me again.

"You don't have to, Byron."

"Medea?"

She held my face gently. "Byron." She paused, a small rivulet of her juice creeping out from the corner her mouth. "We created you, and you can create me."

"What?" I shuddered, but somehow knew she spoke the truth, somehow one of those repressed intuitions of mine agreed with her.

"I'm dying." She blinked at me, and I knew she couldn't see me anymore. "You can grant me life . . . existence."

"Medea, no!" As I held her hands, I could feel her growing still in my lap. "How can you say this?"

"Byron . . . I don't want to be without you. Sometimes, a feeling, a hope to share with someone, can transcend all sanity, all duty . . . I don't want to be without you."

"And I don't want to be without you," I whispered.

"Then . . ."

Suddenly she had no voice, for there was no life to transmit it, no breathing to carry its message. Nothing.

"Medea? Medea?"

Don't leave me! What do I do, Shaman? What do I do?

You weren't always this way, her voice spoke, turning a corner.

"NOOOOO!" I cried, but found myself biting her neck, exactly where Our Mistress had pricked her.

There was very little juice, but somehow, that's not what I wanted. In a complete paradox, I wanted to give her something. What? What?

But the answer lingered there. Not my emotions for her exactly, not my own purloined juice, but part of me, part of my essence, the god-soul, the Dark Instinct. It awoke from within me like never before, like *it* knew it was time to procreate instead of hunt, fuel my body with power and make another exist in its wicked dream. I could almost feel it blooming within me, an explosion that knew no boundaries. Like a cascade of cold flame, something siphoned out of me and into her being, almost gone except for a few sparks of fighting life.

I don't know how long it took, but it drained me as much as it gave me a new perspective. Through the ceremony, a black guilt slammed my senses, spreading like a frigid sliver across my belly.

I don't want to be without you.

My friend . . .

When it was done, I placed her on her bed. The Shaman did not move. Had it worked? Did the transformation need *Luna*'s christening and *Sol*'s curse before it came full circle?

"Medea," I said, wanting to savor her warmth one more time, knowing that would never happen, either way.

A storm of sorrow rose from the basin of my throat, ready to expel into the milky air, but before that could occur, a giggling behind me stopped it.

I pivoted. She was there. She had been there the whole time. Now she made herself present in her kingdom of frost.

Yes, she was blue and beautiful and ancient, wearing gowns of light, jewels of liquid energy. They were real this time, as real as I could understand. She was real, she was reality, towering above me, surrounded by clouds of dusty ice, a morning star of forbidden desires, Our Mistress, The Moon-Queen. She did not quote any dream sequence, she did not speak through cerebral invasions or celestial gatherings in a stadium. No, her gorgeous, metallic lips spoke with the almost timid voice of a young maiden, hiding little of her sardonic demure, her old sharpness.

"Bravo," The MoonQueen said, regarding me through cobalt eyes. "Bravissimo! *C'est magnifique, Mon Cheri.* You have done it!"

I tried to escape the deity's glamour, the hypnotic, astral gauze of her being. I pictured Medea and the war I had just arrived from.

"I have done it?" I questioned. "I have done it? That's all? All of this was some field study to you? To see me betray my species and uncover the Warm One's plans, to witness another Stargazer cursed with your Dark Instinct?"

She clapped her hands and held them in delight, eyes shifting to cloudy indigo. "Byron, Byron, Byron, sweetest of my offsprings. You don't understand, do you?"

"Unless somebody tells me and stops asking me that, not really." She hovered closer to me. I had to hide my eyes from the brilliance.

"I am old," she said, her voice a cutting gale. "Older than you know. A hundred times your life span is but a short dusk

to me. When civilization was young, I was already menstruating worlds. I have been here since the beginning of time,
Byron. My motives and those of the other Giants are perhaps
beyond you, but I wonder sometimes."

"What motives?" I asked, resentment bubbling like a
geyser. "The Holocaust, this little civilization in the wastes?"

She nodded. "Everything, Dearest. You could say it was a
little experiment, a little move of the pieces in creation's chess
game, if you know what that is. We existed well before,
Byron, but a change had to occur. I grew bored, little child,
and boredom is the death of gods. Maybe it was just my destiny."

"Well, I'm glad I could be of service," I said sarcastically,
lowering my head. I felt so tired, all of a sudden.

"But you were." I could feel her resonant, silky speech in
my head, her breath all over my skin. "You always have been.
Now, I know the extent of the Warm Ones' powers, faith
which only grew stronger after we enslaved them. Such a pity.
I preferred crosses and ankhs than this malignancy that not
only hurts us but our handiwork. But adjustments must always be made, and I owe it all to you, Dearest."

"You disgust me." I tried to match her gaze, but found phenomena obfuscating.

She tilted her head. "Careful, *Mon Cheri*. I created you, not
the Warm Ones."

"You did, all right," I barked. "You gave me such a great
ride, Mistress. Thanks for the sham. I'll leave the puppet
strings on the way out."

Her tone seemed genuinely honest, but I knew honesty or
truth were also playthings to this being. "But you weren't a
puppet, Byron. You're still my greatest one, my favorite. I
wouldn't have allowed you to attempt creation if I didn't
adore you."

"So what was I before? What was I when I lived and

breathed normally?" I asked. Hollowness filled me instead of anticipation.

She smiled, revealing perfect fangs, glowing, almost translucent. "Don't you remember your dreams?"

I opened my mouth. Yes, I do, a voice told me.

"Of course you do," she said, "and you must have known I can enter any Stargazer's mind, for I give them immortality. You must have known."

"Damn you." I looked away, more tears leaving me in heavy globs.

"Your dreams, Byron, what do they tell you?" I felt her hand on my face, forcing me to watch her.

"A city," I said in stutters. "Burning. I'm a Warm One. People, trying to save people. Stargazers angry at me."

"They should have been," she whispered, and it cut my insides. "After all, you caused the destruction of Utopia."

I wanted to exclaim, but found words lodged in my chest, found perception spinning in a whirlwind.

"Yes, Sweetest," she hissed, and rivers of glowing mist came from her. "Byron, leader of the rebellion, exploiter of the Stargazers with doubts, the one who played the same trick on us that we did during The Holocaust, causing the city to burn to naught."

Visions fluttered before, the city . . . fire . . . me this time standing at the apex of various semicircles, including the one where I was to be judged.

"Yes, yes, Dearest," she said, tilting her head to cackle at *Luna*, who stood high, ready in her descent to the horizon. "You were so full of passion and lust for what you believed. When we captured you in the ruins, how could I have accepted The Elders' judgment? How could I have let them destroy you? You were too valuable, and I had to make you mine!"

"That was punishment enough," I croaked, recalling a family I must have had, a lover, friends, a little girl with curious eyes and the same hair color as Clannad . . . all gone . . . through the fire . . . through the desire of freedom not unlike Medea's . . . trapped in ice by the sighs of The MoonQueen.

"It wasn't punishment," she cooed, for the first time showing any real emotion. "It was a reward, Byron, my sweet. You were to be the shadowy phoenix of what you once were, a valiant paladin for my cause, and I have watched you closely since your renaissance."

"I'm nothing," I whispered, knees scraping against the sharpness of the ground.

"No, you are something," she said and started snickering insanely, orbs bloating in lurid energy. "Look around Xanadu. Did you think I would make the same mistake and create Stargazers of great ability again, so that they might grasp mortal feelings or philosophize their way to doom a second time? Haven't you ever wondered, Byron? Haven't you ever looked around and thought why I had chosen mediocrity as the best way to create continuum?"

"Hey," I said, wiping my face, feeling then very, very awake. "It's your little experiment. Your little game."

"Call it survival, Byron," she said. "Call it something I've had to do for a long time, a demon in a universe of beauty and grace, much like you, with no choice of who I was. The joke was also played on me."

I rose to my feet. "So you decided to play one on creation."

The MoonQueen shrugged, toying with one of her curls of billowy-white. "Perhaps, my sweet. Perhaps. I reminisce much, Byron, I dream of happy and sad times, I can actually relive them if I feel like it. But I never look back. Time is not my keeper, and neither should it be yours."

"I don't like you," I said plainly.

She only smiled, and I thought my pupils might burn away right then.

"What next, Mistress?" I inquired. "What's next on the agenda?"

The MoonQueen pursed her lips for an infinite moment. "You know what is next, *Mon Cheri*."

"The choice is mine."

"It always has been. Haven't you learned?"

"No, I guess not. Call me stubborn, Mistress. I still don't like you."

"What is your choice?" she asked sharply. "I am your mother and I cherish you, Byron. To be by my side is eternal delirium. Every ruler needs a steward, a gallant champion, and I realize now that it can only be you."

I looked out to the wilderness, to *Luna*'s honeyed aura, beyond all this cold and stagnation. I thought of Medea, and the rest was easy.

The MoonQueen growled at me when she saw the answer on my face. The breeze rose. Temperatures died more. A storm blew inside her domain.

"Fuck you," I said, and snow covered me.

3

I think I put up a fight. Not much of one; it all happened too quickly. Even if my body hadn't been mutilated and bloated in radiation, even if exhaustion didn't nag at me from every pore, I still shouldn't have pitted my strength against her might. Medea might have been embarrassed that the savior of her species from the idols didn't meet the legend's expectations. The MoonQueen smote me down with little effort, and suddenly we soared into the night haze.

There I was, inside a radiant comet of scintillating colors, darting high into the violent clouds, traveling far away from the city of Xanadu. She held me with a grip that couldn't have been broken by a thousand blows of a hammer, she took me to an unknown and final location.

This was the end, and I was a Heretic in my finality. If I was lucky. I couldn't do a damn thing about it, and maybe I just didn't care. Little came to me except the palpitating light of her being and the memory of people I couldn't place anymore.

We must have hit incredible speeds, we must have sojourned far. I don't know why. I just knew. I didn't care. The only thing breaking the fury was her voice, so clear, pretty. Gloating, too.

"If it's any consolation, Sweetest, a wise person once said it's the journey, not the destination that matters."

We descended, rocketing toward what I could discern to be endless sand dunes of rusty hues. I knew the night was ending. I knew everything was ending.

"Jesus wept. I preferred to laugh. And that to this night has made all the difference."

The MoonQueen held me out steadily, right after holding me close to her bosom in a bone-crunching, last embrace.

"Good-bye, *Mon Cheri*," she roared through the maelstrom around us. "Always remember me in your dreams. ALWAYS!"

Then she released me, no, threw me like a projectile. The direction pointed downward.

I came to myself, just briefly, just slightly. It was temporary, though, for the impact sent me reeling to an almost complete darkness, to an endless *Moratoria*. I slammed into the packed sand and sank and sank several feet under. The only few things inside me not broken finally gave away.

Then there was nothing, except that fading light down an annoying tunnel and the whisper of a distant, remorseful wind, here in the wilderness.

BOOK II: HERETIC

CHAPTER 10

The little girl with the curls of crimson, freckles of sallow orange, sits on my lap.

"Daddy, Daddy," she says with excitement. "Roshanon Tower is burning. I can see it out the window."

"It is?" I ask, pretending surprise.

"Yes, yes it is." She points out to the opened window. We should close it soon, since they've lowered the ozone levels all over the city in order to subdue us. Even now, I can see little welts appearing on her thin neck, fatigue setting in too early in the evening.

"Don't worry." I hug her. "The fire won't get here. Roshanon Tower is by the river, far away, practically in Stargazer territory. We'll be fine."

"We will?" She puts tiny hands on my grizzled face. "What is territory? Can we go see it?"

I laugh and hold her again. "No, you don't want to get your dress singed, Darling. It's not our problem."

"Singed, what is that?" she questions earnestly, still trying to understand the large world her senses give her every day. She'll be six in a few months, in March, as my father used to call that month.

I almost answer, but the other female in the house peers her head through a doorway. I hadn't heard her footsteps on the hardwood or even the sizzling coming out in acute aromas.

"Byron," a woman says, hair of the same color as the little girl's, plush lips and a noble chin. I can remember the generous body hiding from my sight.

But I can't recall her name. Their names.

"Byron," she says again. "Dinner will be ready in a few minutes. Do you have time to eat with—"

"Are we having beans again?" the child asks, making a smelly face.

"Don't interrupt your mother . . ." What is her name?

"Well, dear?" the woman questions.

I sigh. "I don't know. I have a meeting with them. They might be coming here. I'm supposed to get a message on my mailbox."

The woman frowns, in full view as she walks out of the kitchen. "You're letting them come here?"

I nod and don't know why I'm saying these things. "I have to if necessary. Times are getting tense. We're almost there—"

"But here, Byron? Please—"

"Are the monsters coming?" the girl interrupts again, jostling in my arms.

"No monsters, dear," I say and look directly at the woman. "We can talk about this later, after . . . she's gone to bed."

The woman glances away. Her shirt is buttoned low, slight perspiration on her upper chest. She wipes her hands with a towel.

"I'm sorry, Byron. You know how on our toes we've been lately . . . how living gets harder with all these cuts—"

"It's okay," I say, raising the girl in the air. She's getting heavy. She giggles playfully. I never want to let her go. "Do you ever get that feeling you're in a dream?"

"What?" I hear her voice.

"What, Daddy?" The child wiggles in the air.

"That you're not here. That reality appears a little too thin."

"Silly, Daddy," the girl says, trying to get down.

I look at the woman. She's back. She snorts. "I don't know, Byron. It seems you've been somewhere else lately. You've always been somewhere else. But we understand the pressure."

Before she walks back into the kitchen, she stops to say another thing, just as now the kid and me are mock-wrestling on the floor.

"Byron," she says.

"Yes," I sing, trying to pin my daughter down to tickle her.

"You're a good man."

A man.

Man.

Thanks, I don't say, not being able to move from my grave.

2

No movement. Except a distant roar, like the sea's, like a bonfire in some canyon. It was the deep wind, far away.

No movement. Blotches of amber. Gritty sensation in my mouth, my throat. A plucking heat kept on reaching me in waves.

And I wondered why I craved black beans.

Black beans?

No movement.

More waves of heat and sound clip me. I was rising one more time, but how could I?

No movement.

And I rose up the well of oblivions.

3

The doorbell rings. I'm surprised it still works. Nothing seems to work in Old Town, where we all live.

My daughter is asleep. My wife, who was reading a book falling to shreds, stands up quietly and goes into the bedroom. I open the door. I'm glad they didn't come in through the window or something.

It's him, shorter than me, brown hair, and the skin of a wraith. With him are two more of his kind. All three are dressed in black and have cloaks. All three nod.

"Evening," I say. "Come in. Make yourselves at home."

The one in the center, my "friend," enters with a greeting, followed by his companions. I see it, though, slight flinching of their nostrils. They smell it all, who's here, who lays in the dark.

"I'm sorry about the time, Solsbury," he says. He always calls me by my last name. "But you can understand the importance."

"Have a seat," I say, motioning for the sparse furniture. They're polite, they sit. "I wish I could offer you something," I add with a dry chuckle. What are their names?

"No, thank you," he says, and the others grunt.

"I didn't think so," I say, still on my feet. "Which always makes me wonder . . ."

"Wonder what, Solsbury?" he challenges, folding his hands.

"Why the allegiance?" I ask with a steady grin.

He grins back. "That's why I like you, Solsbury. Direct to the point in the most blunt ways. A true mark of a warlord."

"Thanks," I say, "but it's a valid point."

I take out a pack and offer each one of the contents. They decline in stiff waves, I burn it up. I'm not supposed to smoke in the project, but I think my wife will understand. I'm sure she's listening to it all.

"It is a very valid point," he says. "Why fight for the truce, when we can hunt you so freely every night? We rule you, and our territories are marked by the Arkansas River, which I hope will be renamed soon. We can cross it every night, while you have no bridges over the toxic waters even if you could fight us."

"Tell me something I don't know." I walk to the window and look out, as if expecting to see a spy or something.

"Things are changing so quickly," he continues. "Our kind has been able to cross the land in search of pockets of weaker radiation. Newer, better cities than Utopia are sprouting left and right, in the mountains where valleys and canyons can block the fallout, in the coasts where the shore has cleaned up some of the mess. Lost people of our kind are finding us, we are ensnaring more of your kind across the country.

"Things are changing and have changed, Solsbury, and sometimes rapid change makes one wonder and reflect to great depths."

I snort with a raised eyebrow. "I still can't believe your nature has changed. You're killers just as we—what's the new term on the streets: Warm Ones—are killers. Can you really fight your cravings? Can you really not hate what you were once, what you still desire to be?"

I see the shocked expressions on his companions. Yet he doesn't falter. He enjoys our little discussions.

"Maybe you're right," he says with a halfsmile. "But your kind will not last forever if we continue reaping you. Your clan is lucky because they live on the west end and have good fighting skills. But by the river, the neighborhoods are drained and we must feed farther and farther."

"I can take care of myself," I say, but I'm sure they don't believe me.

"That's not the point. The point is that rationing your juice would be very wise. There are two arguments, besides all the other moral ones: One says we can decree you to give a certain amount of your juice every night, have it shipped to our land."

"And the other?" I ask, seeing if the rumors are true.

He doesn't answer just yet, looking for something in his henchmen's eyes.

"The other?" I repeat. What was his name?

"The other, Solsbury"—he stares at me in wavers—"is that we round you all up and set you in concentration camps, breed you, raise you, and slaughter you. That's what The Elders are pushing for."

"Are you?"

He shrugs. "Both methods have merit. The former one is more . . . uh . . ."

"Humane." I finish his sentence with an arid smile.

"Yes, humane," he says slowly, not understanding the word at first. "We're working on it, bear with us."

"But you must stop the rebellion," one of them says for the first time.

"The rebellion?" I echo.

"You know what I'm talking about," he presses. "Do you think we're blind? We know, Byron Solsbury, that you're one of the main leaders of the terrorism, maybe even the head itself. Your little attacks during the day do nothing but anger The Elders."

"Don't know what you're talking about," I say nonchalantly. "And even if I did, do you think we're going to sit here and let you guys feed on us and turn us into walking dead?"

"He's a hothead, Proxos," the third one says, talking to the leader. "We should have dealt with somebody else."

"Quiet," Proxos orders. That is his name. "We will deal with whomever I wish. Do you understand?"

They obey by their ensuing silence. He's still looking at me.

"So, do we have a deal, Solsbury?" he asks sternly. "Roshanon Tower was our main outpost in your territory. Detonating by remote control, something we didn't know you had mastered, when it was in operation was cute. It has put us on our toes."

"Join the club."

"Do we have a deal?"

I cross my arms. "I'll see what I can do."

"No," he hisses. "We must know, right now. Things are delicate, but we want things to flow even if it's for practicality."

"You're dead, Proxos," I say flatly, and the two glare at me. "You have no place on this world."

He forces one laugh. "And you will be dead soon, but won't be around to see it, Solsbury, if you don't watch your step. The world has changed. We need your species to live and we will live, too. Don't make me spout some of the nonsense we've been writing lately. I need to know."

I throw my smoke on the dirty floor and stamp it with force. I keep gyrating my foot on the filter, letting anticipation hang in the air.

"All right," I say, not glancing up. "You've got a deal, Elder. Do your work, gentlemen, and we won't get in the way."

"Thank you, Solsbury," he says and stands up.

"You're welcome," I say with a strange expression, "Proxos Commodore."

4

I recalled his name.

No movement.

Bones hadn't knitted together. Skin was still falling in dried flakes. I came in and out of delirium, only hearing the wind, the minute shift in the hot dunes.

No movement.

Brain spasms in the last flickers of light. But I was dead. I was dead twice.

No movement.

I recalled his name.

5

I leave her after a while. They themselves had left through the windows this time, roaring into the twilight, and I went into the bedroom. She sobbed in my arms, fearful of them, of what might happen. I tell her there are too few choices anymore. This is a different world. We make love. We try to understand creation. She sleeps, and I go to make a call.

In front of my screen, I dial a secret-access number, knowing they've bugged almost every line for those few lucky ones with computers. I'm sure they all must know I'm partially behind all of this, but they're cocky and Utopia can be a confusing place.

A husky voice greets me on the speaker. I greet it back.

"Can't believe you let those pricks in your house," she says. "Wouldn't let them near my lover, or children if I decided to go straight."

"That's nice, Wendy," I say, placing another cigarette on my dry lips. "Send me a videotape sometime."

"I'd love to, Byron. So, what's the deal?"

"What deal?"

"You're obviously alive, so there must have been a deal. Are we with them or what?"

"Oh, that deal."

"Yes, that fucking deal. What's going on? I've got bombs all over the fucking city. I got my demolition crew ready to flatten the sky."

"No deal. That's the deal."

"You mean, we don't have a deal with them or you don't want me to carry the operation."

"Yes, Wendy," I say, rubbing my eyes.

"So what do you want to do? Invite them all over for tea next Sunday?"

"No, babe. We go all the way."

"You're kidding," her voice booms in enthusiasm. "You wanna do it? Carry out your father's plan?"

"He didn't die in vain, Wendy. Nobody will when it's all over."

"That a boy, Byron. The tunnel's ready. We've checked. We got the ammo. We got—"

"I know, I know," I interrupt, not feeling so exhilarated as her, hearing my daughter softly snore down the hall. Her sinuses have been plugged up since the bastards decreed more filth should pass the Ozone Fields to weaken our collective state. "But I'll wonder if all the bunks will work when the shit falls all over the city."

"Only one way to know," Wendy says. "That's why we've argued this crap for the last twenty years, man. Gotta do it, I say. Risk it and hope we dug deep enough holes."

"Okay," I say with a sigh. "Get the word out, get the crew together, and I want you there in thirty-six hours. Use the new time-detonators; I don't want any kamikaze shit. I want you guys out when the Ozone Processor goes down."

"Hiding in the tunnel might do it. It's a hundred feet beneath Arkansas River."

"No, get out. By then, you'll have vampires up your ass. Get out and hide in bunker A-12, the closest one to their land."

"Vampires, uh? Haven't heard that in years, Byron. Your dad used to use it all the time, and he wasn't even one of those pre-Holocaust quacks who couldn't take it. He was a good man."

"I know." I nod in the dim light, so alone in the den. "And I'm a good man. Yeah, right. That's why I'm going to stay back and look over the evacuation process." I knead my temples. "I think I can get sixty percent of the population to relative safety."

"You're being optimistic, but I agree you need to stay behind. You're too important and too smart. We'll need you when it's all over."

"I'll be there."

"I think I'm getting a trace, Byron. Better let you go before we get pinched."

"Later."

The line goes dead.

I didn't go to bed just yet. I wasn't going to go to bed. I simply sit on one of the easy chairs by the window and wait. Wait for what? What am I waiting for? It's late in the night and soon it will be . . .

6

Movement.

    There was movement.

    From within me? From without me?

    Sand shifts . . .

    Is it you? Is it you . . .

7

In a few minutes it will be morning. *Sol* will come out, or what was that word my father used? It was hard to tell with a cigar always in his mouth, big, proud, with military tattoos and fire for a voice.

"We were flushed from a world of shit," he used to say. "Into a sewer of hell. Which is worse? You got it. Funny how it's the world where you have more to gain and less to lose."

I had heard once that part of the monsters' intentions was to blot the sun out with the ash and chemicals, giving them a full conquering spectrum. It hadn't worked. You could hide the other stars, erase the heavens, but not It and not its effects.

Why am I so excited, though, sitting here all alone while the world sleeps and the hunters pillage the city? Why do I wait for it to come out of the polluted horizon? *Sol.*

Even now I can see a trim of gold somewhere. Even now my heart beats with anticipation. It's coming. Why am I so excited? *Sol.*

Movement.

Sand shifts, fingers of light break the monotone, the flat darkness etched across a desolate sky. Wind blows. It's coming. *Sol.*

I miss my daughter.

Movement.

It's almost glancing over the flatlands. It's inking life to the stale canvass. It's coming! And I'll see it as if for the first time, as if for the last time. And I won't be dead twice and my daughter will be with me and I'll make love to my wife and I'll be whole once again.

8

The sand got in my eyes. I shut them. Darkness. All an illusion. I couldn't see, but I shut them. Was that the tugging of the wind, as pebbles blew over my face?

CHAPTER II

It wasn't the wind blowing. It was musical, tympanic. Fire's stepbrother.

Water trickled to my left. I sniffed, for the first time being able to smell in a long time. Aromas came gurgling to me, vexing in lashing tones. Coolness, I could smell. Not the frigidity of where I'd taken my last stand, but gentler.

The next thing I noticed was the hardness of the surface where I rested. Stone. Cool stone. And water continued trickling.

I think my eyes were open, but even my good one didn't work. The same with my body. I couldn't feel much, and maybe that was a blessing. Nerve endings tortured, spine and veins severed by broken bones and exterior weapons. I'd been taken through a few grinders, it seemed. Even a Stargazer has his limit, when his god-soul says, that's it, I'm not repairing you so you can fulfill your eternal destiny.

A sharp smell came from my left. No, it wasn't a smell, it was a sound, a rustling sound. I wanted to open my mouth, but my jaw was cracked at several places, more than likely from taking a nosedive into the dunes.

I flinched internally. Something wet spattered on my lips. At first, I thought it was the water.

All of a sudden, my throat started convulsing, as if telling me something. The god-soul, that Dark Instinct, which had kept me going in the sands and now needed to be satisfied, definitely told me something. It was as if it had usurped part of my personality, corrupted it, and now spoke with a true voice instead of an inner awareness.

Feed, you bastard. Feed.

Lips wouldn't move, and I wondered if I had any.

Okay. Sift. Sift, damn it.

Through the cracks of something, the liquid started going down. I felt pain then. It hurt like hell.

Feed.

The liquid kept coming in small spurts. I was feeding. It wasn't water.

Then it stopped.

"That's enough," a voice said. It hurt my head. "We don't want to give you too much yet."

Bastard, the god-soul said, but I was already feeling tired.

Then something large covered me, and the voice fell dormant, too.

2

The process continued. Eventually, when brain cells decided to cross the picket lines, I understood I was being fed every night before and after *Moratoria*. A little at a time, slowly increasing the dosages until I was propped up in caring arms and cups were being put to my lips. Then something covered me, a large slab of solidness.

My senses started to cooperate with my brain cells. The endless darkness became a blurb of smoky grays, smells separated, pain increased and pulsed until vanishing, tics of movement appeared occasionally.

Strangely, I didn't dream anymore. Just *Moratoria*. Like it should be.

Sometimes he would talk to me, a voice not used to hearing itself. Kind of shy, kind of dull. It was never anything interesting. It was mostly about me.

"You're starting to move. I actually found you in a different position tonight."

"Starting to eat properly. I'll soon let you eat however much you want. Looks like one of your fangs is fully grown."

"Good evening, Byron. How was *Moratoria*? You'll recover soon enough."

Just feed me, the god-soul complained.

The gray palpitated. A silhouette offered me food.

Jaws worked, but lips, full lips, mouthed nothing interesting. Brain threatened to go back on strike.

"Don't push it," the silhouette said. "Not yet."

The next night it hit me. How did he know my name?

3

It was stone. Crudely made, but a nice replacement for a cupola. Hands rose, shockingly skeletal, and crossed ailing vision. Touch. I felt it.

Mmm. Probably about four or five hundred pounds of it.
Normally, I would have been able to slide it off without a
problem. Now it was a prison as much as my body was.

I mimicked a sigh and lay there, until he came for me like
he did every evening.

4

"As you can see," he said, holding me up, right in front of an
ebony-trimmed mirror. "You will be whole in no time."

I wish I could have shared his optimism then. But as I was
trying not to lose any fluid through my eyes, a deep shame
settled on me like a quilt.

It was me all right, or more like a comical scarecrow, thin,
emaciated, with blotches of irregular skin, mocking scars, and
a sunken face that once might have been handsome. It was me
all right, not the audacious Warm One that masterminded the
destruction of the Stargazer capital, not the brazen artist that
infuriated so many people and challenged The MoonQueen.
No, it was just me.

At least the outside matched the inside now.

He must have been surprised to see me whimper. He lowered me on my back.

"What's wrong, Byron?" he asked, still an outline, someone who knew my name, who I found also familiar. "Been
through a lot? I still hear things from the city-states on occasion when I travel, but a Heretic is very limited, even for one
of my age."

I whimpered again.

"Here," he said, voice trailing off. "Let me feed you. It will
make you feel better."

I was propped up in my tomb once again. He handed me a
clay cup with an old straw. I sipped, ignoring aching veins,
while he sat by my side.

"There seems to have been some trouble in Xanadu recently," he spoke casually, legs crossed, I could barely tell. "The city was in some uproar for a while. Things have settled in a different way. Besides that, much journeying occurs between there and New Atlantis. Much construction also. Knowing you, Byron, you must have been behind some of this."

I nodded tersely.

"I'm sure you'll let me know sometime," he said. "Not much to do here for entertainment, except to hunt for *Rukas* in the mines below."

I spat out whatever juice was in my mouth. I told you, the god-soul nagged, that it tasted sour and it wasn't your senses!

I stared at him. Contours stiffened. I recognized him. The cup dropped somewhere.

All he did was shrug, stand up, and say, "Must do what it takes to survive. Being a Heretic is not much fun, but you'll also get used to it."

He left me to grimace alone. At least I wasn't feeling sorry for myself anymore.

5

Stone shifted before my caress. I was doing it. With a sonorous rasping, it slowly moved away from the tomb. I was free. My body was free.

I stood up slowly, regarding my surroundings. The whole time I'd been in a deep cavern, probably one of many in his abode. The ground cupped downward, stopping at a basin fed by a couple of underground tributaries. The water smelled clean.

Not much else in the cave. My bed, the pond, stale humidity, and the sultry trickling. And now me, standing, pacing, still so tired.

For a while, I admired the water and its song. I envied it. Water didn't have to live with memories even though they filled it. Water didn't have to feel remorse, to miss things, for all things were from it. Water created, it destroyed, it served its purpose unknowingly. Water cleansed.

I came out of the trance when I was already knee-deep in the basin. The Elders had always told us that water was an enemy of our species like fire, bringing random and horrible effects on our beings. As always, I knew it was another lie they used to keep us from enjoying such a scarce commodity. It rose to my waist, to my chest. I waded in a kingdom of ripples and thick sounds, sinking lower. I heard silence and it was good. It cleansed. Water.

I rose in a haze of pulpy bullets and rippling smithereens, arms outstretched, emitting a sort of relieved grunt, which bounced off the moist walls for a long time. Then I fell back in, waded for a while, and casually walked out as naked as when I'd gone in.

He stood by one of the entranceways, arms folded, leaning on a heel. His face brimmed with slight amusement.

"You are yourself again, almost," he said. "Six months unrotting yourself, Byron. Not bad considering the pummeling you took."

I didn't say anything, lost in the drip-drop of my person, lost in the river's voice.

"That considering you must have been hibernating in that dune for at least another six months," he continued. "Not an unknown feat for a vampire, excuse me, a Stargazer to do in times of dire need or damage."

I avoided his gaze, thinking of that word, thinking of my father. He knew I would.

"It's good to see you, Byron," he said, "even though you've changed since we last met."

I caught his gaze. I nodded slowly.

"It's good to see you, too," I said, "even though you've changed, too, Master Proxos Commodore."

CHAPTER 12

That's how I basically started my stay as a guest, a companion to the Heretic in his hidden home away from the home we once had. "It's not so bad," he would say often. "Stargazers are solitary creatures by definition, though they're quite possessive when they attach to something. This civilization idea we had has its merits, but I wonder what it does to our matrix."

Proxos resided in a chain of caverns several feet underground, away from the brutish climate still castigating the earth for its sins. He didn't live like animals: furniture, apparels, and artwork adorned the place, besides the clean water and the *Rukas* roaming below us.

The ex-Elder was right about the banal existence of a Heretic. All he did, and soon all I did, was learn how to breed the wild *Ruka* population, find trivial hobbies, and tend to the place. Occasionally we went on walks or flights in the night, aided by certain insulating suits he owned that shielded us from the radiation's shifting heat.

And we talked a lot, sometimes rehashing the same conversation, trying to anchor each other and our situations. It's too bad he didn't smoke.

"How did you locate this nifty little abode?" I asked him one night, collecting stalagmites, another one of those hobbies to smother loneliness.

Proxos held up a cone of ruby pastels, brow crinkling as he wondered whether to add one to his medley. "I had a few of these places before and after The Holocaust. Being a noble granted me freedom to purchase certain properties outside Utopia, in case of a rainy night. I'm sorry, Byron, that expression means an emergency."

"I guess the rainy night came," I commented, wondering what rain might look like, sitting in front of him, also holding a stalactite, this one of bright bone-pallor.

"They always do."

I didn't say anything, concentrating on my object. This was sure boring, but it seemed like a good way to pass the time, to lose yourself in the mundane. Proxos liked it.

Something caught my eye. I had to blink several times to pinpoint the slight reflection on the smooth surface of the spike.

"Proxos."

"Mmm." He slid another one into a leather bag by his sandaled feet.

It hit me I hadn't seen my reflection since that night of self-pity, and that memory had been quickly flushed away. "What color is my hair?"

"It used to be brown when you were a Warm One, a shade darker than mine. Did it change afterward?"

"Not to my knowledge."

He buckled the bag and eyed me, a smile threatening to burst from thin lips. "Well, my dear, it looks like it certainly changed after I found you. It's bleach white."

I laughed or coughed or both, running my hands through what must have been milky tresses.

"It can happen to . . ." And he went on that tirade about times of stress or damage.

"Just like Shib," I whistled, shaking my head.

"Yes," he said softly, "I do believe my old colleague had an experience like that once, sometime during the Burning Time in Bavaria."

I didn't know what he was talking about, but I certainly disdained sharing a quality with old Master Shibboleth.

2

Our conversations didn't span any depth for the first year or so. I was still healing and didn't want any stress. Proxos, I believe, was content with another of his kind here and perhaps wanted to extend our communication for as long as he could.

In addition, I had to get used to feeding on *Rukas*, a process that left me in sour moods.

Communication centered around the long walks we took in the middle of the night. There, wrapped in metallic clothes from an unknown material, we spoke and trundled through the dunes and whetted rock, against inflamed wind or sandstorms. Sometimes we reached the base of the mountains and halted, Xanadu just on the other side; other times we skirted shaven ruins of pre-Holocaust times to look for baubles. Proxos knew all the ways, this, his stomping ground for a hundred and more years. My stomping ground now, too, forever and ever, amen.

"Hey, Proxos," I mentioned one evening, both of us standing on a large mound of always-hot sand, admiring scarves of lavender clouds flowing in the sky that tarred *Luna* into a sanguine sphere. "Correct me if I'm wrong, but aren't you supposed to be dead? They'll have to change the name of the station, oh Elder."

He snorted and leaned on his staff, an object he carried to be dramatic.

"They have changed the past on more than one occasion, Byron," he said. "Aren't you also supposed to be dead, Revolutionist? Wiped out from memory for the health of our progress?"

"You're right," I said with a chuckle, sitting down on the sand. "I guess we're both dead now."

He joined me on the ground. "We've been dead. Better make the best of it. I have for thirty-two hundred years."

"Damn," I said. "Did you ever think you'd end up this way?"

"Never," he said. "I never thought of anything but how to fulfill my hunger. It's *your* head that always has to go in different directions except where you are now. Believe me, I knew about your fate back then, even though I was already banished and deceased for all purposes. I heard about you on occasion, from other Heretics running madly in the night, from rare intercepted transmissions, and from other sources. I knew you'd brew trouble. They should have destroyed you back then, but Lilith obviously had a warm spot for you in that icicle she calls a heart."

"Lilith?" I echoed.

"That was her name back then, at the beginning, when the mad-god created her and tossed her to some horrible limbo she was able to escape from. Some legends say she is a white witch who actually escaped from another world of endless snow and mythical beasts such as satyrs. You know how folklore can warp itself. I knew her as Hecate when she gave me new life."

"And you followed her all this time?"

He pondered for a moment. "Back then, if I can still recall, I was nothing more than a slave with a penchant for geometry to some sodomitical king. I wasn't going anywhere, and the other gods were punishing my civilization for silly reasons. My people's time was all but over—a flash for others to remember. I visited her temple in an island called Leros for advice and succor. I was chosen for no other reason than luck, if you believe in that. She made me a god and morality was different back then, so I didn't have too much of a problem. I didn't actually serve her completely, though. We ran into each other here and there, and I followed whatever whim she had at the time."

"So there haven't been these great Elders serving her as acolytes from the beginning?"

He laughed, a hearty one. "Dear, no. Just a few fellows who crossed her path when she was having galactic p.m.s. We were rewarded nicely, though, but that's about it."

I was having trouble understanding some of his remarks, not a first, but my curiosity told me not to worry about it.

"Why did you do it?"

"Do what?"

"The Holocaust, Proxos."

He didn't answer then, different expressions etching on his face.

"I don't know," he said, for the first time realizing I was watching him attentively. "Survival, I guess. Maybe boredom. Amusement? Vengeance? I don't know. It just was, so go ahead and get your little cynical opinion ready if you want. It's hard to explain why you helped destroy a few billion lives and Demeter's kingdom just like that, you know."

"Do you really think The Killer of Giants would have wiped out the whole world?" I pressed.

"I don't know. Nobody really wanted to find out."

"Maybe you were just following orders," I said, giving him my cynical opinion.

He stood up. "And maybe I could have let you perish in the sand when I happened to hear you by accident, Byron, especially for basically stabbing me and my cause in the back after our truce."

"I was just giving orders, Proxos," I said with a wide grin.

"Whatever. At least your first comment worked for the Nazi troops. Come on, we better head back before *Sol* decides to fry us."

3

As time continued I learned more while trying not to challenge Proxos that much. I actually enjoyed his company and grew fond of him. He was more down to earth than his old associates, less eloquent or pompous than Shib or some of the others. He wasn't political like many of the rising Stargazers, like Mephisto. He was just a Heretic.

"I've met a few through the years," he would tell me, only really getting talkative in our treks or perhaps when we ate by a fire (a habit he had as a Warm One way before electrical light was invented). "I've also met Warm Ones, scattered around the land. I've eaten a few of them, but most are grossly deformed by the radiation, basically mutated savages. They taste rather foul, so I would advise you not to chomp on any if you run into one. I hadn't had gas in millennia, but it happened."

"What about the Heretics?" I asked him that time, while thinking the warped Warm Ones had to taste better than *Ruka* juice.

"Oh, just fools who got in the way of The Elders' revolution," he answered. "The MoonQueen sometimes prefers just to rip them apart herself for sport. You know, her mind is Tiffany twisted." He started laughing (nothing like people who laugh at their own jokes). I repeated the question.

"Most of them are as much victims as me, more or less," he said. "Sometimes they're just a random pruning of our ranks in order to create new ones or proportion food supply. Usually, by the time I reach them, they're insane with despair, ready to dig themselves to oblivion. They never take my invitation, especially the times I made the mistake of telling them my name."

"Superstitious Stargazers," I whistled.

"I assume they go raving mad and probably don't survive,

not taking any care in this weather. The few who do eventually become as mutated as the Warm Ones, monsters lurking in the sand or scavenging the ruins. It's rather ugly."

"So, you're basically the only civilized Heretic?" I asked, taking another pungent swig from my cup. "Aside from me."

"I was the only prepared one," Proxos said. "Like I said, I had these little hideaways all over the world. I came to this one after they expelled me."

"They didn't like your hairstyle?"

"Not exactly. They were extremely upset at the fact that I had a faction dealing with the revolutionaries. They thought, and rightfully so, that I had some weak spots for your kind— after three thousand years most of us tend to mellow out. When the Ozone Processor rose in flames and caused a small nuclear detonation, they destroyed my allies, tried me quickly, and made me a martyr. They threw me out into the wilderness and named a station after me."

"Nice," I said. "And then you came here."

"Yes," he hissed, "and then they brought you in to be tried. The rest is history. I would have loved to have left you drying in the dunes, Byron, but when I saw you, when I thought about what they did to you—"

I finished his sentence.

"—you knew that was punishment enough."

He sipped on more blood, admiring the fire.

4

The MoonQueen had remarked about chess, so Proxos explained it to me. Weeks later, he brought in a dusty box from his cellars and asked me if I wanted to play.

I'd been sitting by the basin, trying very hard to suppress all the memories overwhelming me. I'd learned so much in so little time, trauma dislodging traumas in a bedlam of recol-

lection. Now I spent much effort covering it all up, playing
the Heretic. I'd vowed not to think about my Warm One existence, my feats, and even her. Medea. The name brought pain,
the acerbic taste of failure. It also brought the taste of Clannad, the Slaughterhouses. I wanted to forget it all, dissolve it
in ambiguous contentment. Proxos had done it, perhaps several times. Even Lilith had mastered it, hadn't she? I was
Byron, the Heretic.

Forever and ever, amen.

It didn't take me long to master the game, and I became a
challenge after the tenth time he beat me. Chess was great to
loosen his tongue. Whenever mammoth sandstorms ripped
the area or the radiation count heated the wastes, we would
play strategy on a stone table he carved himself.

I soon learned of another strategy: The Holocaust, the
greatest covert strategy in a world unbelieving of Stargazers.

Apparently, The MoonQueen's idea sprouted when the
Warm Ones mastered the might of atom-splitting. It dangled
on her thoughts for years, as she spent her time in her beloved
winter kingdom somewhere in a place called Antarctica. She
passed it on to some of the older ones through her thoughts,
but it was still only an idea.

Twenty, maybe thirty years later, The Killer of Giants
began to spread across the world. It was then that she made
those thoughts potential. The other ancients, different creatures with different powers roaming the world, did not seem
to care. Stargazers really cared. Thus, The Elders were formed
and great machinations given birth. It took them time to understand, infiltrate, and embrace all the technology. In fact,
one of The Elders, Balkros, had been a high-standing military
Warm One in the former empire we now abide in. He was also
a dangerous and perhaps psychotic person, whatever that
meant, so when Shibboleth himself turned him into a
Stargazer, it was not a problem to make him see Our Mistress's vision. No problem at all. By then, on different corners

of the earth, as nation warred against nation, as Warm One killed Warm One, the web was woven and the noose tightened. A few thousand cobalt-salted warheads, an infiltrated silo, a blip on the radar here and there, and the sky burned for nights.

"I was in charge of taking over Utopia," Proxos said, moving a piece. "Getting everything in order for the new world."

"Sounds familiar."

"And fortunate, at least for you. By the time New Town was ablaze, a group of Ravens caught your ally, Wendy, and her friends and ripped them to shreds."

"So I guess she decided to stay in the tunnel after all." My hand shook.

Some of The Elders perished during and after The Holocaust. What mattered is that The Queen of Darkness and her vision lived.

"Oh, yes," he added, "and we had to keep confidential the secret of creation, leaving that to Lilith alone. After all, our kind needed leadership in the form of a deity, not to mention population control. Those with the knowledge and big mouths were quickly destroyed right after The Holocaust."

"And I'm sure those unfortunate enough to hear about the secret of creation met the same fate," I commented sourly.

He raised an eyebrow. "Ignorance is bliss, Byron, as an ancient saying goes, but knowledge is power. You figure out the rest."

Proxos also told me that it was very likely that not all of earth was ravaged by the atomic gales. One of The Elders' secrets was that eventually they would be able to find those areas of the world and reap the Warm Ones there. Then the true empire would grow. But first to wait, to build, to consolidate power in creatures that preferred chaos to order.

"Checkmate," I said. Proxos regarded me quizzically because the game was not even near being over. He was right.

5

"Proxos?"

"Yes?"

"Have you ever thought about destroying yourself, ending it all? There isn't much purpose in our lives."

"There's that head of yours going again. No. I've existed long enough to not worry about time. Only the moment."

"That's my problem. The moment. I feel I never had the moment. It was taken away when I was just savoring it. Why? Your move."

"If you never had it, it never was, Byron. Get over it. You're probably mad you failed twice, but at least you tried. Good move."

"I still miss, though . . ."

"That's the existence of a Stargazer, Byron, and if I can still remember, that of a Warm One. We miss, we yearn, but with our kind it is much more severe. We miss life, we miss death, we miss satisfaction. I, for one, just miss missing, Byron."

"Then it's all over . . ."

"Forever and ever—"

"Amen."

"Unless you wish it to be all over, Byron, then wait till *Sol* arrives and end it all. I tried it a few times throughout the centuries. Never had the nerve, though, but I think it would have been beautiful."

"So, you don't remember what it looked like."

"We miss, my dear, we miss . . . check . . ."

Amen.

6

Two years passed. We existed. By then, I was comfortably numb, an expression Proxos enjoyed using. We talked. We walked. We existed.

Once a week, what my companion called Saturday night, we had a treat. I had thought I'd almost learned everything about the caverns and the surrounding areas, but I was obviously wrong. He walked in holding a bottle, while I was attempting to fix some loose wires on one of his hard drives. "Here," he said proudly, "it's a treat for us, for your good behavior."

"Excuse me?" I looked up from the CPU.

"It's Warm One juice," he explained. "I keep a secret cache in a supercool freezer. I only use it on special occasions."

"What's the special occasion?" I questioned, fangs already dripping.

"Why, your good behavior. You haven't betrayed me or started any *Ruka* revolutions."

I laughed, he poured, we toasted.

"Oh, yeah," I purred. "This is so good."

"B negative," he agreed. "Tart but with little aftertaste. Could have thawed it a little longer. Don't drink it too quickly and don't expect it too often."

"You're the master."

"And get ready to dream," he added.

"What?"

He explained that *Ruka* juice never induced the visions Stargazers had during *Moratoria*. Warm One blood, on the other hand, granted broad imagery.

"At first, during the revolution," Proxos said, "I thought that the only way to sate our kind was with direct feeding. That, of course, changed. After all, I've heard that the Dark Instinct is an eater of souls, that we mollify ourselves on the passing of their lives, make them part of our tragedy. But symbolism is more important than substance. It's meaning, Byron. Their juice is just that. Eaten away from their receptacle, while it's cooling, doesn't give us as much of the meaning, the hunter meaning, which perhaps is one of the reasons why our society is so brittle."

"I've heard other theories," I said, eyeing a mirror by the door. I'd let my bleached hair grow long, usually leashed by a black ribbon. The features were harder. Two years. But it still was me.

"I'm sure you have. It's still all so new, this collective society. All theory. Perhaps I'm wrong, maybe we just need the nutrients to fuel our undead bodies, our shells no longer able to re-create blood cells, our hearts a useless muscle. But I believe the juice, the blood still symbolizes the life we perhaps crave. It gives us meaning. I know one thing, though: Warm One blood is our dream, now more than ever."

"You're making my head hurt, Proxos."

"Good. If anything, Mr. Solsbury, don't forget this. We're notable creatures. Hunting for prey, flying, changing shapes. Bah! Mere apprentice shit! We have the gift of a Goddess. Yet Lilith has kept a shroud over us for such a long time. We're notable creatures, our potential so undiscovered in our blind hunger. What we can do . . ."

I rolled my eyes, cursing myself for letting his tongue get free again without much challenge.

"You've had plenty of time to discover this 'potential,' Proxos. Why aren't you in charge of some creation?"

He shrugged. "Perhaps for the same reason I couldn't end it all, Byron. Just drink your juice, damn it. And get ready to dream."

"I can't wait," I said sourly, but wouldn't stop sipping on what he called a wineglass.

We, then, shared a bit of moody silence. I knew it wouldn't last, Proxos's contemplative expression already wrestling with something new.

"What's funny is that I can't recall dreaming until The Holocaust occurred," he said. "Perhaps it also has to do with the fact that we all lost something we now try to make up in *Moratoria*. Before, it was like just being . . . dead, you know."

"Like drinking *Ruka*'s blood," I said.

He didn't say anything, musing in his own silence. But I had read all of his warnings, or perhaps they were just mine.

7

I did dream. I dreamt of so much. The city burning, me rescuing people, running madly with my mortal family . . . the little girl on my lap . . . Clannad, eat your dinner . . . Tina pouring pints in glossy surroundings . . . and . . . and . . . Medea.

Medea!

Through the tunnel of shimmering memories, a voice called me, distant, a faint echo in a storm of revelations. For a moment, I thought I could go there, ethereally anchor myself to my thoughts and slide toward it. It called me.

Suddenly, I thought of fire and ice, and shivered backward, knowing who it might be, who it probably was. My creator. My destroyer!

Ripples of panic filled the images, and the voice shouted with more strength.

Never . . . amen . . .

I struggled upward, and away from the tunnel, and reality exploded before me.

Suddenly awake, I found my bed open with the covering slab on the ground in pieces, and I was standing ready to jump into the basin.

I didn't jump. I went for answers.

8

I had overslept *Luna*'s ascent by about an hour, which is very rare for my kind. If anyone would have even said that 'stress' thing I would have slugged them.

The cavern seemed different. It was still dank, but the sounds had changed. The usual whistling that snakes throughout the tunnel and crevices was replaced by a deeper, faltering moan. I felt the ground hum.

I found Proxos in one of the smaller chambers, a section of natural balconies where he had all his machines. He was in front of one of them intently scanning a primitive radar that worked only half of the time.

"Commodore," I said, floating to him. "I think Lilith might have tried to contact me, I—"

"It's coming!" he burst in agitation. "It's coming, by Zeus. And this one's a big one."

"What's coming?" I asked, blinking.

He looked at me, as if for the first time knowing I was here.

"It's coming! Get your suit on, Byron. Hurry!"

"Proxos, what are you—"

"Hurry, fool." He imploded in mist and swept into one of the rifts on the floor.

I thought about shrugging or just staying there with my jaw hanging, but found myself doing exactly what he told me.

Knowing his style, I met him at the entranceway, the end of an uneven tunnel. I started questioning him, but he started on his tracks. I followed, annoyed, thinking about my dream. That soon ended.

The first thing that took my attention was the pulsing wind. The land was usually covered with such currents, wiping forces that could take a Warm One off his feet and severely mangle him. To us it was merely tough walking or flying. This dwarfed it. We walked practically slanted against the flow of air.

We trudged for about a mile or so in a haze of sand and rock fragments, barely looking up. I wondered how resistant these suits were, even though the heat from the radiation appeared less than it usually was. We headed away from the mountain range to the flatlands.

"It's a tornado storm," he yelled through his screened mouth-opening. "A big one, probably the biggest I've ever seen."

"A what?" I shouted back suddenly recalling some research I'd done back in Xanadu for one of the guilds.

"They hit open areas once in a while," he said, stumbling

against the increasing gusts. "Rare, but sometimes you can find one."

I thought about asking why anyone would want to find one, but a sheet of air nailed us from all sides. We teetered in place, and I pointed in terror at the sky. The gales, clothing themselves in debris, took shape before us, dozens of them. They took the form of massive funnels, whirling in the heavens, pruning the land.

They headed in our direction.

"Get down, Byron!" he screamed, words barely discernible through the rising concert of perceptions.

"Down where?"

"Anchor yourself." I saw his silhouette drop and begin excavating into the loosening surface. "Go deep. If we get hit directly, we're done for, but you'll see . . ." That's the last I heard of him. The sky blasted in fury, the funnels wobbled monstrously toward us.

You'll see how I rip *you* to shreds, I thought, but I mimicked his actions.

In my greatest Stargazer arrogance, I would have never challenged this. Digging a few feet in a matter of seconds, I braced myself from wave upon wave of heinous wind, each time stronger. I heard ground ripping close by and felt the storm aggressively challenging gravity to pull me away. I clenched my jaw as a million objects struck me, as reality was absorbed into a sound so loud I thought I might go insane. I wanted to place my hands over my ears, but knew that risked taking to the skies in a flurry of brutal pummeling.

All around me, the ground shifted, no, it practically was pulverized by the beating of the funnel's drum. For a second, I dangled in nothing, suspended with hundreds of pounds of ground, a bubble in a sea of compressed air. Then, so quickly my senses didn't register it, I was tossed into the air, crossing an expanse of gust and rubble. I heard Proxos scream, but then he was drowned in a detonation of basso rumbling.

I thought about screaming, too, but my body couldn't obey. Like a marionette, I flopped along the contours of a large curve, gaining dangerous momentum. Shards of everything pelted me from all sides.

This is it, the god-soul told me. Shit, fuck, shit, it's not even *Sol*, for hunger's sakes.

Or was it me, I wondered for an instant, momentum taking solidness. Once again I was a missile on a downward trajectory.

"NOOO," I objected in the celestial roar, but this time I wouldn't give up.

My first instinct was to rise, but that would have been useless. Instead, I surfed on the overbearing current, bouncing on the arms of the gusts. I was still spiraling the wrong way.

This is it . . .

Immediately, I was motionless. I did it. I landed safely. No movement. Nothing. I did it. No sound. I see . . .

The second bubble burst, and I smashed into the ground along with several tons of dirt and a loud BOOM!

Not again, a voice inside told me, and it pulled a dense curtain over me.

CHAPTER 13

It wasn't so bad, thanks to my amateur gliding. Just like last time, Proxos came to my rescue. He unlodged me from a compacted mound by my arms. The dolt had the nerve to chuckle.

"I guess I should have taught you how to fly correctly through a tornado," he said, lowering me gently. "Not that I've done it often, but still—"

As he spoke, my brain scanned my body in a millisecond. Everything seemed basically intact, not too much was broken. Then I swung backward at the ex-Elder.

My blow caught him with obvious surprise, and that was probably fortunate. His jaw didn't dismantle against my knuckles, but his whole body pivoted obscenely and bounced backward a few feet. By the time his resilient body started trying to get on its feet and his mouth question me, I had dusted myself off and was slowly charging him.

"You bastard!" I spat, noticing that one of my fangs was loose. "You could have destroyed us, you maniac!"

He coughed up some dirt and simply pointed upward. I thought it was a distraction, but suddenly I noticed a radiance from above, a light I'd never seen.

I raised my head and beheld infinity.

"Jesus Christ!" I said, my entire being filled with its true purpose, for which we all yearned.

High above me a mantle of creation's handiwork twinkled at me with innocence over dark blue, stretching across the heavens in coy grandeur.

Stars. Hundreds of them. Thousands of them glittering the night away, pinpricks of pure light like a gauze of enlightenment.

My jaws moved, but no words would dare come out. Proxos stood up, and a gentle cold settled upon us.

We gazed at stars.

Even *Luna* appeared majestically clear, perched in nothing, a ball of creamy light, marred by faint blotches. Yes, even then, I knew its light was fake just as my life was fake. We served her, but it is the stars, these stars, we yearn to gaze upon since they are a glimpse into what the world looked like before, when nature and creature coexisted in harmony. Their light is not ours, but we wish to admire the other *Sols* in the universe. Stars remind us of what we were, what we might be, all in a brief twinkle.

"After the tornado storm," Proxos said in joy, not sobbing like I was, "the sky clears for a while until the filth returns."

"Then we can gaze at stars," I said softly. "Thank you."

"You're welcome," he said, and we shared the constellations above us in silence, our thoughts, our desires, our hopes dancing there in the astral rapture, trying to bounce off each flicker of their illumination, each surreal spasm.

The stars shifted, a scintillating dance. *Luna* moved, trying to gain our attention but we beheld the altering mantle only. We could have stood there forever, ignoring our hunger, uncaring of the chewing coolness, forgetting ourselves totally. That was the best part, forgetting ourselves in the vast performance above us.

I never thought I could feel so small and large at the same time.

"You miss her," Proxos said or asked, his voice crisp like the openness before us.

I wanted to close my eyes, but it seemed like a sin to miss a beat of creation's mystic folklore.

"I miss all three of them," I said sharply, "they're all dead."

"She might not be."

I lowered my head slightly. "Either way, she's dead. How do you know these things?"

"I told you I've watched you throughout the years and have connections."

We didn't talk for a while. I could see already a haze at the edges of the canvass which would soon warp the area. Then I wondered if anything would be the same if we could all gaze at the stars, for Our Mistress had lost that joy a long time ago.

"I don't remember much about my last moments as Warm

One," I said suddenly, "or the moments after being endowed with immortality."

"Few do," he said. I felt his gaze caressing me. "It's normal considering the trauma. Probably the best thing for what happened to you."

"Did I put up a good fight?"

He sighed. "You always do, Byron. It's your style."

I smiled under the stars, not my usual sardonic expression, but an honest, carefree one I knew my daughter once possessed, one I used so rarely. My thoughts came clear yet without voice, so full of perspective here.

Proxos must have seen that smile and the sudden decision behind it. He probably had expected it at some point.

"You're going back?" he questioned.

The smile grew.

"Why?"

I might have shrugged. "Maybe for the same reason you destroyed a few billion people, Proxos. I don't know. It's my style. I could say that it's because I want vengeance—they took away my family, my humanity, they cursed me with perpetual hunger, and then they took away a friend of mine. But it's more than that. I want justice. This . . ." I waved my hand at the sky. "This is why we were named. But it's a lie. Our leaders never wanted us to gaze at stars, they never wanted us to attain our dreams, our hopes, our innocence. As they covered the world in ash, they wanted to cover our souls in it, too. And you know why?"

"Why?" he said, probably knowing the answer.

"Because we really *are* ash, Proxos. We are the darkness and we are the enemy of the living universe. Medea was right, we are destroyers by nature. We don't deserve to be at the head of evolution or creation. We'll just devour both in time. They must be stopped. *Our* kind must be stopped."

"And how are you going to do this, Sir Knight?" he asked with annoyance. "Take on the Raven army? Challenge The

MoonQueen to a duel of chess? You may have destroyed one of our kingdoms, but there are no Ozone Processors in Xanadu, no divided Stargazers."

"There's always a way," I said. "Even when there's no way, it's a way."

He grinned, although his nostrils flared. "You're a fool, Mr. Solsbury."

"Maybe."

"It'll be risky."

I nodded. "I wouldn't have it any other way."

"It's a good thing I'm here to help you," he said softly.

This time I closed my eyes. "And this time there will be no broken promises, Proxos Commodore."

And we stood there, watching the sky change, watching ourselves change, but realizing neither had changed that much since the beginning.

2

"First things first," Proxos told me the next night, both of us in fabulous moods. We shared Warm One juice and dabbled in more games. "You'll have to find one of my contacts, one of the Stargazers still loyal to me."

"Or at least sorry for you."

"Your barbed wit only disguises your lack of talent at chess, Byron. Now, listen to me, I'll give you her name, address, plus secret ways into Xanadu through abandoned tunnels and blemishes in the structure. They're all found in the arms of the city leading to The Farms. Never go through the cupolae because their radar is pretty accurate that close, do you hear?"

"Yeah, yeah," I said. "But tell me one thing, speaking of radars, won't Our Mistress know I'm there? She's done it before, very recently I believe."

He took a generous gulp before speaking. "You don't know if it was her."

"Then who else . . ." I internally answered my own question. "No."

"You created her," he said. "You're attached forever in a way you probably didn't want. Remember, we're eaters of souls, symbolized in the blood that pumps from the heart. There are some Stargazer tales of how we are actually permanently attached to everyone we hunt, and that was the burden we carried in the old nights before rationing, besides the hunger."

"That couldn't have been," I said, but found myself biting my lip.

It was her. Somehow we had touched in *Moratoria*; perhaps a subconscious part of mine had searched for Medea to touch her.

"Don't overestimate Our Mistress too much," Proxos then mentioned. "She can't keep tabs on everyone at the same time. Her power is breathtaking but she is not totally omniscient. If she knew about my contacts they'd be Heretics and I'd have already had a little and final visit from her."

"Maybe she just doesn't care, Proxos."

"That's possible. But all you need to know is that when she does know or care, when she *believes* you might be a threat to her hive, you'll be attacked from all sides. Then you better get out before she hits you directly. Believe me, Lilith rarely manipulates anyone more than once—she's beyond petty challenges."

"At least it's a start." I nodded, not letting any odd emotions diminish my conviction. I was going back.

"So what now?" he inquired with a patronizing tone. "What will be your next move when you get back?"

"I've got a few plans. You said there are no Ozone Processors, but there are nuclear plants, factories, and other things that can go 'boom.' There are plenty of options, but I need to get there first and then I'll let you know."

"How?"

"The same way you talk to your connections."

"Smart-mouth. Okay, and I'll eventually become more active in aiding you. I'll have to leave for a while, too."

"Leave?"

I didn't like the sound of that, of not having Proxos, my savior, where he should be. I still needed a few constants.

He took another sip, as if the juice wasn't enough for the emotional energy he was mustering. "You're not the only one with agendas resurrected by what we saw last night, Mr. Solsbury."

"What are you going to do?"

"I have plans, too," he said. "You'll hear about them when we meet physically the next time."

I half smiled and snorted. "We better. I'm almost intrigued."

We schemed more. We played more chess. Finally, we went for another walk, imagining a naked sky in the blur called the outdoors.

3

Planning took another week or so. When I left, Proxos would stay behind for a while, making sure the place was secured for his sabbatical. I didn't pack anything because I arrived with nothing. All the information about his contacts rested patiently in my head. "You'll learn of my method when you meet her," he told me, walking me up to the entrance. "You'll also learn a few secret hiding places if things get heated. Please don't involve her too much."

"Don't worry," I said, regarding him solemnly. "It's my risk."

He smiled narrowly, suddenly reaching for his pockets. "I know it is. Here, I want you to take this."

It didn't hit me what it was until the weighty, metallic object rested inside my palms, or, to be more precise, what might be inside the case.

"It's a video disk," Proxos said. "The titanium case should take care of any abuse you take while prancing around Xanadu. It's something I kept for one of those rainy nights. I want you to give it to an old colleague of mine."

"Who?" I asked, fingering it curiously, then placing it in my coat.

The narrow smile thickened. "Balkros The Elder, if you get the chance."

"Balkros!" I exclaimed. "Is this a sad attempt at humor, Commodore?"

"Perhaps. It's just a hunch, if things go the way they might go. The old psycho would really enjoy this and it would help our cause."

"How?" I felt like tossing the thing out, instead of even thinking of dealing with the chaotic master. "What's on it?"

"I don't know," Proxos said with a shrug. "And what's in it is a secret, for your own good, Byron. Trust me. Don't even think about accessing it, for only Balkros could understand or fathom the implications of the data."

I shook my head and calmed at recalling the stars and the laughter we'd shared. The haunting fact that I still was the plaything of the higher powers just seemed too sophomoric these nights. "Just a hunch, right?"

The smile vanished, replaced by a slow nod.

"One more thing, Byron. Are you going back for vengeance and justice, or are you really going back to see her?"

I dodged his gaze.

"I don't know," I said. "It's obvious she is still . . . she still exists. And it's obvious we are connected, despite what I did to her. We were connected before that."

"There's a word for that," he told me. "Do you know what it is?"

I hate you.

"As a Warm One I knew that word." I sighed heavily. "But now I am ash, Proxos."

He grabbed my arm. "Good, don't forget that. Avoid her and avoid everything you might have held dear in Xanadu. Let her memory and that of your family fuel you, but that's it. If you have any chance to destroy the kingdom of destroyers, which you probably won't, then you must be a destroyer without any distractions. Do you understand?"

His expression showed he didn't believe my slow nodding. We planned more.

I thought about a decent good-bye when it was time, a fat thank you or something. Nothing came out; my throat constricted around the words. Proxos noticed this and pointed out into the wilderness.

"Go, Mr. Solsbury," he said. "Go on the wings of Hermes to the City of Domes and bring forth a new age. Somewhere in between, we'll see each other, I think."

"You've always been a good comrade, Prox."

"You would have made an honorable lover back in my early nights."

I tried to smile, but couldn't. I pursed my lips, placed the visor over my eyes, and blew into the night murkiness.

It was a hundred and fifty miles to my destination. Though it took The MoonQueen mere minutes to traverse that distance, flying would still take me a good four hours going against the wind and sweeping over the hills.

What Proxos didn't know (and me, too, until the moment) was that I wasn't going first to meet his contact. There were scores to settle, intuitions to be satisfied, and, more than that, I had to do things my way. It might be a quick, messy ending, but so what.

I flew high after a while, directly heading for the higher

places in Xanadu, to see an old pal of mine, knowing that Proxos's estimation about being caught this close was exaggerated. It wasn't their technology, it was that arrogance thing.

CHAPTER 14

The amber glass had the misfortune of meeting me again. The same place I entered a few years ago had long been fixed. It burst into shards around me, and I stood in old Shib's office. It was empty. I knew that.

Before leaving Proxos's caverns, I was able to get into an old database in his computers. The schedule told me tonight was The Fusing, and no Elder would miss it in order to spout caramel dogma to the population. Proxos's information had a good chance of being right—the last time the religious itinerary had been changed was forty years ago when a massive power outage crippled the city for about a month, the reasons blamed on an unusual electrical storm scalding the entire land from coast to coast.

To confirm this, I had buoyed just outside the window, making sure all the offices and chambers were empty. They were.

I said I had come empty-handed for all practical and impractical purposes, but that wasn't entirely true. From one of my large pockets, I retrieved a stone about three times the size of my fist, a meteor Proxos had found for one of his many un-fulfilled hobbies. I dropped it on the ground. It was a stretch, but the odds of a lonely meteor striking Xanadu were much higher than an intruder daring an uninvited entrance into an Elder's office. More than that, Shib's computer would buy me even more time than if I'd wandered the city searching for in-formation.

Using the information I stole from Balkros's database back before leaving to investigate The Farms, I broke a few of Shib's codes. I couldn't get too far into his massive banks, though, since many of his codes seemed to have been changed.

"Strange," I mused out loud, fondling his drawers for a cig-arette. No smokes, either. Shit.

I switched to look at the news of the night and whatever else I could find. It flashed before me like a gust of melan-choly, and I almost forgot to turn down the speakers.

I had no choice than to giggle a few times at the news. Yes, things had definitely changed around here in such a brief time.

Since the massacre, the Northwest Farm still remained closed. The Slaughterhouses stood idle and the Warm Ones awaited with their newly acquired power. It was almost like an old city of pre-Holocaust times or even Utopia. I almost wished we could have used our faith back when I was a rev-olutionary, but religion was all but nonexistent in those early post-Holocaust nights. It hit me then that my father always carried a cross in one of his pockets, even though he didn't know what it fully meant.

Stargazers were now relegated to commando tactics of in-vading the town to poach Warm One stock. A new covert branch of Ravens was created to find food until the wise El-ders found a way to reclaim The Farm. I doubted they ever would, since they would never turn down the ozone in the place: Warm Ones were too much of a commodity, especially now that rations were even lower. The price of juice had skyrocketed, wounding the service industry, making a lot of lower-caste Stargazers very hungry very often.

"But we're a society of equality," I said with another snicker, seeing how the actual population of Xanadu had dropped without reason. I knew the reasons, and they were probably out in the wilderness right now.

One of my plans nagged me from the back of my head, and it wasn't the god-soul: Spread the faith of the circle to the other Farms! Make the Warm Ones independent!

"Maybe," I whispered. "But it would leave things like in Utopia: Semi-independence and full-interdependence for both factions. I have to go farther . . ."

Another slab of news appeared, and this one completely surprised me. Forgetting about my plan to create mayhem in Xanadu, I noticed they hadn't forgotten theirs. In fact, they'd gone for it completely and regardless of the shocked economy. It took them from the time I left until I returned to finish the great plumbing job. As they dreamed, one could wake up and have a (rationed) cup of juice in the evening from the cupola.

I didn't know why they went ahead with it, but I guessed they needed another way to conform the Stargazer population. In addition, this way the juice supply could be better inventoried through expensive data banks found somewhere in The Citadel. This process had almost broken the back of Xanadu, but Elder commercials told of the rewards this would reap. Tighten your appetite and grow into the future, an advertisement said.

I shook my head, accessing more data. Different plans, none very attainable but one would be attempted before I was captured or thrown out again.

I heard a voice, distant, perhaps down the hall. It couldn't be! Only the secretaries and a few Ravens were ever allowed to miss The Fusing. This voice said something to the receptionist and neared the hallway.

Time to go, I first thought, turning off the machine and rising. Wait a second, it was a female voice, not Shibboleth's.

No one would come into his office . . . unless they had permission. Shit.

Then another thought made itself present: The voice, it was familiar, like a half-recalled dream, words not discernible.

I put my hand over my head, not knowing what to do. The footsteps were getting closer. It couldn't be . . .

The footsteps disappeared. I took a deep breath, even though I hadn't actually used my lungs in a long time. Obviously my head was playing tricks on me. Some blasphemer must have left The Fusing early in order to catch up on some work or something.

I sat down. A little more research and then I'm gone.

As soon as I slid into the chair and relaxed, the door opened and I'm sure a Stargazer floated in, having heard me when I heard her.

2

"Shibboleth?" a voice said, so well-known yet so tinged with the iciness of death.

I turned, the name on my lips catapulting out, all intention of escape taking a detour.

"Medea!"

You weren't always this way.

It was her, but it wasn't. Hair had grown, bobbing on her shoulders in glossy black; her eyes, once that honest brown were my grim color, and her skin was very white, flat white, like finely burnished china.

"Shibboleth?" she repeated, mouth hanging open, revealing the twin marks of a Stargazer. That wasn't all that glued me to the seat. It was something else as well, something that sent a cold rage slithering down my stomach.

Medea wore the robes of an Elder. The joke continued.

"The hair, the features." She tilted her head without an iota of recognition. "They are the Heretic's, but I don't think you are him."

"The Heretic?" I stammered, knocking over the chair as I stumbled to my feet. "Shibboleth?"

"Who are you?" she asked, her sternness softening for a second. "What are you doing in my office?"

"Medea." I looked away, not being able to see the perfect specter of unlife before me, my perfect creation obviously usurped, my friend.

"Why are you weeping?" she asked, not losing any of her bluntness, only the memory Our Mistress had strangled. "Who are you?"

I met her gaze in blooming aching. I smiled with sadness, I heaved with yearning.

"You could say I'm a dream, Medea," I said slowly. "A dream that is never too far away, if you only call it."

She placed a hand over her mouth. "The dream! I remember . . ."

"Don't ever forget it," I said and went for the window. Quietly I said, "I hate you."

And I fell down the curving wall, teetering for a while until I had the strength to fly toward my original destination, Proxos's connection. Medea didn't follow me, immobilized by my words about dreams. Thus, I flew alone and the only thing that brought any comfort to me was the fact that it seemed Shib had been doomed to my same fate. And he *had* served Lilith obediently.

Guess you must have grown "soft," Shib, old friend.

3

"I didn't know Proxos had sent you here to mope around," Drisha told me, placing a diluted meal of B-positive on the table. "Did you do the same thing at his place?"

"He didn't send me here," I said, head resting on my hand. "And I'm not moping. I'm thinking. I'm planning."

"Planning what?"

I didn't answer, eyeing the corpulent Stargazer. Right then, I knew why Drisha was so keen on Proxos. As she'd told me on various occasions during the few weeks I'd been here, her existence had to be an accident. She wasn't svelte or striking like much of the population; as a matter of fact the first time I met her, she reminded me of my old friend, Wendy. Drisha was plain, homely, and sexless. She didn't have Wendy's fire, but a kind of subdued pragmatism. Drisha was an outcast in a species of outcasts. It was obvious why she respected Proxos, the old ex-Elder known for his fairness and generosity to all aspects of Stargazer society.

Drisha told me she was around my age, born sometime at the end of the fall of Utopia, probably created to quickly fill their dying ranks when I began the Revolution. I didn't tell her that, of course, but I doubted anything would have changed if I did. Drisha's existence was as simple as her demeanor, and only her loyalty to Commodore and passion for trains gave her any true emotion.

My host dwelled in a rustic village close to the Northeast Farm. In a not so distant past, she drove the trains back and forth from The Citadel to The Farm, uncaring of the cargo. All she wanted was to drive. About fifty years ago, when computers and electrical trains were implemented, she lost her job, her mind not up to the new technology. Drisha worked odd jobs for the Transportation Guild these nights, fixing things here and there. Her home rested at the lip of a village of tunneled neighborhoods on the side of the tracks underneath the gigantic tube. She liked it; I was already getting sick of the constant noise.

"Nothing," I said with a tired smile. "Just wondering if the little station down there might need a ticket handler in one of the booths."

She sat down by me and filled our glasses. "Everything is done by computers, Mr. Solsbury. Whenever there is an outage or similar problem, I'll sometimes help out."

"You can call me Byron," I told the plaid-dressed, strawy-haired Stargazer.

"Master Commodore always told me to call you Mr. Solsbury."

I laughed. "The scoundrel."

"You better eat quickly," Drisha said, sipping on her cup. "The juice we get here clots too quickly. Not enough chemicals I suppose."

"Drisha," I said, looking at my food. "You're too kind. Maybe I should leave. You don't have enough food for two people."

She shrugged, staring into space. "I'm always helpful to Master Commodore. He was very kind to me back then. It's a pity that everyone thinks he perished. Even so, I can't fathom what goes on with our beloved leaders and Our Mistress. I don't question their motives, and I know the shortage will end soon, Mr. Solsbury."

"You're right," I said, trying to mask my sarcasm. "They won't let us starve."

"No," she agreed plainly.

After our meal, Drisha left me alone, saying she had to help one of the crew clean up part of a wall that had been damaged by a sandstorm. I bid her good-bye and sat in front of the computer idly playing some zapper game.

I started getting a headache, another reflex of another life. The so-called plan swirled before me.

I had no idea what to do.

I had spent the first week inspecting the various industries of Xanadu. I'd looked up files and structure plans for the nuclear and chemical plants. It should have been as easy as it sounded when I had planned it with Proxos, for The Elders had seduced our population in the same way we'd corralled the Warm Ones. In the past, most workers came in and out undisturbed, most guilds left their facilities open for visitors. We were a species of gods, of perfection.

Things had changed.

Traveling into Xanadu was difficult now that the authorities knew I was present. Legions of Ravens religiously guarded the perimeters. Eavesdropping on several of the engineers, I learned that complicated sensors and lethal traps designated for Stargazers lined the hallways and plant floors. There was no way I could do it alone, no way to devise an intricate scheme to make one of those places go "boom," especially the areas where the "boom" might be strong enough to rip out the heart of this city. I needed help for my vengeance and justice, and I wasn't going to get help unless Proxos suddenly appeared. Even with his help it was unlikely. The Elders had quickly tightened security, perhaps even before I arrived. Unlike Utopia and The Farms, I was a very visible foe in people's minds. I was a Heretic, after all, the second most reviled thing in Xanadu besides *Sol*.

On top of my frustrations with plotting my attack, I still couldn't get Medea out of my thoughts. Proxos had been half right about me coming with intentions of seeing her. I had arrived here to destroy the destroyers, but I had wanted to at least see her one more time (I hadn't expected it to come so quickly, but nothing surprised me anymore in retrospect). Couldn't I have both? I wondered. After all, she was an Elder, she had influence and perhaps something else from her prior lifetime. Did part of her humanity still exist? Could I bring it out like she had done with me? If I did, would she be my partner like she had that night when we battled in between two worlds?

"Come on, Byron," I told myself with small head shakes.

I didn't want her to be part of my vengeance. She was another ghost, another daughter I'd left behind. It had taken me more than a century to recapture my humanity and I still hadn't completely tethered all the old memories and emotions. Then again, it was her who challenged me, who brought out something in my unbeating heart because of who she was and what she represented. Could I do that to her?

"And doom her a second time," I groaned. "Like it happened with you."

I played different computer games for another eight hours, heard some news, and went early to *Moratoria*, part of me looking for a new plan to get back to chess games and midnight walks in the wastes. There was no point in seeking her, no point even in defying this society.

The only problem was that the Byron in me told me another thing as soon as blackness settled on my deceased visage. He told me about gazing at stars.

4

The stars burst before me, a symphony of horns blared in infinity. It sounded like something I'd written a long time ago when I first came to Xanadu, a passionate, prodigal son of Lilith.

I'm dreaming, I told myself, and a tunnel of watery light dipped under me. I followed it, vaporizing, turning into an echo, liquid voice in a well of sounds. Plop. Plop. No, you're more than dreaming, you're using a power you didn't know you had, didn't know you could use. Plop. We are connected after all, and Lilith isn't the only one with this power. I can use it. Plop. I can speak through it, follow the thread of connection. Plop. Plop. I can speak to you.

Where are you, Medea?

Who is it? a voice answered, spanning eternity, spanning nothing.

Medea.

Plop. Plop.

Is it you, dream?

It is. I've been searching for you since the beginning of time, I feel. I need you. I . . .

What?

I hate you.

The tunnel shook in racks of jittery feelings, trembling memories.

Who are you, what do you want? Leave me to rest.

I wish to speak to you.

You are speaking to me.

(And touch you, and breathe you, and hate you more.)

I wish to speak to you.

Where?

The date was set, the questions left unanswered, and I floated back through the cavity of hope, somewhere in a little dream.

5

When I woke up, Drisha was surprised to see me dressing with hurry. She asked me where I was going, pausing from ironing a load of more plaid-clothes. I'm sure she was sick of my erratic *Moratoria* patterns, but so was I.

"I'm going to The Citadel," I said, hopping as I tried to slide a boot up my shin. "To the Mall."

"Good place for a Heretic," she said dully, probably not realizing she'd made a quip.

"I'm in the mood to skate," I said.

"Can I come?" she asked shyly, bloated cheeks expanding slightly.

I regarded her with a sense of sorrow, realizing the only sorrow I should have was for myself. I was completely ignoring Proxos's advice on ignoring what I held dear. Not only that, but I was going into a potential trap like an amateur and

I didn't care. I just didn't care. I had to take that risk, any risk, because I wouldn't have it any other way.

"Another time, I promise. Have to meet an old flame."

The cheeks relaxed, her hopes returned to the pressing of garments. She didn't look up until I left.

"A what?" Drisha asked, just absorbing my prior comment.

"Fire and Ice," I said, going for my coat, thanking Proxos he had my style of wardrobe in his cavern. I fingered the disk-case in pseudo-comfort. "I don't know who said that. I think it was a Warm One."

Her lips rubbed in disgust, but at least there would be no more questions. She wouldn't even answer what train I should take, thus I took to the air once again.

Fire and Ice.

CHAPTER 15

The Mall hummed with gay noises. In the center, circling Stargazers sheared a chalky rink. Some skated more than others, most used their innate flight to aid them in the labor of showing off.

I wasn't participating, leaning over the plastic railing, comfortably smoking a cigarette I'd sponged from someone. Being spotted wasn't one of my main concerns, here with the shops, fake plants, and the myriad sounds sieving through speakers or television sets all around. I doubted anyone would recognize me with the powder-white hair and etched features adding age to what should have been an eternally thirty-something face. But that happens when you spend a few months in a sand catacomb.

This area brimmed with traffic of all sorts. Despite the dogged times in Xanadu, the population took to the tunnels and walkways and stores with the intention of escape. Many scientists had decreed that the normal thirty-five-hour work week was too short, but hey, we were a species of gods, of immortals. Even with all the time on their hands and aching stomachs, a little window shopping or ice-skating helped one forget just a little.

Still, I could sense the quiet despair of the Stargazers flurrying by me. Like Proxos had said, we were solitary but very territorial creatures. The territory was barren of food, and we still had to act civilized. Already, the news boomed of rogue Ravens trying to "hunt" off limits for themselves. The Elders wanted this shown to make an example, but I'm sure it would work the other way. Drisha had told me more and more "tourists" were tarrying to The Farms. I wouldn't have been surprised to see a black market of poachers arise from the law's sewers.

That wasn't my concern, though. My concern, as the cigarette crackled semi-quietly between my bleached fingers and dark shades hid my scanning eyes, was to meet someone. Once again, we were to meet like perfect strangers, me wondering if what I so rapidly felt for her was true care or just an admiration of what I once was in another lifetime.

I saw her leaving one of the tube-stations in the corner, between a jewelry store and a tattoo parlor (the newest fashion in Xanadu since my banishment). Of the jets of gas spurting out, one of them liquefied and solidified into the female named Medea. Wisely so, she wasn't wearing her Elder robes, but a flowing dress of lipstick-red that somehow didn't fit her, even in her changed state.

It didn't take anytime for her to see me. She walked coy-seductively toward me, and again it just didn't fit her. I started getting annoyed at this transformation, trying to tell myself it just didn't matter anymore. Things had happened, and it was time to try and righten them as much as possible.

Another thing that annoyed me was the fact that I'd already noticed hidden Ravens in the crowds, surrounding me. Oh well, better to be direct.

2

"Good evening," I said, pivoting away from the ice capade, stamping out my smoke.

She looked distastefully at my butt dirtying the glossy tile. Then she dove right in. "You are not Shibboleth, even though I never met him. I thought perhaps he disguised himself slightly in order to gain entrance."

"Sorry," I said, wanting to place a hand on her shoulder but knowing only one temperature would answer my senses. "Not Shib, though I've met him."

"Who are you? How can you reach me through *Moratoria*?"

I leaned on an elbow on the railing, trying to appear relaxed. The Ravens were closing in.

"Well, I guess I do share a quality with old Shibboleth, who I'm sure was dismissed as another example by Our Mistress. I thought I'd get all the press for the Northwest Farm."

Her pretty eyebrows crinkled slightly. "You? Are you . . ." She wouldn't even say my name, what a good little citizen.

"Byron," I said with a slow nod. "We've met before, Medea."

"We have, Heretic?" she hissed with revolt.

"Yes, we have. Another time, another life for both of us. The situation is very similar, but we can't hide the way we feel, what we were and are to each other."

"You talk like we have some sort of bond," Medea said, searching my eyes for something other than painful light.

"Sure, I created you," I said, not really liking the irony of this.

She shook her head, as if too impressed by radical words to be angered. "Only The Queen of Darkness can create our kind. She created me, Heretic, and your existence is forfeit for being here."

"Then why are you talking to me, Medea?" I asked, grabbing her arm. Yes, it was cold but the yearning in me only grew. "I can prove it, you know. You weren't always this way."

She had been looking around quickly, as if ready to give a signal. My last sentence wrenched her attention completely.

"Prove it," she said, glaring at me in pouting challenge.

That's more like you, I thought.

"Oh, I will," I said steadily.

"I doubt it, Traitor," she snarled.

I turned her struggling arm, pointing at certain marks. "Nice scars, Medea, very, very faint, coincidentally on the exact places a Warm One tattoo might have been. A little surgery, and you're almost like new—"

She pulled free. "Your insolence has no bounds, you—"

"Ever wonder why you were almost bald when you came into being, Medea?" I questioned, taking a step forward to make up for her angry retreat. "Ever wonder why you spoke a certain way or had certain likes and dislikes without foundation? Come on, Medea, think, damn it, think!"

She stopped and stared down, hands clutching themselves, senses closing in like a fan.

"Who are you?" she asked again, this time with trembles of frustration.

I held her shoulders, forcing her to see me. "Medea. Medea. It's me, Byron. I made you when you died. I—"

"Liar!" She struck with both arms, sending more than physical pain to my body. She took two steps back with a pointed finger, uncaring that heads turned and listened to our conversation. I could see the conflict in her twitching eyes, the frustration bulging in her thin neck.

"You are nothing more than a traitor who slew his own kind in the name of animals!" Medea screamed. "And it is my duty and pleasure as an Elder to vanquish you personally."

I sighed, a circle of space forming around us.

"You're probably right," I said without much emotion. "Give it your best shot, *Shaman of The Circle*."

Even though those words struck her like a sidewinder, she still was able to give the signal. I knew this would happen. I thought of Proxos's advice again and the fact that I was the second most stubborn creature I'd ever met besides Medea.

3

I didn't make a move. I didn't attempt some plucky escape. I stood there and allowed four Ravens to surround me. Two grabbed my arms, one stood in front of me holding a *radiovac*, nothing more than an overgrown vacuum cleaner used against Stargazers in mist form. The last one waved his arms and took care of crowd control.

I didn't know if they were surprised I was surrendering without a struggle, but I sure was mad they'd sent only four against me. Four, can you believe that?

"You were foolish to come back," Medea said with a tight smile. "You were more foolish to even try talking to me, an Elder."

"I speak the truth," I said, not wanting to elaborate anymore. "Search within yourself and you will find you're existing in a lie, Shaman."

She slapped my face, almost daintily. The soldiers held me tighter in case she wanted to inflict further damage.

"Get this embarrassment out of here," Medea ordered. "Take him to a holding tank and keep an eye on him at all times."

"Wait!" I exclaimed, suddenly feeling like I was really here. "You're forgetting something."

Medea slightly leaned over. The Ravens relaxed their grip.

"What is that, Heretic?" she asked.

I didn't answer, my silhouette did, as it began to gurgle and lose form.

They took the cue well. Medea took a step sideways, allowing the one with the *radiovac* to take aim with a gleaming tube. He positioned it ready to suck my gaseous form into a metal backpack. A whirling noise rang, and the crowd, forced to continue its march, stopped for a moment to see the effects.

I didn't flow into the tube. My body was dragged by the strong vortex of inhaling air, for it had returned quickly to its formal shape. The Ravens fell for it, and the one trying to devour me barely saw my knee dig into his face.

I did turn to fog this time, as the others tried to grapple me and Medea screamed in rage. Losing their prey, the two stumbled against each other. Surprising everyone even more, I materialized in front of Medea with a quick wink.

"Should have brought more against me," I said and planted a generous kiss on her face. She stumbled backward, giving me a chance to avoid a Raven jumping on me. I tossed him aside and didn't have time to see him ram into the other two, still trying to gain stance.

I took to the air, leaving Medea with a hand on her mouth, frozen against her rage. Stealthily, I flew toward one of the terraces, a place of empty bars, and searched for the first tube I could find. I could already hear the Ravens on my heels and more alarms sounding.

But they wouldn't find me. Like I hadn't been there, I quickly oozed into a tube that led to another mall. There, I glided downward and lost myself in a large store known for its exotic juices. There had been a sale, so it was no problem to blend into the struggling Stargazers trying to buy diluted, spiced blood at incredible prices. The last part of my plan, an hour later, transformed me into a *Ruka*like creature with leathery wings, which sailed over the top of the Mall's dome.

I should have been ecstatic at my victory, at the seeds I'd planted. I wasn't. A sense of loneliness dribbled within my chest hours later when I walked the large tunnels, trains and carts whizzing by me. I'd beat The MoonQueen's little creation, but it was shallow. They knew I was in their territory and getting caught was a matter of time. The only nice result from this was that even now that I did not hunger for her juice anymore, I still owned the same strong emotions for her being. Perhaps that wasn't so nice, since it only made me yearn for what we never had, what we never could have had, for destiny kept tossing us into different lives, different worlds where we were so far away from the other in many ways.

4

Drisha didn't say a word when I came in. She'd been working on another model train set, her only true hobby. She wasn't bad at it, but I'd seen better at shows in The Citadel where great metropolises were built with elegant but impractical railroad systems. At least she had something to give meaning to an otherwise useless existence.

I mumbled something and got changed, preparing for incoming *Moratoria*. Commuting by flying and skulking to The Citadel took a good portion of time, time that was running out very quickly.

When I came out of my chamber, no more than a small hole, Drisha confirmed any suspicions I might have had with one sentence. Another witty remark she probably didn't care she'd said, as I slid in front of the computer to get some last-minute news.

"So," she said, still not raising her head from her model. "I hear you're a celebrity."

CHAPTER 16

I was a celebrity. My face, posted throughout Xanadu in billboards or news flashes, showed a Heretic in the midst, the vilest sort besides a destroyed Heretic. There were no rewards or threats, the population knew to report me if seen and let the Ravens take care of the rest. Very simple and very simple to find the white-hair, striking fiend.

It was a good thing Drisha was loyal to Proxos. The chubby Stargazer purchased plenty of disguises for her famous guest. I lay low for a few nights, not knowing that things would get much worse very soon.

2

About two nights after my meeting with Medea, Drisha informed me she had been contacted by Proxos. I'd not been in *Moratoria* very well, strange voices breaking the vast expanse of slumber. Maybe it was the Shaman of The Circle, maybe it was The MoonQueen trying to mock me again. Either way, I did the best I could to block my senses.

"How did he contact you?" I asked, across the table from her, sharing a light meal. "I've been burning with curiosity."

Drisha shrugged lightly, twitching small, round lips. "It's supposed to be a secret, Mr. Solsbury."

I laughed. "Commodore and I have no secrets, we just keep things from each other in order to be dramatic. Come on, tell me."

She looked uncomfortable, but probably knew I would hound her the rest of the evening.

"He can speak to me through *Moratoria*," Drisha said slowly.

I thought for a moment and said, "You mean you have a bond?"

"Yes," she answered, dipping her finger in the bowl to savor the last scraps she'd purchased (even though her apartment had plumbing, it only worked periodically out here away from The Citadel).

I nodded, more to myself. "In other words, he created you. I see."

She stared at me with flat perplexity. "He created me? What do you mean? Only Our Mistress can create us, Mr. Solsbury."

I opened my mouth, but halted any speech. I understood that Proxos probably kept this from his "friends." It just wasn't necessary.

"Master Proxos and I have a special bond," Drisha said defensively. "All friends have these, Mr. Solsbury. They're never too far away from each other, you know."

"Of course," I agreed with a smile.

"Lord Commodore once told me about a legend before The Holocaust," she spoke with some excitement, a first. "He said that Stargazers have two souls. One, the cowardly one, hides from *Sol* during *Moratoria*, for it is not of this world. The other, the noble one, the one that truly gives us our power, travels during the raging of *Sol* across space, untouched by anything, all the way to the other side of *Luna*."

"Interesting," I put it, missing old Proxos and his dry persona. I wanted to ask the god-soul which one it was in jest, but it was content as long as he was sated in his consuming and its husk was well tended.

"There, he told me, there is no back part to part *Luna*, only endless darkness filled with the noble souls, who share wonderful tales and create their own adventures in infinite space."

"So that is where we . . ." I paused to find the word. "When our time is over here."

She narrowed eyes in contemplation. "I have never thought of this that way, Mr. Solsbury. I guess that is where we eventually go, our noble souls."

"And our cowardly souls go into the ground," I added with imagination. "And somehow, by losing something, we Stargazers become whole again."

"Yes, maybe it does." She grinned with small teeth and would stay that way for the rest of the evening.

"I envy you, Drisha," I said sadly, and totally forgot to ask her what Proxos had said.

3

The next evening, I did ask her. By then, my hopes all rested on Proxos. Either he might help me, or I would join him in the wilderness.

Drisha was outside the villa down at the tracks, a small figure under a looming, rugged arch of pale concrete and dangling lights. I walked over to her, passing the small station that was no more than a hovel next to the dozen steel lines carrying progress back and forth. The Stargazer in charge of handling the rows of computers inside the ticket booth didn't even glance at me since I was dressed in a gray jumper suit and wearing a red bandana over my hair.

Drisha grunted when she saw me. She had been hammering away at a loose board in one of the more primitive tracks, probably one of her menial assignments for the guild.

"By the way, do you recall what Proxos said in your talk?" I inquired, feeling somehow exposed in the middle of the tunnel.

She glanced up briefly, face slightly covered in dust. "He didn't say much. Just that he is tied up in what he is doing, I think. He will make it here sometime."

"That isn't much," I said, disturbed, but knowing Proxos's presence wasn't important to her, for they were never too far apart. "How many times has he come here?"

"Not many," she said, banging the large, rusted nail into the mock-wood of the beam. "Maybe two or three. I don't know. Oh yes, he also said he . . ." She paused, face contorting to a brief confusion she wasn't going to worry about. "Said something about helping you find the end to everything. I think . . ."

I sighed, suddenly not liking the weight I'd put on my shoulders. The end of everything. I must have lost my mind somewhere in the sand dunes.

"Maybe he said—" Drisha started, stopping immediately and flinching. "What's that?"

I could hear it, too. A humming sound, gyrating vibrations coming less than a mile down.

"Sounds like a train, Drish," I commented, taking out a cigarette from a pack she'd been nice enough to buy me.

"That's strange," she said, getting on her feet. "The 20.15 doesn't come for another fifteen minutes, even with the winter-schedule change."

"Maybe it's late," I said, walking back to the villa.

"But it sounds like it's on the wrong track, too," I heard her say. I didn't answer, leaving her to deal with her crisis. I wanted to tell her I was soon not going to be a hindrance on her anymore. I'd wait till the end of the night.

A whistling and sonorous howl filled the tunnel, just as I walked up the stairs to the complex. I needed to go inside quickly in case I was spotted by some bored passenger looking out toward me. Something nagged me and nagged my body to halt. I turned toward the station, trying to recapture part of a recent conversation.

The 20.15 doesn't come for another fifteen minutes, even with the winter-schedule change.

"Ah, shit!" I hissed, dropping the smoke, trying to catch the growing light coming my way. I stood frozen on the steps, part of me wanting to run, part of me concerned for Drisha.

Without thinking about it, I started screaming her name, waving my arms frantically. She was waiting by the track. After hearing my voice, she calmly walked toward me.

"Drisha, get away from there. Come here *now!*"

She shook her head at me trying to signal her. Maybe it was nothing, but an alarm had sounded from every pore. Maybe it was nothing . . .

The train, a small one, slithered to a halt, screeching majestically, dust rising like a storm. As the windows took form, motion causing them to be but globs of color, I noticed many shapes facing this way. Drisha just stood right in front of it, her flannel gown and short hair lashing against the erratic air, looking at me with a droll expression.

When the train came to a complete stop, she glanced back briefly and choked on her own chagrin.

Doors and windows were blasting open, Raven after Raven, most of them armed, puked out of the ebony machine, flying, spurting, running toward my direction. They probably were all chuckling at the fact that my shouts and waves had just given them my exact location on this zone.

But I was glad I had done that, for the soldiers ignored the terrified Stargazer. Time to make my move, I thought, disintegrating to fog. It would be harder than they thought, for other Stargazers oozed or ran out of the tunnel-encrusting apartments, wondering or dreading why this little army came to their quiet abode.

Bodies, cries, and gases flew by me, all trying to avoid the black wave covering the villa. Instead of walking toward the few allies at the sides, down the train tunnel or upward, I zigzagged into the complex through windows and vents, hoping to catch an escape from behind and into the outdoors. I discerned various voices, praying that the soldiers would expect me to follow the occupants of this complex. From all the voices of anger and fear, one stuck out when I had almost reached the cracks in the deepest apartment.

I heard Drisha. What was she doing so close?

Then I listened to the ghastly torrent of fire. Flamethrowers were being used.

"Not my house!" her voice shrieked somewhere. "My models, please don't hurt them!"

More voices drummed my senses then, angry voices, along with the sounds of destruction. Damn it, Drisha, you shouldn't have come back . . . run . . . get away!

I found myself taking solid form, shattering a few ceilings, and flying above the villa. Only about ten feet until rock marked the roof of this section. It gave me enough acceleration to whirl around other floating Stargazers and Ravens. I aimed for the apartment building with the most fires. Mortar and Sheetrock gave away to my body. So did a lagoon of flame.

"Drish!" I yelled, landing in her living room, baptized in ebbing heat. A Raven, who must have had the misfortune of running into her as she entered, trembled on the floor by the entrance, trying to move with a snapped spine.

"Drish!" I yelled again, hearing more flamethrowers and shouts of victory outside. They must have known where my host lived. Somebody at the top must have known that there was a good possibility I would have helped her.

My host appeared from her room, holding a large box, half of her body singed, peeling to the bone.

"My models," she choked. "Must save them, Mr. Solsbury."

"Drisha, no!" I snarled, reaching for her, sensing the foundation begin to rumble and forms surrounding the whole place. "Let's get out here. Forget them, Drish—"

"My models," she squeaked, reeling at the damage sustained. "Must save—"

The wall to her side suddenly collapsed under a battering ram of flame. Shrapnel and tongues of fire struck her, smashing the box to cinders, throwing her off her feet.

"Drisha!" I exclaimed, horrified at the dark figures marching inside in a single line, stoic expressions behind thick goggles. Something yielded behind me with a crash.

She should have stayed on the ground, she should have given up. Instead, the Stargazer rose to her feet, hands with little flesh poking at the ashes of the box. She never saw the second strike.

"My—" I thought I heard her say when six streams of liquid heat covered her simultaneously. I thought I might have said something, but the vast inferno rose like a wall, making me teeter backward.

Survival taking over concern, I stumbled, senses numbed in pain and confusion, and let my being turn to mist before I became swallowed by the waves of fire.

Everything turned to slow motion, phenomena grinding against too much action. I thought I saw more walls fizzing into wreckage, more silhouettes rushing toward me, more blazing punishing Drisha's simple home.

Then I saw a familiar face, grim in anticipation, holding a long, bright tube toward my fleeing form.

It wasn't a flamethrower.

CHAPTER 17

My father, strong and big, a mustachioed, cigar-smoking, curse-sputtering veteran of some pre-Holocaust war, always held me in wonder with his little sayings. He was as raw as he was astute. He had as many friends as foes in his lifetime, in the two worlds he had lived in, and all heard his little sayings.

"The blood is on their hands," he once said, Old Town celebrating the fact that he single-handedly defeated a Stargazer, a god. Like everything else, memories flashed like spurts of bad reception, distant fizzles in the mind's camera. I couldn't recall how he killed it, being no more than twelve, but I somehow never forgot that saying or the pride it brought me that day.

"How did ya do it?" his friend and accomplice, Tom, asked through naked gums. "Did ya drive a stake through its heart?"

"No, you asshole," he said, laughing, and I remember my mother's hands sliding over my ears. "That crap don't work anymore, probably never did in the first place. Goddamn bitch probably has all the hearts of these pricks hidden up her—"

I heard my mom shout at him about his mouth with words I couldn't understand. If it wasn't his mouth, it was his temper, or just his uncouth comments. I don't think they were together anymore, if at all. We lived all together, though, until the night my mother was taken by my present species, trying to find books for me in some abandoned library.

My father crossed his arms, a statue of pride. "Don't matter what I say or what I do. Blood's on their hands."

Thinking of him, I wished I could have looked at my own clawed hands and imagined the blood there, the blood of the lives that had fallen because of me, innocent ones who simply had the misfortune of coming under the shadows of my misbegotten schemes.

I also wished I could have spoken an apology to Drish, even as she wandered to the dark side of *Luna*.

But I had no hands and no lips. I was vapor trapped in metal. I didn't know how long a Stargazer could survive like this, but I knew my being was dissipating in a very unromantic way.

Shit, I thought, knowing where I got the foul mouth from.

2

I touched my eyes. I had eyes. I existed again of stony flesh and spiritual juice, not realizing I had been blown out of my container. The next thing I did was gaze at my hands. No physical juice, but there was blood on my hands.

The blood, specifically Drisha's and perhaps others from her complex, was also shared by the figure standing in front of my cage, thin bars separating us in a simple room.

"I'm glad you made it," the figure said with an almost concerned smile.

I didn't say anything, too weary to open my big mouth.

"There is food on the table next to you. Please don't touch the bars, it's about fifty-thousand volts of soberness." She pointed at the circuit box several feet away from the cage. "The roof of your cell is nothing more than a *radiovac*, which will turn on as soon as you try mist form. You'll have to be in *Moratoria* in crouching position. It is humiliating and perhaps a little draining, but it will serve our purposes, Byron."

"Thanks," I said. It came out more like a sigh.

"Get some rest. We have much to discuss."

Medea walked out of the room.

"Shit," I said this time.

3

Moratoria was more than a little draining. In a cage, somehow closer than I should have been to the outside, I cringed and ached all night. In fetal position, I was swept away by heat and shapeless dreams. I remember crying out to a mother I still couldn't place a face to, and another one colder than death itself, emotional vacuum in a world of misplaced feelings.

Luna eventually came, like she did every night, our true mistress, earth's secret handmaiden.

And so did Medea.

I couldn't help think of how gorgeous she was, my little pet once, my creation. She stood paces away from me with a condescending smile. Damn her. Damn me for thinking of her beauty instead of the fact that my existence was as forfeit as Shib and The MoonQueen had wanted in the past. I was at her hands.

Behind her, also bragging the same shade of a smile, stood Black Gomez. Although wearing an Elder robe, his annoying personality was reflected in laced trim sprouting underneath his sleeves, powdery makeup and lipstick, and a few painted dots on his long face. For reasons that couldn't include his fashion or his bravery, I'd never liked Gomez, the former mayor of New Tenochtitlan and a young Elder chosen after he escaped the Cataclysm of Tears. Right then, I realized I'd wasted my years simply disliking him.

"Very well done, Master Medea," he said. "Our Mistress knew who to replace Shibboleth with. You've done nothing but impress The Council in your short tenure."

"Thank you, Master Gomez," she said.

"This is the first and hopefully last time a Heretic has dared to invade our capital. I've always been a firm believer in public executions, Byron. What do you think of them?"

"Not civilized," I replied.

He laughed, tilting his head back, waving one hand on a floppy wrist. Medea only stared at me, crossing her arms.

"I'm afraid The Elders have always agreed with that," Gomez said, his mirth vanishing like a whim. "But this is a serious matter, Byron. You are more vile than the vilest of the vilest. You are an embarrassment to our cause, a tired bruise on the side of this society. Perhaps you can set a precedent, eh? Perhaps I can persuade Medea and the others to make an example of you, once and for all."

"The Elders have never believed in public examples," Medea said. "Nor potential martyrs, for that matter, Master Gomez. I think information is the most valuable asset the Heretic has. After that, forgetfulness is his and our best reward."

Gomez snorted, pointing at me. "But this . . . this thing, Master. He razed Utopia, he caused the destruction of a Farm. He even dared confront—"

"Yeah, I confronted her," I said, not liking that I was being spoken about as though I wasn't here. "And you know what, Gomez? She let me survive each time. Which is more than I can say if I ever get my claws on you."

The Elder's mouth closed, his cheeks vibrated. He still retreated a step. Before he had mustered enough indignance to give another one of his speeches, Medea had lifted a hand.

"The Heretic is correct," she said firmly. "But we have agreed to deal directly with you, unless Our Mistress states otherwise. So forget any prior deliverance." She turned to her partner. "You are right, Master Gomez, he is a vile one, so I suggest we get this over with."

"Your suggestion is noted," he said, folding his hands. "Again, you impress me. Please, go on. I will enjoy this."

"Why did you come back?" she asked me, wasting no time.

"I forgot a belt with sentimental value," I responded.

"Answer me truthfully, Heretic. Aren't you hungry? I can see it in you. I didn't leave much food out last night, barely enough to wet your mouth. You're tired from a humiliating *Moratoria*, starting to pain in certain places. We are patient. A starving Stargazer is not a pretty sight. The Dark Instinct would rather be free than allow its desire to go unfulfilled. They say the mind succumbs long before the body. Two nights, perhaps? Three?"

I grinned, trying to mask the truth she had made clear. I also made something clear.

"What's the difference?" You're going to destroy me. One way or another. Slow or quickly. I'd like to do it slow and hard."

Black Gomez gasped, mouthing the word "beast," but Medea remained unruffled.

"Why did you come back?"

"To beg for forgiveness," I said.

She took out a canister from her robes. Opening it, she held it toward me. I cringed, knowing what was inside. Something akin to electricity crackled in my veins and scissored my midsection several times. My chest swelled with hot emptiness. My head spun and my body wanted to do the same. Yet, I stood firm, ignoring the quivering, the voice of my Dark Instinct.

"It's good," Medea said, taking a small gulp. "You can have it, Heretic. We just want some answers. I will ask you this one more time. If you don't cooperate, we'll leave. Understood?"

I wanted to say something nasty, but the god-soul kept shouting at me to attack the bars.

Feed, bastard!

"Why did you come back?"

"Because I missed you," I uttered without forethought.

Gomez cackled, holding his stomach. The other Elder pursed her lips. I wanted to match her gaze, but found myself leaning over, usurped by a deep drumming.

"This is too much," Black Gomez said, opening the door. "I would like nothing more than to stay here and witness this spectacle, Master, but I must put together a video clip on this story."

"Of course, Master Gomez," Medea said.

"Since Balkros is less than indifferent to the Heretic, he is all yours. The Council will expect only the best results when you're done. Good-bye, Byron, you *hijo de puta*. It was a pleasure seeing you hurt."

"Pleasure's all mine," I groaned.

"Place all your belongings on the table," she ordered when he had left. I had taken the opportunity to sit down. "Remove all articles of clothing."

I glanced up, trying to conjure any anger to fight this slow draining of dignity.

"No," I said. "I have nothing you need, except the truth."

"Quiet with that!" she snapped. "Do you ever desist? You know what will happen."

"I'm not afraid, Medea. You were never, either. Do what you have to, and forgive me for not caring anymore."

I lowered my head between my knees, hearing her growl. The growling turned into laughter. Before I had dared another look, she had sifted in mist form underneath the door.

The canister lay a foot away from the bars. I snatched it quickly, not knowing or caring if this was just a tease. I drained the contents into my body and howled afterward in what was the slightest of joys, the greatest of reliefs. Barely a pint. Enough to get me by. Another night.

4

"I've done some research on you," Medea said mechanically the next evening. "You were right about Our Mistress sparing you. That's very odd, and none of the others seem to understand. Can you tell me about it?"

She showed me another canister. I half smirked. Through the agony I'd been fighting, the endless starvation swelling within me, confiscating thought and stamina, I knew I would have answered that in any event.

"She didn't spare me, Medea. I survived."

"None can survive her wrath, Heretic. The Elders had thought she had simply erased you. After how you challenged Xanadu, taking your defiance of The Farm directly to her, I just don't understand. She wouldn't have made anyone a Heretic for that."

"Well, she did," I said, wrestling with my throat that kept tightening against my vocal cords. "I don't know if she spared me, but she did make me a Heretic. Maybe she didn't, maybe it was just you fellows in The Council."

"It doesn't make sen—"

"Nothing makes sense, Medea. That's why we're here right now!"

"Do you love her?" Medea suddenly asked, I think surprising herself as much as me. She had used that word Proxos had alluded to and I recalled as a Warm One. Any discomfort was temporarily washed away by shock. I answered after a minute, lost in eyes that for once had faltered in her rocky determination.

"No, Medea," I said slowly. "Please, don't you—

She raised a hand, a small hand, which I had clutched so nicely in other lives.

"Never mind," she said with some embarrassment. "It's all irrelevant now. I am out of order. All that matters are the important questions."

She handed me the canister, which I emptied swiftly. I then sighed and pretended to admire the ceiling of my cage.

"You're right about that, Medea. A cigarette would be great, you know."

"A cigarette?"

"You don't know what one is? Insulting your own intelligence isn't your style."

She also pretended to watch the same ceiling. "Whining isn't yours. The time isn't right . . ."

"For what? Cigarettes?"

"It isn't right," she said. "I must go. The time isn't right."

She left before I could slouch down again and murmur the 'great' word. I was alone. The night would continue. The Dark Instinct would rise from its demanding well and flog me. Medea was just baiting me with morsels of juice, knowing the hunger would exact a large toll. I had already paid much of it.

Proxos would think I was a fool for ending here, if he wasn't angered about Drisha. Between here and the tame freedom I had enjoyed in the wilderness, Medea filled my thoughts until my head stung.

Relax, you bastard, because that's all you are. My bastard! It's all about feeding. You're a hunter. A caged one, but a hunter.

"Thanks," I said, lowering my head in the ending spectrum of the twilight. Taking some of my god-soul's advice, I tried to concentrate on other things, build enough will to fight the hunger when the juice I had downed dissipated into my divine body.

For some reason, in my situation, I found it easy to thread a feeling to a feeling, still recalling much of what Lilith had submerged, corrupted and my entombment emancipated. Through my years as a Heretic, I'd been forced to achingly pick them out of the scab that she'd left behind, the wound she thought, like my brethren, should have never healed. The feeling now was desperation. Desperation born from the sensation of powerlessness, imminent anguish. I'd only really felt this way once, this impotent and hopeless, and I believed it still wasn't as bad as now because I had still held the capacity of a warrior.

I thought of Utopia. My home.

5

The chimneys of the Slaughterhouses, the tornado storm, the battle between worlds, amongst the two species where I'd saved and destroyed. They couldn't have matched in pure brilliance and force that of which rose above the horizon.

Wendy's mission has succeeded, I can tell from my home, watching a celestial flash sear the sky sometime during a cloudy day. All the inhabitants of my project are in the basement, including my wife and daughter. I stand alone in my apartment, my home, and watch behind thick goggles the first explosion topple the Ozone Processor. It occurs in the middle of the day, since Wendy and my soldiers couldn't have gotten there at night with the security. It took them six hours to get deep within enemy territory. Part of me curses the fact that I had acted sometime in early spring, when daylight is still short. The vampires have lost their protection now, much of their buildings ready to catch the sweeping fire, so it's still a success. For now.

When the third explosion glimmers, caused by a chain reaction affecting their other plants, I go to retrieve my clan. All the way down, I bark orders on a cellular, which steals transmissions from one of their satellites. The bunks must be readied. In less than an hour, Utopia will be lashed by radioactivity, nuclear fallout, and Jesus knows what else. I don't know who Jesus is, but my parents always said he was a liberator.

I recall talking to my cousin, my right-hand man, who curses me for doing this now since his mate has just given birth. I tell him there will never be a truly good time, those two words left behind in the atomic storm that separates ages.

"Just get your own project to safety," I snap. "You'll be telling your children stories of this feat one of these days. Get to work."

Everything goes smoothly. Soldiers oozing from the basement, we lead our people to planned paths. The basements serve only to protect our eyes from the withering light at first. We need to go deeper, to hide behind feet of concrete with hidden reserves of food. We don't have idols, just our inner faith. Faith that will make sure the fire this time swipes them in the crippling manner they did to us. Across the city, hundreds of these groups like mine are rushing for final sanctuary.

My daughter cries heavily through much of the ordeal. I should have sent her away with the clan, but I need my family's strength. Since it's still daylight and the monsters sleep, all I need to do is bellow orders on a street corner at a busy intersection, communicate our strategy to the thousands waiting at the many projects, and try to make sure we get as many as we can underground. Everything goes smoothly. The girl latches on to my legs most of the time, while my wife stands next to me. Herds of people pass us, holding sparse belongings, urging their children. Then the sky darkens, and it still isn't night. Then dusk inevitably comes, and we can hear loud sirens in the distance.

"Oh, God!" my wife gasps with realization. "We're leaving our home. Byron, we're leaving our home."

"I know." I place an arm around her. "It's for the better. We'll have a better home. We'll end this all, once and for all."

She pats my cheek with her hand. Her look seems as childish as my girl's, with the same context of blind hope.

"You think so? It's all going to end, Byron?"

I kiss her, warmth to warmth.

"It's all going to end."

"But I don't want it to end, Daddy," the girl says, tugging at me. "I want my toys. We left them back there."

I grab and sling her to my chest. "Daddy will make you other toys . . ."

What was her name?

". . . we're going to a better place. Do you believe Daddy?"

"Yes," she says timidly, looking up at the frothing sky. "But I want my toys."

"Daddy will get you some new ones," my wife says,

stroking her back. "But we must go. You must behave, dear. You promise."

"I promise," the girl coos. "It's getting so bright, Mommy."

We take our course, already behind the rabble heading for their shelter. Night settles like a warning. As I predicted, none of the streetlights flicker on our side, the electrical plant already handicapped by our assault. I haven't heard from Wendy yet. She'd better have taken my orders, the damn dyke.

I had anticipated many things, but not this. As the last character of day vanishes, just at the last second, something interrupts our pilgrimage. We never noticed it at first, finding ourselves on our backs, my daughter crying in fear.

An earthquake.

Hearing my wife trying to calm the little girl, I know it isn't natural. The ground mutters with impact, cracking old houses, severing streets.

Trying to urge them on, hearing more explosions now on our side of the river, I notice the sky turn lighter, much lighter. I push my family ahead, telling them we need to catch up. We are lagging too far behind our clan. The shelter.

"Look, Daddy," my daughter says, her tears so easily lost in curiosity. "It's a comet."

She is right, but so wrong. It is a comet, a radiant missile of blue flame dissolving cloud and smoke in its wake. It rises so high, so majestically over us, descending right in the area where many of the shelters had been forged. Behind its light, I hear a shriek of venom, so loud we fall on the ground a second time with covered ears. Windows shatter in tall buildings.

The light vanishes, and then more brilliant explosions before us. By then, as my wife and I are sprinting, we can feel the hot breath of the destruction of New Town and so much more.

Growls, immense growls, coming from the sky, coming from everywhere. I'd never thought they could be that fast, but this is a time of emergency. We must hurry, I must get my family to safety.

"Byron," my wife shouts. "There's people over there. They're trapped. We must help them."

"I . . ." I say with a swallow. "I . . . we can't."

"Byron!" she urges with narrow eyes. These are our people, her expression tells me. She's right. I need her strength, her quiet stamina.

Before I can think of any reason to be wise and escape for the shelter, I'm helping people from smoking ruins at our wake, those still alive, directing them out of this growing pandemonium. There's so much to do, all around us. The earthquake . . .

I glance at my wife. She nods, eyeing the violent sky. We have to go.

I find myself darting through alleys and buildings, eventually taking to the sewers through a manhole. I sense angry presences above us, joined by ash and bursts of fire. It is all ending. It is all beginning.

"We're almost there," I shout, hoping they didn't see the many bodies scattered in the waters, people, my people, who have given up or succumbed to the encroaching hell. My daughter has buried her head in my chest, my wife is gripping my hand.

"We're almost there."

I see a sapphire flash in the distance, perceive another tremor. We collapse into the dirty waters, but continue. I ignore my family's crying. We're almost there.

The shelter should have been closed, the reinforced iron doors only admitting one with the right knock. They were secret, but they were open. Perhaps the others were still waiting for me, their leader, the one who had caused all of this. Perhaps . . .

I lower my daughter. Diedre takes her with a blank expression.

That was her name.

"Stay here," I command. They must be just waiting for me, but no sound emanates from the other side. I push my head in, first noticing a large crater on the ceiling, trimmed in ice.

Whatever had come in had left very directly. It had left a scene that could never be forgotten, in a hundred years, in a thousand, in the vast abyss that is blissful denial.

"Jesus Christ!" I hiss, seeing so much under the few lamps over a low ceiling, what's left of it, of the large chamber comprising our shelter. Much of the illumination is out, though, as odd icicles cover the roof, frost matts the walls.

"Jesus fucking Christ," I say, and my wife whimpers on the other side.

Everyone has the same, final decoration. Some sit, most lay on the floor, a few still stand, trapped in a gloss of winter. Yet each owns a gash somewhere on their throats, deep, ending, their blood already coagulated by the cold. Eyes look toward me in certain surprise, as if they hadn't known what had entered and stolen their lives. I had just spoken to many of them, my daughter had recently played with many of the children here.

I want to walk in, inspect the adjoining chambers and storerooms, but know with all of my dread what I will find. The same looks. Cold. Ice. My people.

I slam the door closed. Only about twenty minutes. I had been behind them that long. How could have something done this so quickly? Eight hundred people. I should be part of them. Twenty minutes, but their faces informed me they probably had died in less than one. It isn't a Stargazer. It's more . . .

"Byron," Diedre begs. "What happened in there?"

I inhale a deep breath and clench my fists with all I have. Father always believed in action, not inaction. A warrior acts, doesn't think, doesn't need to feel.

"Let's go," I say, grabbing my daughter. "We'll go to another shelter."

"I'm tired, Daddy," the girl says. "Why can't we go in there? I want to play with—"

We're on the run again. We climb through the manhole, ashes and arrogant heat covering our city. Chaste fire burns in structures around us. Screams howl in the distance, reflecting anger or doom.

"Just a few more blocks," I yell, hearing darting forms above us. I try again to go in between alleys and narrow streets, but walls have disappeared in so many places.

"Byron," Diedre says. "Can't we just lay with the corpses? Pretend we're dead until daylight?"

I shake my head. "No. It's not safe. Good plan, but not safe."

"But we won't make it," my wife says. "It's too far away. We should—"

"No!" I repeat. "You don't understand. This place won't be livable very soon. And they're coming, and they'll know, Diedre. They'll know we're . . ."

Smoke laughs at me steps away. It gurgles. It changes.

It stands in my way, a fat one, mouth matted in fresh blood. My wife screams, while I toss my daughter back to her.

"Going somewhere, my precious?" it says, flexing its claws.

"None of your business," I say, taking out my weapon, a gun, that's what it is. Another of those blue flashes appears somewhere behind him, high above the clouds. Then it descends rapidly, vanishes. I know it will rise again in a minute, leaving more winter, more destruction. It's her, the one in the stories.

The monster eyes my weapon with little concern. It leers at me, showing stained fangs, a serpentine tongue dripping with something that didn't belong to it.

"Do you think that's going to hurt me?" it asks dramatically, taking a step forward.

"Exactly," I say, and shoot him through the left eye. Its head cocks back, and then falls forward to covering hands. A scream of rage follows.

"You son of a bitch!" it bawls, showing me its mangled face. "I'm going to—"

"Language," I tell it, knowing the idiot would have wanted me to witness the damage, as the vampires always want to show our kind how nothing can really take them out.

I shoot him this time in the right eye.

We continue, leaving the monster behind swiping blindly at thin air.

"You hurt him, Daddy," my daughter says, face over my shoulder. "You—"

"Quiet . . ." and I say her name.

What was her name?

Perhaps it's the sight of the neighboring shelter, underneath a building that's been shaven entirely from its foundation and crumpled to one side. Perhaps it's the oily smoke rising from it, revealing its fate and the ones it housed. Perhaps it was just the red specks of eyes appearing through the darkness. But I don't catch her name.

I do catch the rising desperation. Something had gotten to it. If we descend we will find similar results to our respective bunker. My plan, what had happened to it?

What happened to it is the blue comet, now descending toward us. I drag my family through a building, to the next block, hearing growls of monsters that appear at each interval, doing nothing but corralling.

My body beams in sweat, muscles complain in throbbing jolts, but I continue. My chest feels like an oven. A warrior acts. A warrior . . .

A few dash in our way. Many have missing limbs, bones grinning through melted skin. Some hobble on twisted limbs. It doesn't matter, they are still angry, dangerous. I blast them off their feet and hurry. My wife sobs in frustration. My daughter is very quiet.

It all ends somewhere in the ruins of some edifice, fire crackling around us, radiation making me sleepy. We are covered in ashes, soot, and desperation.

We are also surrounded by those crimson eyes. All around us, while the comet hovers over us with a haunting melody. I can't run anymore. I have to act. My family at my knees, I take my stance, weapon held out in one hand, my other still holding a cellular that has no dial tone anymore.

"We can't fight them, Byron," Diedre cries. "We've got to try and run. Oh, God!"

There is no God, I think, there is only them and the inferno I have created. What happened to my plan?

"I love you very much," I say shakily, replacing the magazine of my weapon. "Don't forget that. No matter what. No matter when. I love you two so much."

"Byron?" Diedre looks at me oddly. I hug her and then hug the little girl. Deformed figures are beginning to close in, out of the shadows, out of the flames.

And suddenly, there she is before us, beautiful and ancient, wearing gowns of light, jewels of liquid energy, taking form from an eternal snow that is her being. Behind her, the monsters crowd obscenely, keeping their distance.

"Daddy," my daughter says with a big smile, eyeing her with fascination. "Look, it's—"

"I love you," I repeat, looking directly at the queen-bitch. "Never forget that."

And I fire my weapon.

6

And I screamed in rage, sending this vision back to limbo from where I'd picked it. I couldn't take it anymore. It was so clear yet separated by a membrane of states, reality and the recalled vision. And in this state the rage came because I couldn't fully cross that membrane. I recalled the notion of sweat, the kiss, the fire. I saw how hard I took oxygen in. Tiredness.

Yet, I couldn't capture the true taste of her saliva, her warmth, the warmth of the fire, the aching muscles, nothing, absolutely nothing, here, trapped on the other side of history.

That hurt more than the facts, the memory, which I'd kept in check on the base of my skull, inside this divine body, that yearned, that craved the blood, its warmth, its symbolism of all that once lived.

"I loved you," I said, finally invoking that human word, kneeling in my confines, close to *Moratoria*. The needle had been thread, puncturing the membrane open to allow a pinprick of light, sliver of remembrance. Nice metaphors. Terrible situation. I was so hungry. Weary, beaten. Right then, I only wanted to cross the membrane, to understand those things that had been stolen from me, that had made me a thief. I knew I couldn't cross further, deeper, for the queen-bitch had taken it all away that night, along with the last remnants of what happened in the end. And my new beginning.

CHAPTER 18

"Good evening, Byron," she said, standing inches from my jail. It hit me then that she'd used my first name instead of some derogatory pronoun. "Ready to talk?"

"Been ready since the meeting at the rink," I muttered. If I had *Moratoria*, I didn't feel it, exhausted, mood as sunken as my eyes must have looked. Thinking of that night, the first time I had battled Lilith and her brood, hadn't helped. Even the god-soul was quiet somewhere in the recess of my darkness.

"I know," she said, "and I'm ready to talk now."

She placed her fingers on the bars. Nothing happened. I closed my eyes and groaned internally.

Medea laughed. "Not so smart as you thought you were. Could have been gone by now."

"Where?" I asked, as she unlocked the door and motioned me to follow her. We entered another room, more spacious with several lavish computers only a high-standing member of Xanadu could have boasted.

"Sit," she commanded, and I did. She placed a large bowl of food on the console. As I fed, she pressed a few buttons. The screens burst to show news flashes. By the time I'd heard the first minute, an empty bowl lay on the floor and my mandible had separated from my wet fangs.

"They think I'm destroyed? That I perished during that raid on the village?"

Medea, standing behind me, placed her hands on my chair and said, "You can always change the news when you help control it. We all wanted it this way, except for Gomez. It's a pity about the village, but a firm example had to be set. We lost a handful of Ravens and about five Stargazers including your friend. But at least Byron, the Heretic, was expunged forever."

"He was?" I shuddered, once again feeling like I wasn't in this city.

"Yes he was, after he was found. Your one mistake, Byron, was assuming that because you created me you could only speak to me during *Moratoria*. One of the first things Lilith tells us when we take the robes of the Rose is that she can reach *any* of her creations at anytime. I pinpointed your relative location by sensing you."

She knew I created her? She believed it?

"Who?" I simply asked, testing what she'd just said.

Her hands crawled over my shoulders, which were ballooning firmly from the energy replenishing the starvation damage.

"Who helped us cover this up? Ravens have their oaths, and I promised The Elders to have you perish immediately after I had finished interrogating you. Like I said, the rest believe you burned along with the one called Drisha."

Her fingers plucked at my hair. My lids felt heavy, my chest hollow.

"You were lucky Mephisto is once again a Raven," she continued. "In one of his first assignments, he paid back his tortured debt to you, as he put it. An arm for an arm, he said. As for me, I told The Elders you succumbed to the tormenting, that you weren't as strong as everyone thought you were. They didn't really care, even Gomez."

"Why, Medea?" I asked shakily.

One hand turned my chair. I faced features holding little rancor, no apathy. I faced an expression that once held color, that once owned capillaries brimming with juice and emotion. Now the features were divinity, a fine statuette in the universe's museum, but there was a ghost of a smile.

She caressed my face with her palm. A magnetic residue brought me closer to her. Could this be just taunting? I thought but didn't care. If this was as close as it would get, so be it.

"Byron," she said, and licked my name from her lips. "You should have kissed me before you tried talking to me, you fool."

"You know who you are?"

She nodded. "I am like you now, Byron."

I held her in my arms before kisses took away any communication and said, "You were always like me, Medea. You'll always be like me!"

"I hate you," she said, and held me tighter.

2

We sojourned to yet another chamber of this secret enclave of Medea. This time to a luxurious chamber of silver trim and satin sheets. We stared at each other, slowly undressing the other. Once she had touched my face underneath a temple and awoken something in me, now it seemed my touching of her mouth had done the same. We went further. We went to forge our friendship, to bring forth more of ourselves.

Why are we doing this? her expression asked me.

Because we may never again, I told her with my eyes. Because this is an expression of what we once might have shared and should have belonged to us. Because we're imitating what is right.

Our thoughts became voiceless rhythms, as we lay down and acted that play of creation, so forbidden for our kind. It wasn't like the savage encounter with Tina, it was gentler, painful, eternal. We made love like shy Warm Ones, like two rivers eroding grime and joining in passionate flow.

Medea didn't ask to see it, though. She bucked under my onslaught, purring when I filled her again with juice, with my life, a second time. And this time she came to me fully known, fully willing. We felt ourselves crossing that membrane, trying to recapture what had been stolen by Lilith's granting of the Dark Instinct.

Then something burst inside her in molten delirium. She urged me on, grasping me tighter, and I rode with her until she calmed under a waterfall of serenity.

When it was done, we did not release each other, waiting for another wave of fruition, not wanting it to end. We continued. We loved each other. After the third time, Medea wept. For even now, our actions were but reflexes of other times, other places when our bodies pulsed with true yearning instead of hunger, when the colors of the sky were hope and we might just gaze at one star. We imitated, we expressed, we hoped but it was still just a reflex. We would never truly recapture what we never had. But we would try, and try again.

I cradled her, not saying a word but allowing for her flow of sorrow to lather her senses.

"You know what, Byron?" she asked between sobs.

"What?" I stroked her rich hair.

"You're much better than the Shaman."

I started laughing, a hearty cackle, and held her up. She giggled back and my thoughts spoke once again, sharing in just many ways we could share.

Oh, Medea, I lost you and now I've found you. It seems I've been searching for someone like you for an eternity. I've lost so much through time, but I've found you.

And I'm never letting you go.

3

Desperation was completely washed away on amorous shores. Yet I was worried Medea would be missed, for we spent *Moratoria* together. She informed me that one of her duties was to take care of all the reserves of juice being pumped into The Citadel. While I was gone, massive filtering and storage systems were built under the city, right smack in the center. Her job at the beginning was to look over the construction. When the engineers and workers had finished, they were eliminated and complex computer systems set up by Balkros himself. All she had to do was process the information and make sure everything worked correctly. It was a system that had worked flawlessly in New Atlantis. The worst thing that could happen was a leak somewhere, easily detected by scanners, or a general malfunction that would only cause Stargazers to get off their butts and find food outside.

Medea spent half of her time down here overlooking things in solitude or at her office in The Tower doing much of the same.

"Being the new Elder means having the lesser responsibilities of the seven," she said, standing naked across the room, letting me admire her ivory contours from the bed. "It's not lesser, but the others thought this job was below them."

I grunted, lost in her curves, enjoying watching her run around the room inspecting consoles, straightening up, or just showing off. I believe Medea had never really been coveted before until I came into her life—as a Warm One, she burst as a religious icon at a young age, as a Stargazer, she was The Princess of Plumbing, as her peers called her. Like me, she never really had normal choices.

"Of course," she said, crossing her arms. "Coping as a new Elder is now the least of my worries. You have awoken me, or something in me. I am a Stargazer now, Byron, but I realize I was once a Warm One. You created me."

I sat up in the large bed. "I understand your situation, but remember the Religion of The Circle . . . The Blood of The Circle. We have no real place on this world. We are immortal and are hecklers of life. That isn't right."

"I'm remembering everything, Byron," Medea said. "It wasn't exactly your kiss, Byron, that brought me back, although I'd like to think that, but you caressing me with your thoughts and feelings through *Moratoria*. Part of you woke me up from a nightmare only to be in another nightmare. It all started sifting back even before we met at the Mall . . . it was hard to hide it from everyone. I'm sorry, Byron, about the rest . . . I needed time."

"I know." I closed my eyes. "You have to just sit there and let it come back. I still wonder what happened to my family, if my line might be somewhere out there. It's all lost, but somehow we must find it again, Medea. Ignorance is bliss."

She cocked her head. "Who said that?"

"Nobody," I said with a sad grin. "Just some old friend in yet another life."

"I hate you, Byron."

"I hate you, too," I said. "And nobody else, Medea. Only you, do you understand?"

She turned to look into the mirror, just to give me a nice view of a smooth back, chiseled buttocks, athletic legs, and that well of true creation somewhere in the center.

"Yes," she whispered happily. Her expression eclipsed. "I recall The Circle, Byron. It's still in me."

"What is?" I asked, but the answer was there. It had always been there.

"The Killer of Giants, Byron. It's still there. I can sense it. I know it will destroy me eventually, when it desires. It could have been last year, it might be tomorrow. Why would The MoonQueen allow my existence?"

"If you have it," I said, "then perhaps I have—"

"You would know, Byron. The god-soul can sense and inform anything that is its bane, especially when it's within you."

"You're right," I agreed. "But also somebody else . . ."

She turned briefly to catch my expression. We shared the monumental thought.

Then she returned to her lonely expression on the mirror, leaning over slightly.

"No," she hissed. "It couldn't be. She is too mighty."

I left the bed and went to her. My hands touched her shoulders and lowered until holding her hips. She bent over more.

"Medea," I said, allowing vibrant energy to fill me. "I have survived much. There is still much we don't know about Stargazers. We're notable creatures."

"You believe so?" Medea questioned, bottom slightly caressing me like a feather.

"Yes," I groaned, pushing myself against her. Wetness gave way to pleasure, fold and flesh joined in tingling. "There is hope. We cannot give up."

We've come too far, I thought, bucking against her. And, although her face showed desire at the thrusts, her sight did not leave her fanged reflection.

This time, when we climaxed, she growled and thrust her hand through the mirror, shattering it in a haze of sparkling shards like temporal stars.

4

Afterward, closing in on the threshold of *Sol*, I asked Medea what exactly had happened to Shibboleth.

"No one has really told me in detail," she responded. "But there always has to be someone to take the blame when something bad happens. An Elder rarely has to do that, but Crow was gone and the situation with The Farm was very embarrassing. After all." She shrugged. "He was responsible for your mission."

"I see," I said while patting her head.

"And I took his place."

I shook my head. "How odd."

"What is also odd, Byron, is that I have discovered that I was also supposed to be in that cage with Clannad that night."

"That is definitely odd," I mused. "I guess Our Mistress simply wanted to make sure no revolution began and the mission was accomplished, one way or another."

Medea was frowning, as if wanting to change the topic.

"I guess Shibboleth thought you *had* finished the mission and he sent for the boy. You know what else is odd, Byron?"

"What?"

"I miss going to relieve myself. I miss it a lot, of all things. Can you imagine it?"

"Forgot what that even was in Warm One terms."

"Byron?" she said, lowering her head to my chest.

"Yes," I whispered, worried at her low tone.

"I want to help you in your vengeance. I know you want to end it all, whether it's you or Xanadu that goes first. I can feel it in you. I'm part of you, forever."

I didn't say anything, holding her tighter. I was also part of her, and I had a feeling about what was coming next. My question had opened this up.

"But I'm not doing this for you," she said.

"I know, Medea."

"I'm doing this for Clannad."

"I'm sorry . . ." My voice dissipated against the shame of recalling that night after the battle.

"For Clannad, Byron. I understand. To end it all."

5

She was gone by the time I rose the next evening. As an Elder, duty called, roles had to be played in the vexing rigors of Xanadu.

I didn't do much. I ate. I paced the vast confines of this abode, this small factory that served little more than to capture the juice from The Farms and irrigate the Stargazers of The Citadel. I watched the news: Northwest Farm still isolated. The Elders thinking of simply destroying it and sending expeditions to find more Warm Ones in desolate areas, maybe ask for help from thriving New Atlantis. I thought about playing some video games.

You won't make it, my god-soul told me then. *Every time you attempt victory, it turns into failure right in your bastard face. You're not even a hunter, just a silly scavenger at best!*

Angrily, I began accessing Medea's data banks, which were vast compared with what I'd experienced. There were no passwords or codes down here, where Medea and a few assistants were allowed from time to time. I knew where to search, what to do.

"I'll make it," I said to the god-soul. "We'll both make it. And one of these nights I'll travel alone to the other side of the moon and I'll take Drisha skating. I'll leave your coward essence behind, uh?"

It didn't answer, knowing what I was finding. Not only the way to end it all, but perhaps a way to save Medea, to save ourselves.

It was all improbable, but this civilization had been improbable from the beginning.

I didn't see Medea for two more evenings. We shared ourselves, and then we talked over our strategies.

CHAPTER 19

They were called the Purification Wells. Stretching for a few dozen yards, a lattice of metal squares about a foot in diameter was fed juice from various sections. The juice in the pool was cleansed of lead or whatever impurities it sustained in the Slaughterhouses or through the voyage. Then it was furnished with different chemicals to preserve, oxidize, and slightly dilute it. Finally, it was spurted into various holding tanks in Xanadu to benefit whichever Stargazer turned on his tap. All of this was overseen by state-of-the-art computers that also rationed the ever-hungry population.

I stood on one of the steel bridges cutting the glittering field. In the mesh, juice bubbled and shifted in endless humming. I was glad I wore nose-plugs, for the desire would have been unavoidable. Even then, I felt like jumping in and sinking in one of the squares, dropping into the massive puddle of food. I clutched the railing, knowing my knuckles couldn't whiten anymore. Above me an immortal society starved and thrived, below me life, stolen from the innocent, drained and was sterilized. In between, I endured once again. Perhaps out of annoyance, I tossed my cigarette into the Purification Wells. An electronic voice warned me through speakers about a glitch. Something spurted yellow liquid, and I'm sure my butt was dissolved.

I walked to the edge, too confounded by how much this must have cost to care about eating. Who cared? Economies were illusions blanketing survival. Stargazers survived when they weren't even alive. So many paradoxes.

Before I could further be gripped by the pseudo-philosophical mood, one of the many doors slid open and Medea entered. She didn't enter alone. A sense of familiarity tickled my thoughts when I saw her drag in a massive cage. In it, a herd of Warm Ones crouched against itself. No awe there, just terror.

"Are you sure you want to do this?" I asked for no reason other than the looks on the Warm Ones' faces.

She followed my sight, then shrugged with coldness. "Why do you ask, Byron? You know many lives have to be forfeit for more to be saved." She giggled at her remark, but her eyes reflected my own sorrow. "It's the only way. It's only the beginning."

"And we must move fast," I said, not telling Medea about how the previous night I'd felt another presence searching for me. Our borrowed time was coming to an end, I knew.

As Medea walked to the computers in order to shut down some of the purifying chemicals just as a precaution, I went to the cage. The Warm Ones, thin, shaven, and, of course, tattooed, shuddered and moved away from me.

"I am sorry," I told them. "You must be sacrificed for your kind to live."

One of them, a female that must have been nearing thirty, broke away.

"Please, sir," she said, barely able to speak through trembling lips. "Spare us! I am of age, but the others are still young."

"You don't understand," I said. "We are on your side. We do this to end this horror, this slavery. We must do this for the good of your species."

"Do what?" Her eyes widened in terror. Some of the others started weeping. "We do not want to die. It makes no sense, sir!"

"It will make sense," I said sternly. "Your remains will be tainted with a malady that will hurt my kind, bring your kind freedom. Your death is not in vain. You must believe."

"Please!" she cried. "It makes no sense. Why kill us at all? One life lost cannot save another, it makes no sense!"

I opened my mouth, suddenly realizing I was sounding like an Elder. What was she talking about? It did. One life lost . . .

"But it will," I stammered.

"You have no right," she shouted, and the others joined her at her side, pleading, supplicating, hands outstretched.

"But it does!" I shouted back. "Think of your children, your family in the future, think—"

The cage door opened and closed.

"They don't care, Byron," Medea said, inside with them, eyes glowing, fangs glistening. "I never did when I was one. Clinging to life is all a Warm One can truly do."

What should have seemed so natural, so beautiful to my being, wasn't. I turned my head when Medea attacked the ten or so Warm Ones. One by one, their desperate screams overtaking the hum of the fields, they were harvested. One by one, they witnessed their own devoured by Medea. Some struggled, some tried to help the others, most just waited in terror for their turn. After five minutes, I felt a wet flow on my boots, speckles of wetness strike my face. Ripping sounds made me hungry. After ten minutes, Medea started cackling. I lost track of time when a slurping sound was all I could hear.

The cage door opened again, and I beheld something that brought a fear I'd never experienced.

It wasn't the gutted, pierced, still tepid bodies that did it. It wasn't the damp mess staining the metal of the floor.

It was the bloated, obscene giant staggering out, five times the size she should have been. Her skin glistened in pasty blue, fat breasts melted into a fat stomach, veins swelled from membranes, threatening to burst at any second. And much of her did, I thought. When she opened her mouth, jets of blood squirted; even her eyes were painted in fine pink, tearing uncontrollably.

"Looks like I ate too much," she rasped, intoxicated by the life in her. "You're going to have to be stronger than this, Byron. You're going to have to be stronger than ever before."

I know, I thought, taking a handkerchief from my jacket and putting it over my mouth. Through the nose-plugs I could sense her aroma, even in disguise I could smell The Killer of Giants growing within her at this volume.

For an instant, she smiled with sadness. "What's wrong, Byron? Am I not beautiful to you anymore? You created me."

I didn't comment, standing up straight and staring at her. She was right, I had to be stronger.

But that wasn't her concern. Medea blundered toward the fields, slowly floating over the stairs and small wall. I thought she might crash at any moment. Her eyelids fluttered, as if the strain was ready to consume her at any moment. With effort, she slashed her own wrist, then punctured her neck in order to allow the escape of the poisoned juice. Then the strain consumed her.

No section here could have allowed her girth. She simply dropped into the lines, smashing a grand opening, vanishing into the bloody stew. I went to the edge and waited and waited. The computers didn't object. I waited.

After a while, I thought about jumping in or using the scanners to find her body. I waited. Suddenly, my keen ears heard something at the far edge. I flew there quickly and saw a body struggling at the edge. It was a smaller one. It was Medea.

I picked her up in my arms and flew to the sides, uncaring the syrupy matting got on my clothes. I thought she was laughing at first in my arms, but as I rocked her gently I knew that wasn't the case.

"How many times more do we have to do this?" she asked and kept on crying.

2

That's how the first part of the plan started. It was a plan that made Medea essential because of who she was, a Stargazer with an enigmatic disease, and an Elder with influence. This was a plan I'd hidden even from myself; I'd never fathom to attempt it.

She pursued her butchering for the next few weeks, whenever she had time to come under the city and check on the Purification Wells.

"I wonder if we'll get caught," she mused.

"Sooner or later," I commented. "Why do you wonder?"

Medea told me about a meeting she recently had with The Elders. In a secluded chamber in the middle of The Tower, the leaders gathered once in a while to discuss the running of Xanadu and to a lesser extent New Atlantis, where their puppets ruled. At a C-shaped table of dull silver, they sat and argued and viewed a massive screen and argued some more. Five were present that night, Balkros, Black Gomez, Tugros, Tsing-Tao, and Medea herself. Of the other two, Qumbre had left to the other city-state and Yammamoto had perished weeks ago, his position unfilled.

She said that a little conversation with Balkros had made her nervous. The Stargazer with the prolonged features and long, flickering tongue leered at her. He leered at everyone, his speech unpredictable, disjointed sometimes, but with always piercing eyes under a mop of slovenly hair.

"Everything fine, Medea?" he asked with a guttural chuckle, as she slid next to him.

"Greetings, Balkros," she said, "and yes, everything is fine."

"Are you sure, Princess of Plumbing?" he pressed, left eye twitching, spittle clinging to fangs that seemed too large for his mouth. "I want to make sure everyone is fine. Don't want trouble, don't want waste."

Medea sighed. She knew it was better to handle it her way—direct, instead of brushing him aside. After Shibboleth had been disgraced, weird Balkros had somehow taken unofficial and complete leadership of The Elders. Though one of the younger Stargazers, crossing him was something few ever did a second time. Besides his sharp mind at computer science, he was incredibly sadistic even by Stargazer standards. I recalled going to one of his "balls" years ago, nothing more than an orgy of gore, a circus of Warm One torture and Stargazer dueling.

"Balkros, please get to the point," she said curtly.

He leaned over the table, eyelids trembling, as if a massive headache had invaded his cortex. Then, like nothing, he appeared fine.

"The Matrix," he said, referring to his personal computer, connected to basically everything in Xanadu, "detected a few glitches in the wells the other night. Seems to be a nightly routine. Do you know about it? We don't want any poaching or polluting, Medea."

"I know about it," she said. "I've already contracted a scientist to come see what the problem is. Everything else is in order, so it must be something minor."

"Of course it's minor," he said with a snicker. By the time the other Elders had taken their places, Balkros was trying to suppress his mirth and giggled all throughout the meeting. The agenda mostly concerned the sudden quietness of The MoonQueen. They didn't get anywhere, deciding that maybe she was in one of the mystic trances that sometimes lasted for years. Losing Shibboleth, the best at communicating with her, definitely hadn't helped. More initiative was needed, they all decided, to get over this recession.

After the meeting, Balkros spoke to her while they walked down the hall to their offices. "Please let me know if I can assist, Medea, or if you need one of my people or the Matrix to help you."

"Thank you, Master Balkros," she said, "but I have the situation under control."

"I know you do. It was my project before the bitch created you. Very important job, but she didn't think so. She has me overseeing some research team to begin studying Stargazer organisms. Secret, very secret."

"I know, Balkros. It is Our Mistress's will."

"I still feel attached to it."

"Yes," she said and turned the corner.

I worried about it, but knew it was of no use. We had done huge damage by then. The second phase I had to thank Medea again for, although I was to carry it out.

She told me that months ago, The Elder Yammamoto had been assigned to deal with the Warm One situation in the Northwest Farm and make sure he didn't become an example like Shib. He acted much more aggressively, sending wave upon wave of Raven in guerrilla tactics, trying to slowly break their morale. It didn't work, obviously, since Medea's fall and their new weapons had forged their determination. They would all die rather than become food.

One night, to prove this point, the Warm Ones attacked the steep wall of Commodore Station. With ropes and flamethrowers, they took over a crane and brought more into the station. Yammamoto, along with his henchmen, rushing toward the Slaughterhouse the animals were attempting to destroy, were caught in a barrage of fire while entering the threshold. As his body collapsed in fuming disaster, a group of Warm Ones surrounded him and brought down their axes. Hours later, the Warm Ones already retreating back in victory, Medea, who had been inspecting plumbing in the tunnel a few miles away, came to the station with reinforcements. She found half of Yammamoto's body crawling on one arm to imaginary safety.

"He still exists," a Raven told her, poking at the remains, which couldn't listen anymore.

"Doesn't look like it," Medea said with distaste at the charred, quivering mass.

"But he will regenerate, thanks be to Our Mistress," the Stargazer said.

"No, he will not," she said and shoved her boot into Yammamoto's indiscernible head. It imploded with a popping sound. The soldier ogled at her in pure shock.

"Well, what are you looking at?" She scraped the gunk from her boots. "There is work to do. I want all the cranes permanently disabled from now on and all Raven missions suspended."

The soldier would never mention this to anyone. She quickly confiscated the fallen Elder's possessions (or hunting trophies, as he used to brag to the others) at the station. She didn't know why she'd done it at the time, except that it was a chance to rise a notch in The Council. Now she knew that part of her had coveted Yammamoto's stolen idols that once had been her truest hope in another life.

And so did I, riding in a train to yet another Farm, holding two suitcases tightly, Medea's accounts so vivid in my mind. I hoped she never saw my past like I could see hers.

"You have a total of six suitcases," she had told me the previous night, as we lay in bed in light petting. "Two for each

Farm. I've written all I know about The Circle on various disks in different formats."

"Don't worry," I said, kissing her shoulder. "I've also written it down. By the way, the mention of disk . . ." I fumbled in my pocket, totally forgetting about Proxos's little gift. It had survived my battles and remained unconfiscated.

"Medea, I want you to give this to someone."

She took the burned case. "Who?"

"Don't look at the information," I said. "It's from Proxos."

"Proxos?"

I explained to her about a host I once had, an Elder that had also taken the blame for something. And then I added:

"It's a gift for Balkros."

"Balkros!" she exclaimed as I knew she would. "Byron, you must be—"

"That's what I said." I gently pushed back the case, which Medea had extended to me. "I don't know what it is, but for some reason I trust him. He said it would help our cause."

She shook her head, although the object slowly went into her own robes. "But, Byron, what do I say to him! I'm weary of dealing with his personality."

"I know, but only you can. I really think Commodore knew you were the key all along. Just hand it to him and tell him you found it in my remains, that you didn't want to handle it if it dealt with computers. It might make him less suspicious if he sees you acting so loyally."

"You're right," she said, looking away. "I must trust you. I don't like it, but I must trust you."

"Thank you." At the same time, I felt a slight lightening of my own chest.

"Your identity has been changed," she said with a sigh, returning to the former conversation. "Not only that, but you have documents signed by me. No one will give you any trouble."

I poked her nose. "I know. We've been through this. I'll be back before you know it."

She released me, sitting up. "But this could be the last time we see each other."

I shrugged, laying my head on her chest. "It always is, Medea. We're never too far apart. I will be back to you."

"Byron?" She grabbed my chin and made me look at her.

"Medea."

"Did it ever occur to you who you are?"

"Believe me," I said. "That's how this whole mess started."

"You are going into the Warm One Farms in order to arm them with faith weapons. When this comes full circle, they will rebel and we might fall. Do you know who you are?"

"Medea, I've been wondering that for—"

"No, listen. Don't you remember that night underneath the temple? The new idols I had made?"

My eyes widened. The side of my face found her chilly breasts.

Sitting on the train, among sunken-eyed, always hungry Stargazers, my people now and forever, I thought about this yet another time, like everything else. But soon the train would make its final destination. I would take to the air and drop the contents to whatever Warm Ones I could find. The contents of the suitcase, the prizes Yammamoto had amassed in his wild hunts.

I would drop the symbols of The Circle, religious icons of power against evil, except one, a crude circlet carved with undulating eights, which I kept for no real reason other than weird comfort, and perhaps I would give them their liberation. That night Medea spoke about hadn't been a mistake, what she created. Yes, I remembered that night and how neither of us could believe a monster would righten the balance, help the downtrodden. The prophecy had to come true.

Every oppressed society needs a Liberator, whether he knows it or not.

CHAPTER 20

I found Medea's motionless form at the Purification Wells exactly a week later. My quest had been fulfilled. I didn't have any real problems getting through the tight security, although my pale locks attracted a gaze here and there. Once I was inside The Farms, I was a blur dropping off those faith-weapons that had been used throughout the millennia against Stargazers. I hoped that all The Farms had the fervor to believe in these relics, many in my image, which would help them to freedom. Either that or the Slaughterhouses working full time, blotting the sky in grim smoke, would release them.

The missions were simple. The hours remaining gave me a lot of time to ponder the situation and my actions. What was I doing? crossed my mind several times. I could have played it safe from the start, slain both Shamans that night at their temple. I could have remained with Proxos for centuries and been half bored. I could have just said no to Crow that evening when I simply wanted a pint of type A-negative and let bygones be bygones. Part of me knew, though, that my actions were not fully my own, my fate was preordained by The MoonQueen, the Mad God, or whatever galactic chess games were being played in the wastes of the world. Even Medea, the Shaman-to-be, had used me for a while. But I had my choices from the start, and those made me into a Warm One destroyer, a traitor to our species, a Heretic, and now the Liberator of Warm One myth. After all, I had been plagued by dreams of *Sol* before going into The Farm. I had woken once before *Luna*'s rise to feel the tentacles of *Sol*. I had perhaps been spared, but why had it happened? Had this been a message from *Sol*, had this been a formal anointing by the enemy of my species?

Even then, I hadn't liberated anyone except myself—and even I still wondered if Lilith was not somewhere behind all this, still laughing at me in her kingdom of everlasting ice.

2

Before descending to the Purification Wells, I decided to take one of my more famous walks in The Mall Zone. Unlike last time, the bright shops, the reinforced walkways, and the other sections were sparse. I didn't have to wonder why. The population was being sheared by the battles in the Northwest Farm; many Stargazers had been exterminated as examples by The Elders, and, of course, Medea's hand must be making its presence.

Some Stargazers looked thin, too thin. Their eyes appeared unfocused, expressions reflected no hunter swagger. I couldn't detect the killer through scent, and wondered how tight the rationing and disciplining continued. What shocked me was the fact that The Fusing had been postponed the last few weeks for important matters. I couldn't hear any conversations asking why this sudden move. No one asked questions, no one spoke much at all. Existence continued, barely. A part of me felt a certain sadness for this "temporal recession" as The Elders called it. We might be monsters, I thought, but at least we spent our time pursuing leisure and pleasure, which I'm sure the Warm Ones had tried for thousands of years.

That's because you're my vessel to consumption, god-soul told me, *now feed me, bastard.*

With that, I thought of an expression my father used constantly. Blowing smoke up my ass, it was.

I made my way to a jewelry shop and asked the lady for a silver pin in the shape of the rose, paying for it with Medea's credit. The thought is what counted.

"The symbol of The Elders," the lady said blandly. "A proud thing to wear."

"It's a gift," I said for no reason. "And it applies more to a friend and me than it does to them."

I rushed out, quickly jogging to the right shafts. I fluttered to the wells. Dropping hundreds of feet almost to the bottom of the structure called Xanadu, I found the right door and entered a card Medea had given me into the slot.

Everything seemed fine in the waiting room. For no reason at all, I checked the computer on the empty secretary desk, which was always that way. No messages, nothing new to report from the Purification Wells. Medea was here, in fact.

She hadn't left for the last twenty-four hours.

"But . . ." I heard myself say, then rushed through the door of the various chambers shouting out her name.

Cursing myself, I closed my eyes and felt her. We were never too far apart. I created her.

A faint voice echoed distantly down the shoal of thoughts. It was her. What was it saying?

Help.

"Where are you?" I hissed.

Help.

Suddenly, I knew. Smashing through doors this time, I ran to the wells themselves. They bubbled in their porous squares, computers glowed digital greens and did their work. Medea was the only thing not laborious. She lay by the edge, drenched in juice, torn clothes, as if she'd just entered and fallen off the stairs on the way out. A cage of dead Warm Ones stood in a corner of the large chamber.

I kneeled and lifted her up. Her eyes flickered faintly, taking their time to register recognition.

"Byron," she slurred. "The Killer of Giants. It's growing in me."

"No!" I said, hugging her, cursing myself more for not fully accepting this. Unlike Warm Ones, it was said to strike quickly and unpredictably, instead of wasting the body. In both cases, it was unavoidable, an inescapable curse by fate or the Mad God.

"It happened recently," she squeaked. "Sapped my strength . . . feel lost . . . Byron?"

I held her tighter. "Yes, Medea?"

"I'm afraid . . . I know what cold truly feels like."

I clamped my eyes. She'd never been afraid of death before. What was happening to her?

"Medea," I said, getting to my feet with her in my arms. "There is always a way. We'll find a way—"

"There is only one way, yes?" a shrill voice told me.

I turned around. No one. Laughter pierced the humming. The computers started glowing in neon teals. A rumble echoed far away.

"Balkros?"

His face began materializing in all the computer screens with that famous leer.

"Hello, Byron," he said, practically panting. "Having a hard time? Need a little help?"

"Fuck you!" I grumbled, already hearing the massive movement of soldiers outside.

He didn't seem too offended. "The Killer of Giants will take my colleague quickly. I have been appointed to study this disease by The MoonQueen, Byron. I have some interesting facts."

"What?" I asked, my mind searching for an escape plan never discussed.

"Rest is good," he said, cackling. "My research shows extensive rest can send the killer to dormancy. Long rest. Like the one you must have encountered when the bitch dropped you into some gritty soup."

His laughter rose, face twisted obscenely. I heard doors sliding open, loud footsteps. Balkros was opening the way with his Matrix for an ambush.

"Too bad you won't get a chance to rest your little love," he said, beginning to blur. "I'll have to find out myself, Byron. By the way, you shouldn't have bought the stupid gift for her. It was all too easy to track your whereabouts."

"Fuck you," I repeated, my mind fumbling for anything, but already armed Ravens filtered in. The crazy Elder had bought enough time in his stalling.

"Good-bye, Byron," his image said as it turned to sparkles. "I will see you in oblivion soon enough."

For the second time, I fell into an easy trap by an Elder.

3

A swarm filled the outer edges of the wells. Raven after Raven, armed with *radiovacs*, flamethrowers, and grappling ropes, stood prepared to attack, prepared to rush the two figures. Carrying Medea, I jumped on the bridge.

How many times do I have to go against these louts, I thought angrily. In my arms, Medea opened her eyes and moved. She definitely knew what was transpiring.

"Surrender!" barked one of the Ravens, unarmed but with obvious leadership status.

"Buzz off!" I told him, only to see more soldiers in the hallways as backup. I heard doors shutting all over the place.

"Surrender, Heretic," the commander said, raising a hand. "There is no escape."

"Is that so?" I derided, looking down at the lagoon of juice. "But I think you need to reconsider."

The Raven leader laughed, and a few joined him. "Is that so? As you can see, you are in no position to barter, Heretic."

"Not unless I drop her," I said, raising Medea over the railing.

Stargazers glanced at one another. The leader cocked his head. "What are you talking about?" he asked.

"You don't know what I'm talking about?" I shouted. "She's got The Killer of Giants, the malady that nearly wiped us out before The Holocaust. It is very harmful to our kind, in case you hadn't checked the history files recently."

"So?" he questioned, but understanding already crinkling his brow.

"I'll cut her and drop her! Stay back! She will fall in and a hundred Stargazers will lose their existences, maybe more."

"You're just stalling," he accused, although his hand furiously waved for all weapons to be lowered. "Probably a lie. This Killer is a myth I hear from some of the older ones, that's it."

"Go ahead and ask Balkros, if you want," I said. "I'll drop her, I mean it!"

The commander pointed at me. "You cannot escape. That is the final order from Master Balkros. You and the traitor Elder will not leave here. The best thing for you to do is surrender."

"So what are you going to do?" I asked, leaning over the edge. "Is it worth the risk, Raven? Why don't you talk to your superiors and figure this one out. You're not going to let us exist once we're apprehended anyway, right?"

He opened his mouth only to shake his head. Taking out a headset, he began talking quietly. Shuffling echoed in the chamber, as a bout of indecision took away all the battle-lust.

"By the way," I said, letting gravity take hold. "You're right, I was stalling. Sort of."

The Raven commander screamed. Even with their guard down, the Ravens swiftly turned on their weapons and doused the area. As I fell the final length of about fifteen feet, sheets of fire stroked the surface and the metal separators. I braced myself against the yielding steel and clenched my jaw at the searing heat.

The blazing and urgent shouting were drowned by a large, thick splash. Metal twisted, vision dimmed, and I was swimming through a small sea of blood, I'm sure one of the best fantasies a Stargazer could have had.

I would have tended to agree, but the aching from taking the brunt of the fire nagged me as I propelled myself through the stuff. More than the pain, the hunger wanted to open my mouth and take it in.

It's poisoned, I thought furiously, edging to the wall of the wells.

Feed me. Feed me. Feed me!

A wave of light-headed weakness mushroomed. Medea held me tighter, sensing my struggle. It sapped me second by second.

I reached the wall, moved by weak kicking. In each of the walls, hundreds of tubes sent the juice to the different tanks or directly to its destination.

Blinking in and out of consciousness, I rammed my fist through the steel mesh of the filter. As soon as it gave away, I let the current take us, hoping the tube I'd chosen wouldn't change size.

We gained speed with the current. It was hard to hear with the viscous substance around us and the pounding in my head, but I didn't think we were being followed in any way.

Forever, it seemed, I lost sensation of reality, immersed in my own craving, which threatened to break my sanity. Nostrils flared, fangs swelled from gums ready to fall out if necessary. Medea didn't move at all anymore.

Feed me. Feed me. Feed me!

I can't! I have to . . . just one gulp . . . just one . . .

Motion was sharply perturbed. Momentum racked my body from all sides. I released her and flailed wildly. We had hit another screen. The current pushed me against it in tormenting crashes. The screen gave away. Hands reached for a Medea that wasn't there. We were thrown into a large tank, I noticed. Consciousness slipped away and hands still felt the blood for my love.

4

It must have been quite a sight. I'm sure he had been an engineer working in the myriad shafts, tunnels underneath The Citadel where only plumbing and wiring and other things existed, even lower than the chambers where we went to *Moratoria* every night. Only a few workers ever went this low, assigned by the guilds to fix or keep an eye on things.

This particular one must have been pacing the crude tunnel when he heard a thumping from one of the tanks where juice was temporarily stored. He must have taken some initiative and climbed to the top where the panels could be unscrewed. As soon as he did just that, I think he leaped down in surprise at the syrupy thing bobbing out. It loosely held another one. It tossed it over its shoulder and tumbled down the oval object.

He probably was too much in shock to do anything else. The thing that was me lumbered away to hide in the deep underground of the city. The scent of juice in the opened tank must have seemed more noteworthy to him in these impoverished times.

5

Hearing the worker's hungry lapping down the tunnel, I didn't know where I was going, trying to recall Proxos's myriad of hiding places, many of those his rustic guest chambers whenever he came to Xanadu. All I really knew was that every hole or shaft in this dark maze gave me a chance to escape a little more in case we had been followed down the tube.

I carried her a long time through tunnel and natural cavern, entering places that many Stargazer writers said were the abode of ancient monsters or animals affected by the radiation. I don't think I encountered any, blankly dazed, body attempting to self-sabotage at each step. Rust and soggy stone mocked me from all sides.

Eventually, I felt *Sol*'s imminent arrival far and above. I placed Medea on the ground and lightly covered her with dirt.

"You'll be fine," I said meekly. She didn't move at all. "Just need to rest, Medea. Do you hear me? Rest and it will go dormant. He's got to be right."

And why shouldn't he be? Balkros was our brightest thinker, no matter how twisted he appeared. It seemed he was also another stagehand in this comedy of raptures. Immortality breeds eccentricity, I could hear Proxos telling me.

"You'll be all right," I mouthed, falling next to her, everything going dense, colors in my vision collapsing against one another. The last thing I was able to do was find her hand and hold it.

You'll be fine, a voice said inside the peaceful whirling smiting all senses and aching.

You didn't feed me, another voice said, *die, you bastard.*

CHAPTER 21

My father stands across the street, wearing an undershirt, brown slacks, and fallen suspenders. He's bigger than I remember, lumbering toward me, continuously masticating on his cigar. I want to look at him more, to absorb his largeness, but my surroundings take my breath away, almost literally.

It's a city I've never seen but I lived in once. It's Utopia before The Holocaust: Full buildings, complete streets, unhindered by parasitical structures built over its carcass. The air smells clean. The sky is blue.

I don't dare look upward. But I'm here. I raise my arm and inspect it. It's pink, full of hair. I pinch it and feel pain. Pain! I take another breath. I'm breathing. Warmth blushes at every corner of my body. The last thing I do is place my hands over my eyes. No juice, no blood, but real tears, salted, mortal.

Have I crossed the membrane?

My father stands in front of me. He's of flesh, too, not a day older than when he met his valiant death. There is more movement around me. The city lives—parks full of playing pups, strange little trains on four wheels whizzing by, pedestrians with full faces and tranquil expressions.

I seem to recognize all of them, especially the ones in the block. Clannad and my daughter are playing some peculiar game of jumping on chalk-squares, while Medea calls to him from a windowsill. My wife reads papers on a bench by a lamppost. I see so many more . . . in a bar with open doors getting ready for business . . . in a calm train station.

"Watcha expect?" Dad asks, hands on his hips. "Goddamn Pearly Gates or something?"

"I . . ." I look at him. I don't smell him first. I don't hunger. I want to laugh, but think I'll cry if I do.

"Better not cry, boy," he says, somehow knowing that I might. "Why don't ya have one of them cancer sticks so we can talk."

I fumble in the pocket of the wool shirt I'm wearing. A weird humpback animal decorates the pack. He lights my cigarette.

"Dad," I say, coughing as I can actually experience the harshness of the cigarette in my lungs. "What am I doing here?"

"Nothing," he says, putting a hand that feels like steel on my shoulder. "Just thought I'd tell you how proud I am of you. You done well."

I shake my head. "Thanks, but . . . I haven't done much except fail."

He slaps my temple playfully. "Shut up, boy. You done well. It's great to see ya grown up. You had a beautiful family and you were almost a cool vampire. Not bad for the Liberator."

He tries to give me a nuggie. I slip away from him. I want to walk to my family, to hold Medea, to apologize to Clannad and all the others. I try to fly to them, but I can't . . . I'm a Stargazer, though.

I stop myself. "Dad. Where are we?"

He shrugs. "Nowhere in particular. Used to call it Tulsa City, boy."

"Where Proxos and the rest figured it had the less percentage of The Killer," I say in awe.

"Bible Belt's always been strong here," he says. "Those pricks spared us and we just had to wait for the piss to come out of the sky. Shit, if I'd known what horror came out of the devastation, I would have killed us all."

"That wasn't your style," I say, stamping out my smoke, staring at the people gathered here. "But here . . . why are they here?"

He doesn't answer right then, pursing lips as if he even doesn't understand.

"It's just a dream, boy," he says. "A special dream. You have to learn one thing, and that is that you vampires were never really killed by the queen-bitch. Your humanity still lives somewhere close to The Light. It's battered, beaten, and drained, but part of it still flickers. Yours has always flickered stronger than most. This is it, and this is its dream. We're the ghosts of that humanity, fragments of people you knew who made you who you are. I shouldn't tell you, but all of these people have died because of you. They're part of you now, even before they cursed ya."

"But." I shake my head. "My family, Dad?"

"They're beautiful." He waves at my wife, who waves back.

"I didn't kill them," I say, not waving at Diedre.

He places an arm over my shoulder. "You had to, boy. When things fell apart, when the revolution took a nasty turn and they surrounded your ass, you told your family how much you loved them, hugged them, and slugged a few bullets in their heads."

"Bullets?"

"You had to, boy. They would have had the same fate as you. You wouldn't let it happen. But, you never had the courage to take your own life."

"It's not my style," I say flatly.

"Not your style," he agrees. "Don't feel shame, boy. Be proud. You done well. We all think so."

"Is that why I'm here?" I ask, wiping more moisture from my eyes. I can't believe I feel my breath on my arms. Something pumps inside me.

"Kinda."

"I miss them all," I say, watching Medea, Warm One Medea, run from the apartment, bald but well dressed, trying to apprehend Clannad.

"You should. I miss you, too, boy."

He faces me. He smiles with dignity. He'll never hold me. Not his style.

"Well," I say. "At least it's a nice dream, Dad."

"And let's hope a long one, boy."

"Why?" I ask.

"It's gotta be. You need to stay dormant until it's over. Keep you serene so that Medea will also sleep, boy. Just relax. Time goes."

I laugh once. "Dormant? Serene? Big words for you, Dad. Are you really my father? I never killed you, I hope."

He slaps me again. "Are ya listening to anything I'm saying, goddamnit? We're all part of you. As fer me, I'm just another lost flicker who wanted to see ya one more time. Or maybe it's vice versa. I'm sorry."

"For what?" I scratch my head. "It's fascinating having real nerve endings again."

"No." He shakes his lowering head. "For bringing you to a horrible world, boy. I was young and thought we could lick these guys, thought the nuclear fallout would end in our lifetime. I'm sorry. This is the kind of world you and your family should have lived in."

"It's okay," I say, patting his right arm. "Maybe in another time, in another world, who knows? All I know is what I experienced; it wasn't that bad."

"I'm sorry, boy." He looks at me strangely. "A warrior is more out of place and time than war itself."

"It really wasn't that bad," I whisper with a half smile. "Come. Let me introduce you to my family."

"I'd love to, boy." He grins that ferocious grin of his. He's right, we're so out of place here in this peace. It was never our destiny.

We walk toward the other side of the street. "I hope you don't mind Medea, Dad. I don't know if you'll approve of her and me considering this situation, but let me—"

A buttress of wind rushes down on us. Greasy clouds break the blue sky in dark patches. I hear cries of fear.

"Ah, shit," Dad says, looking up.

"What's wrong?" I ask, surprised at the rapidly changing panorama.

"It's coming for you, boy. It tried to punish you by sending you to the light, but now it wants you back."

"It?"

He cringes slightly. "Yeah, it or she or whatever. The part of you that's cursed."

"The god-soul," I say, almost angrily.

Die, you bastard! was the last thing it had told me.

Like the breaking of gigantic waves, dark grim clouds wash

over the world, dragging with them an incredible coldness. The wind starts calling my name.

"Dad," I say, watching people scurry into their homes. "What do I do?"

"You're going to have to go to it," he says. "Either that or you'll really become part of this dream, drift away to The Light."

"That's not so bad," I say, thinking that this is so real and nice. I'm real again!

"No. You still got work to do, Byron."

"But it seems I just got here—"

"Actually you've been here about three months," he says, "that dormant thing, you know. Time gets warped. This god-soul thing is a part of you and it won't let you go. But you can use it to finish. Don't lose faith."

"But . . ." I can't argue with him, especially when snow starts falling. I blink, feeling its sharp coldness, wondering if it's snow or ashes.

"Think about Medea," he tells me. "And the rest will be easy."

He waves at something. Around the corner, another one of those vehicles appears.

"It will take you back," Dad says, raising his voice at the gales ripping into the world. The voice, its voice is calling me to its curse, to its purpose.

The thing screeches and halts in front of us. I look at it and then at my father.

"Dad," I say.

"Go, boy." He opens the door and pushes me to it. "Get out of here and finish things up."

"Will I see you—" But he's shoving me in, slamming the door closed. He bangs on the roof and soon momentum is in full swing.

I try to look at his dimming silhouette, at the others, but sheets of powder obfuscate the world I'm in.

I turn to the driver. He shouldn't have been here, but I guess he's just another intruder in this little dream.

"You know where to go?" I ask him.

He winks once at me. "Of course, Byron. Just hang tight."

I lean back and put on the seat belt. "Good to see you again, Crow."

2

Something sniffed my hand. Immediately, I sprung from where I lay, flinging dirt chaotically. The sniffing stopped. Something scuttled down the tunnel.

"Stop," my voice commanded, raspy, jittery. The thing stopped. My voice told it to come. It did.

It was a *Ruka*. The rodent, the size of my thigh, settled next to me, as if knowing its fate.

My voice thanked it, but hands shot out and quickly broke its neck. I brought it to my mouth and bit through the wiry fur, through the rubbery flesh. Its juice, tasting as sour as ever, took away my light-headed feeling and obligated my mind to start working with my consciousness.

After a few tepid gulps, I recalled where I was. I placed my hand over my chest. No beating. Dead silence. I then put a wet hand over my mouth. No warm pattering. Nothing. I was me, a Stargazer. I wasn't in the dream . . . I was . . . still part of the Dark Instinct.

"Medea," I said, shaking the figure next to me. I swatted dirt off the body, dread telling me to close my eyes.

I sighed in relief.

She was still in *Moratoria*, I could tell, looking the same as before. Balkros must have been right. Long resting would stop it for a while. Why had he told me this?

I brought the *Ruka* carcass over her head, squeezing its punctured body. Droplets of juice pelted her lips. Instinctively, the lips move, mouth opened, and tongue took the substance. I pressed it to her mouth. Jaws loosened, fangs were beheld, and she also excavated into the animal, eyes still closed.

Her throat started slowing down its quick spasms. Eyes opened and Medea pushed away her meal.

"Byron," she croaked through a stained mouth.

"Medea," I said, holding her up. "You exist. Balkros was right. You exist."

I hugged her, so glad I had that chance one more time, even though only dead flesh touched. But I knew part of us had to love even though it was just the specter of a past life.

"Byron?" Her voice sounding like herself.

"Yes," I whispered.

Just thought I'd tell you how proud I am of you. You done well.

She looked at me attentively. "That was the worst thing I've ever tasted."

I laughed so hard, gravel fell from the tunnel.

3

Later on, after we'd hunted a few more *Rukas*, we discussed what would be our next move.

"I think we've been in *Moratoria* for about three months," I said, walking up a slant, holding her hand. I didn't know if she knew about my dream. I wouldn't tell her.

"That long?" she mused. "Then should we get out of Xanadu? I'm sure nothing could have changed so quickly."

"You'd be surprised," I said. "Remember the shafts we passed a while ago."

"Yes," she said. "Row Z-12, the lowest living quarters of the city."

"I noticed all the doors were open when we crossed them."

"And? It is *Luna*'s dominion now."

"I know," I said, "but doors always remain shut even after a Stargazer has left it. Remember it is the last form of protection we have."

"You are right. I'm forgetting my stint as one of the rulers of Xanadu."

I chuckled. "Maybe we should check out some of the higher cupolae in order to find out."

"I agree, but we should get proper nourishment first. We're at a juncture where we don't know when the next meal might come, Byron."

"Proper nourishment?" I mused, immediately catching her thought. "Oh, I see."

"We're heading away from it, and it's sealed from all other shafts. Airtight. I doubt I have access anymore. It's probably very well guarded."

"Don't worry." I placed an arm over her shoulder. "Come on. I've got a trick I want to teach you."

4

It took us a while to burrow our way there in the form of what we'd just eaten. I followed her, knowing she had knowledge of accessible spots underneath its floor. Making loud jittering noises we couldn't control, we popped up right in one of the hallways of the Purification Wells. Our shapes gurgled back our natural forms, quickly taking guarding stances. Evolution had taken the rodent's vision away in an age of bright fire, and a keen nose was worthless against creatures that owned no real odor.

Medea and I felt a little embarrassed at first, seeing from a hallway that the entrance was wide open. That turned to surprise, noticing a plethora of our kind's bodies littering the edges of where we stood. Society must have broken down because it had obviously been a Stargazer battle by the signature of flamethrowers on the surfaces and the gross mutilation: strewn limbs, shredded torsos, organ-smeared walls. It was like a grim work of art, a tribute to blind, stern annihilation. The looks on each of the fallens' faces showed defiance, refusing anger even when existence had forsaken them after amazing damage. One, strangely enough, had received no outside damage; he was sitting with his hand directly jammed into his eyes. He had pushed so hard his fingers poked from the back of his skull. His mouth still grimaced at some horror stamped out by his action.

"I don't want to know," I said quickly. "Food. You were right. I have a feeling we'll need all the energy we can muster."

"We must be careful, Byron."

"Careful is my main credo," I lied.

Stealthily, we entered the Purification Wells. A few more bodies littered the area, including that of a certain high-ranking member of the Engineering Guild that had her scalp peeled off completely. A Raven here and there. The screens on the computers processed numbers in digital tones, scanners and dials showed the usual work that occurred here. Many of the doors were broken, walls held holes or claw marks, but not much else.

"It was a battle," I said, "but there's something missing."

"What do you mean?" Medea walked directly to the wells.

I tapped my fingers on the wall. "Where are the victors, Medea?"

"Perhaps there weren't any?"

"Hungry Stargazers don't believe in stalemates."

"I think we better worry about other things, Byron."

I leaped to her side. I didn't see anything too strange. The juice, the blood was still there bubbling, inviting my senses.

Only it was about five feet less deep.

"It's being drained," Medea said. "All of it, at once."

"Where?"

She sauntered to the computers and started shaking her head.

"That's odd, Byron. It's all going Sector G-7. But that doesn't make sense."

"What do you mean?" I asked, still by the wells, trying to fight my hunger.

"That's a contingency reserve. We devised it only to be used in times of . . . emergency . . . not a grave emergency but cataclysmic. All available stockpiles are supposed to flow into it until tapped afterward by any survivors. It's even more underground than where we rested last, Byron."

"Can't you stop it?"

Her voice took on its own urgency. "No. Something else is controlling it . . . from . . ."

She didn't have to finish her sentence. We knew.

"Well," I said. "We better get what we can. It's almost gone."

After tearing the mesh, we hovered over the depleting pool, craning our heads to stick our mouths in the substance. Once again, I pushed back visions of Clannad and my other life and understood that survival was necessary to finishing our quest. Energy flooded us, brightened our minds and bodies. We increased our eating even after being sated, understanding that this place might not be filled again for a long time.

I stopped first, hearing a groan from one of the rooms on the other side of the complex. I glided toward it, catching that it was a single voice. I would have ignored it, but it had familiar vibrations.

He must have recognized my voice as well, his slouched body in one of the utility rooms facing me when I entered. Half of his body had been neatly incinerated, flesh looking like a lather of black mud. Someone had used a pair of broken brooms as stakes and rudely stabbed them through his abdomen.

I cradled him in my arms, knowing that no danger would ever come from him again.

"Byron," he said, tongue visible through a tattered cheek. "How . . . are—"

"Don't speak, Mephisto. It's okay. I'm—"

His fingers dug into my arms. Body twitched.

"We . . . losing . . . broke ranks . . . came here with the engineers to fee—"

"Don't talk." I tried to raise him, but he winced in refusal.

"No . . . listen . . . came . . . fought, Byron. So foolish." His face broke in terror. "He found us, oh Mistress! Thought he was destroyed. He found us . . ."

"Who, Mephisto?"

"Found us," he said, speaking so quickly his tongue scraped against chipped fangs. "And . . . Mistress . . . showed it to us! HE HAD IT, BYRON. HE HAD IT!!!"

"Had what, Mephisto?"

He shook his head, clamped his eyes, and took the opportunity to sob a few times.

"It's okay, Mephisto," I said. "I'm going to take you for some food, man. It'll help you. Before you know it, you'll be—"

"No," he squeaked. "I can't . . . ever again . . . can't . . ."

"Yes, you can. Mephisto, what did he show you? Who was it?"

More sobbing. Part of his body was starting to fall off in crispy chunks.

"I can't . . . Byron . . . please." He took a brave, useless breath, more to give his thoughts a pause. "End . . . end it, please."

"No!" I exclaimed. "I can't do that. Mephisto, please, you are my friend. I can make you better."

"End it!" he gasped with such force, ashes burst from his mouth. If I hadn't been holding him, I think he would have shaken himself to pieces. "I SAW IT! END IT!"

"Do you want me to do it?" I heard Medea ask me at the doorway. "He has no will, Byron."

I shook my head. "But what did he see? Mephisto, come on—"

"END IT!"

"Do you—" Medea started before I raised a hand.

"I'll do it," I whispered, and couldn't avoid Mephisto's look of peace.

Quickly, I twisted his neck. His head tore from his body, sound lagging behind. Then I smashed it against the wall until I felt my palms touch the surface. Wet clumps of him slithered between my fingers. His body shook one last time, his hand raised to me briefly before it became static.

I kneeled next to his remains in respectful silence, wondering if I had just saved him a second time.

"At least he had the courage," I said. "But I wonder why? What happened here?"

"There's only one way to find out," Medea said all too logically.

I turned my head to her with raised eyebrows.

"You're right. Action."

5

In the Purification Well we found one of the many major pipelines that briefly had served to transport our most valuable product. We crawled for a while in *Ruka* form until discovering a blemish and sifted through it in mist form. We decided that normal methods could be dangerous in our exploration of the city.

Our first visit showed us a Stargazer cupola, empty like the ones before, door wide open. The only difference is that smoke gushed in. We walked cautiously outside down the hallway toward the shaft leading directly to The Citadel.

Every chamber was the same, although the ones closer to the shaft burned heavily. We noticed a few unmoving figures.

Once we glanced upward, our curiosity only grew. Something or someone had been dousing this area with fire, probably flamethrowers or . . .

"Warm Ones," I said, "they're known to create crude bombs of sorts."

"They always had them," Medea said, awed at the charcoaled walls, at the several dangling Stargazers on different levels. "In any case, we've missed more than one battle while resting, Byron."

"Yeah, but I want to know what could have done that back in the wells. Mephisto, why was he so . . . defeated?"

She stared at me. "Shall we go up to The Citadel?"

"I guess. Like you said, there's only one way to find out."

She held my hand, and we both rose through the oily smoke and destruction. I didn't mention it, but the possibility of the Circle Icons was definitely there.

6

The Mall didn't look much different. Once I thought it might have brought me joy, but odd sadness pinched me instead.

Fire spread everywhere. Shops were empty, vandalized husks of broken glass and torn walls. Plastic gardens were melted, walkways shattered, and even part of the dome grinned openly revealing the outer one covering the whole Citadel. So much waste. Stores I'd visited, restaurants I'd eaten in, virtual libraries I'd spent so much time in, all gone, swathed in blind destruction.

We weren't the only ones witnessing the bleak transformation. Periodically, random Stargazers darted in and out of the tunnels or halls, avoiding our gazes, with wild expressions in their ravenous eyes. Like us, they ignored the charred and mutilated bodies strewn about. Distorted music played on the speakers; screens, the ones still intact, sparkled grainy snow.

We wandered without a word. Some places were less damaged than others, but some whole buildings, where the guilds once machinated, no longer stood on their foundations.

Our suspicions were answered from the beginning. Nostrils had captured the sweet delight of their juice. We couldn't see them, but only Stargazer corpses dirtied the once lustrous place.

"Where are the Warm Ones?" Medea questioned, sniffing. "I'm sure they would have casualties fighting Stargazers."

"Unless their fallen ones were taken away," I said, looking down at a lake that once had been a place of merry skating. Flotsam, coils of fallen wires, and more bodies floated on its electrical surface. "Taken away to be eaten by our starving population," I finished grimly.

"*VERY GOOD!*" a booming voice said from all around.

Medea and I crouched, urgently looking around.

"It came from the speakers," Medea said, "it sounded like . . ."

She didn't have to finish, because our sights went to the screens perched on the many walls. In each of the unbroken ones, a long face smiled at us.

"Glad you could come," Balkros roared, not exactly him but a cartoonish, computer-generated image. "You missed the party, but even now the Warm Ones are getting ready to raid The Citadel as soon as *Luna* dashes away."

The screen changed. Scenes of Warm Ones rushing down the massive tunnels from the Farms, riding in trains, armed with flamethrowers or religious icons, appeared again and again, transforming to ugly battle scenes. They had not wasted any time.

"That's impossible," Medea said, and I had to agree. It all seemed too easy.

"Oh no, it's not," Balkros said, as the images changed. "You brought The Killer to us, Medea. Hundreds of us, thousands of us were afflicted within weeks. It happened so quickly we didn't know what to do. It caused pandemonium, and it didn't help that our people were famished. Morale was low, yes?"

The screen then showed Stargazer fighting Stargazer, Ravens dropping their weapons in the heat of battle at some station only to converge with others on a dead Warm One. It showed looting, betrayal, true frustration at society's yolk.

"But it's strange—how we could have fallen so easily." Balkros's wicked face sparked back on. "Can a species of immortals succumb to some rabble coming from miles away?"

"Maybe," I said. Medea held my hand.

"You could say I helped put the last nail in the proverbial coffin," he said and burst into manic laughter. Once again, his face disappeared and we saw with terror the cupolae. Doors slithered opened automatically, while a few Warm Ones descended in scaffolds or ropes with one intention.

"The Matrix," Medea hissed. "You opened all the doors! You took away our last protection. The wells . . ."

His face glowered with black delight. "It wouldn't have been fair! Had to be amused, Medea. And thank you, Mr. and Mrs. Solsbury, for my good friend's gift; it helped. Of course, the battle is not done. Fighting continues. The city's in disarray, yes, but not done."

I shook my head at his image. "You're not well, Balkros. Still, I don't mind too much that you beat me at destroying a civilization."

He laughed heartily. "I had to, Byron. Don't want to be upstaged. A Mad God needs his playground, yes? When it's all done, broken down enough, I shall start something new from the wreckage, garner survivors, bring the rest into my state of being, my new vision. A Mad God needs—"

"You're no Mad God," Medea barked. "You're just another puppet."

"You're wrong, bitch," he said, and he showed us another vision. "I'm more than that now."

It was him, surrounded by Warm Ones, chained to a massive crane in one of the stations. As they showered him with fire, the crane tugged upward pulling his head away from a body tied to the ground. I had to spare a chuckle at seeing his head tear away from his body. Other Stargazers were receiving the same treatment.

"But I didn't perish, as you can see," he said with a nasty smile. "Balkros is always prepared for everything. Prepared, yes. I know more about technology than anyone. I have put my soul into this place, literally."

"You mean . . ." Medea covered her mouth.

The word YES flashed on the screen in bright crimson.

"The Matrix and you are one," I said. "I'll never cease to be amazed."

"It wasn't so hard," his voice said, and the televisions showed more destruction. "Took a little inspiration, much invention, and a mound of primeval magic, which is nothing more than the research I took from my work of studying Stargazers. We are a fascinating species, Byron and Medea, so full of potential, so lethal."

"Heard that before. So this is why you did this, Balkros?" I motioned at the havoc surrounding us. "To usurp a people after another Holocaust."

"I did because I could, because I am truly the next step in evolution," his face told us. "The reason for existence and obedience. I am a blend of nature and technology, silicone and soul, real and synthetic. Special, different . . . supreme! I couldn't have done without your help. You might have not needed my help in your quest. I did this for—"

"Just shut up, will you?" I said with a flinch. "I'm tired of the reasons gods have, Balkros. And I'm already getting tired of you."

"I'm sure that goes for the rest of Xanadu by now," he countered. "Then let's get on with the festivities, shall we?"

"What do you mean?" I asked, hearing part of the roof cracking at the seams.

"It's not all over," he said. "The Elders are still barricaded in The Tower. And The MoonQueen hasn't acted so far, Byron. She could have destroyed every Warm One, every insurgent with little effort, including myself."

"So?" Medea crossed her arms.

"So, they must be eliminated. At least one or the other, yes?"

"You're *really* not well," I said.

"And neither is The Princess of Plumbing," Balkros sneered. "She won't exist for long. And guess who can help her defeat The Killer of Giants?"

"No!" I gasped.

His eyes bled dark red. "Yes, Byron. I can. And in return, I want you to do what needs to be done."

"That will not happen," Medea said to a television and to me. "Byron, let's go. I don't want any more risks. I will not deal with this thing."

"No," I said, shutting my eyes with force. "He's right, damn it. It has to end, one way or another. He has the answers, and I want you to live."

"I'm not alive, Byron," she cried. "We're all dead. We're just avenging ghosts, that's it—"

I took a step away from her. "You're wrong, Medea. Part of us, the human part, is still very much alive. If it wasn't, we would have never made the choices we made. In any case, you must let me fulfill my quest as the Liberator."

"You mean?" she whimpered.

"I have to go see her one last time," I said forcefully. "I knew it. I have always known it."

"Yes, yes," Balkros roared. "You will do that. And I shall keep the bitch company and give her the cure for the disease. It's a deal, Byron. I think you know what to do, yes, I think you understand me."

My gaze met the ashen floor. "Yes, I think I do, Balkros—"

"No, Byron," Medea said, reaching out for me.

"We're made from the same essence," I said with a sigh, pushing her away. "Medea, we have to be stronger, remember. We all sacrifice, we're all victims. It's the way it began. Now it's time to end this cycle."

So proud of you.

She nodded, covering her whole face. "Yes," she whispered. "I know. I know."

I couldn't take it. I brought her to my hold, in the middle of anarchy, before one final climax.

"Balkros," I said, not wanting to let her go. "Can we have some privacy, please?"

"Sorry," he said with a chuckle, and all the screens went blank.

"I'm sorry, too," Medea said. "I hate you, Byron."

"I know," I said, remembering what it was to feel warmth. To feel someone's beating heart, to fuel it. "I hate you, too."

She gently pulled away from me. "We're never too far apart, are we?"

"Never."

"Byron?"

"Yes."

She laid her head on my chest. "You had a very beautiful family, you know."

"I know. Thanks."

"Your daughter's name was Eve. Eve Sith Solsbury."

We're never too far apart.

CHAPTER 22

Perspective, use it or lose it, I heard a voice say in my past, maybe something my first mother quoted.

Smashing out of the dome, perspective still lingered the same. Xanadu's splendor was crippled by streams of smoke and distant explosions. If the damage of a quick uprising hadn't taken it down a notch, then the possibility of thousands of mutinous Stargazers and even more Warm Ones did. As I rose with dark laughter, I could see both factions running out into the wilderness, perhaps for escape, perhaps for search or chase. It didn't matter. Same result.

It was amazing how fragile this had all really been, a glorious jewel sprouting mature all too soon. All the city-states were accidents waiting to happen in an age of eternal growing pangs. Arrogance, cowardice, blindness, and more were as abundant here as they must have been before The Holocaust.

Xanadu wasn't done, though. There was one more thing to do. Considering how quiet The MoonQueen was being, it occured to me that this could all be another of her puppet games.

"Only one way to find out," I shouted, radiation and hot wind hammering me, Our Mistress's domain still gleaming in the greenish distance.

I chose the same entrance I had before. This time it wasn't open. No bartender's head hung from the door. I rammed it and gained entrance.

The chamber looked the same. Almost. The temperature still could have killed a Warm One in hours, but water trickled everywhere. The crushed ice looked like spongy mud, the sculptures had lost some of their detail.

I didn't have time to notice more. I walked on a path, knowing it would probably be impossible to surprise her. After a long walk in her museum of frigidity, I came into the center of the round chamber. She sat on a massive throne of ice, resting her gorgeous head on delicate hands.

The MoonQueen seemed not to notice me at first. Her eyes changed colors every time she blinked.

"Byron," she said with tympanic melody. "It's you, sweetest of sweets."

"Yes, it's me," I said firmly. "Good evening, Lilith."

She smiled, and if I had a working heart it would have melted.

"I haven't been called that in a long time," she said, touching a bluish finger to her chin. "I knew you would come back. It was Proxos, right?"

"Yes, it was Proxos," I said.

"Good, *Mon Cheri*. He may be a bore at times, but he is a good balance to your mercurial personality."

"I didn't come here to talk," I growled.

She shifted in her seat while mumbling something, and I found myself taking a step back. There was something different about her, but she still was The MoonQueen. Furthermore, her casual tone, her detached attitude was making me angrier by the second.

"Your city burns," I told her, holding my hands behind my back. "Your people perish. Warm Ones run around the city with ancient magic. It's over, Lilith. Don't you care?"

All she did was sigh. I barely heard it through the drip-drop all over the place.

"Byron, you didn't come here to speak sweet nothings in my ear?" she questioned. "I've already heard that from the fools hiding underneath me. I know these things. I knew of these things, Byron. Let's discuss more important things."

"Important?" I echoed. "Your city is in ruin and you want to talk about romance?"

She shrugged, glasslike face appearing almost devoid of any emotion. "Do you blame me? We can talk about how you avoided me, how you cheated me of my games, Sweet Byron. Unfortunately, I had other things that occupied my mind, letting little purrs like you and Balkros to bloom fully. Such is the way of the Mother, *Mon Cheri*. It's of no importance. Nothing is, except my delight."

"Other things?"

She placed her hands on the armrest and lifted herself up. "Don't worry, My Sweet. I forgave you once and more. You are still my favorite. There is still a place at my . . ."

The MoonQueen paused but regained her stance.

But I noticed it. I noticed.

It was an imperfection. An imperfection that didn't belong to a goddess, that couldn't have existed in true immortality. Her glamour thawed in my soul.

She had stood up with a slight hesitation. As if she was dizzy, as if . . .

"The Killer," I said. "Lilith, Mistress, it's in—"

"Come to me, Dearest," she said, extending arms to me, eyes not focusing on anything. "Forget it all and come to my embrace—"

"It's in you!" I hollered with a pointed finger. "You took the risk, Lilith. You must have changed your mind at some point after I killed the Shaman. That's why you wanted Medea as well as Clannad. You wanted to know if you could fight it, if you could defeat the curse of your adversary, but now you have—"

"Silence," she barked, her chalky expression darkening. "Do not speak of that, Byron. It is irrelev—"

"No it's not," I said, laughing, but kept retreating. "That's why you got Balkros to research our organisms. Even you can't overcome this, Lilith."

"Stop it!" she commanded. The chamber shook, sending a rain of frozen shards on us. "Nothing happens here unless I will it, Byron. DO YOU UNDERSTAND?"

"Sure I do," I sneered, not retreating anymore into the maze. "Glory unto the highest. Looks like it's finally affecting your head."

The MoonQueen staggered lightly toward me, putting hands over her face. "Oh, Byron. Is that why you came? You knew of my plight and decided to take advantage of it. You came to mock your Mother, the one who granted you life eternal."

"No," I said softly and firmly. "I came here to destroy the one who took my temporal life."

Fingers parted, revealing very human eyes.

"Does that mean you won't court me?" she asked coyly.

"I've said it once, I've—"

This time I actually saw her hand move. She had slowed a lot. I still didn't have time to react, the massive swiping sending me across the chamber.

I wished I could have counted how many yards I flew, how many sculptures I smashed, how many bones crackled inside me, but consciousness became a commodity right then.

Shakily, I staggered out of a pile of ice blocks, trying desperately to regain my bearings. At first thinking the ivory haze before was from the punch, I realized it was the real product. A hypnotic tornado of freezing precipitation rose before me, her silhouette in the middle glowing in acute blues. Her eyes blossomed in red, though.

Lilith's voice thundered throughout the chamber, rocking the whole place to splinters.

YOUR FIRST MISTAKE WAS NOT KILLING YOURSELF AFTER YOU MURDERED YOUR FAMILY, BYRON.

"You don't have to tell me that," I said, trying to run away from the onslaught, trying not to see double.

I didn't see the next strike for obvious reasons. More and

more ice shattered against me. The next time I couldn't even get off my knees.

YOUR SECOND MISTAKE IS NOT KILLING YOURSELF RIGHT HERE, BYRON. DID YOU THINK THAT EVEN IN THIS WEAKENED CONDITION I COULDN'T CRUSH YOU LIKE A SIGH? I AM THE QUEEN OF DARKNESS. YOU ARE A PLAYTHING, MY PLAYTHING. NEVER FORGET THAT.

"At least you don't like to scoff," I said in between coughs. The storm of cold energy surrounded me.

YOU'RE RIGHT. BUT IT'S SOMETHING GODS HAVE TO DO FROM TIME TO TIME.

I took the opportunity to take mist form, gain some distance in order to find a strategy. I knew she was beatable if I acted wisely. I even had time to smirk at Lilith. She smirked back.

Nothing happened. My god-soul wouldn't grant me the gift. I tried again. Nothing, except the widening of my eyes. And her voice.

REMEMBER, BYRON. JUST LIKE YOU AND THE LIT-TLE CUNT, WE'RE CONNECTED, EXCEPT THAT I AM THE DARK INSTINCT, THE FOUNTAINHEAD, THE PRI-MAL SOURCE.

I don't know if she hit me or kicked me under the ribs as I tried to move, but this time I broke a few records. I landed almost on the other side, my flight stopped by a curtain of icy stalactites hiding a semichamber housing an elevator.

I must have blanked, because the next time reality made an appearance, I was crawling toward the elevator. I hadn't traveled far and was still mostly covered in the ice.

A gnashing wind fell upon me and flipped me over. Lilith stood over me, skirt raised to show calves of perfect tone, shaking her head slowly. The storm vanished. She didn't even need her primordial magic to torment me.

"Byron, Byron," she said, lifting the hem a little higher to make sure my attention returned fully at the sight of thighs of blue-desire. Something glowed above the hemline. "You really are a funny creature, *Mon Cheri*, all scoffing aside. Do you know that? Even now you're trying to escape in an elevator that hasn't worked for a long time."

"It does work," I mumbled, glad my jaw was only partly broken. "Balkros fixed it. Said it would work . . . could escape."

She shook her head and dropped her skirt. It touched the ground, sending a numbing glaze of cold across the floor.

"When are you going to stop believing those silly little Elders and listen to me, My Sweet." She then daintily stepped on my ankle, pulverizing it. I did my best to hold in a scream. "The elevator doesn't work, and Balkros is just a misguided old coot."

"You're wrong," I groaned with clamped teeth, glaring at her through a kerchief of pain that had finally reached me. "It works, damn it—"

"Byron," she said musically, moving her right foot inward. Various segments of my pelvis fractured. This time I had to scream. She waited until I stopped. "I already told you. Tell you what—I'm going to count to ten with my eyes closed. That will give you enough time to get to the elevator and leave. If the elevator works, I'll let you go. If it doesn't, your existence will vanish in an excruciating way. Don't try anything cute."

Reminding me of my daughter, she took off her crown, placed it over her chest, and covered her eyes with the other hand.

Part of me wanted to just succumb to my agony and let it all go. Yet her counting woke something in me.

"One-one thousand. Two-one thousand."

I flopped on my stomach, groping for one of the icy objects next to me.

"Three-one thousand. Four-one thousand."

With the object, gaining momentum, I helped myself up and used the waning reserves of my strength.

"Five-one thousand. Six-one thousand."

She must have caught something in my mind, a little slow in her infirm state.

"Seven-one thousand . . ."

Her fingers cracked opened a second time, eyes widening at the sight of the gleaming point.

"Eight—" The hand over her face shot out at me, just as I thrust with everything I had.

"Byron!"

Nine-one thousand.

It entered right in the center of the crown, the perfect target for ailing vision.

"NO!"

Her hand never reached me.

Ten-one thousand.

The point of the five-foot stalactite dug cleanly into her chest. It came out the other side with a slashing sound like metal scraping.

"Byron," Lilith gurgled with a brittle smile, lines of aching marring her polished features. "You cheated!"

"You may have taken our hearts," I said, barely able to stand, "but I think you still have yours."

"Fool!" she spat, the chamber rumbling, melting even more. "It's going to take a little more than that, *Mon Cheri*."

She grabbed the embedded object with both hands, but weakened fingers slid from the moist surface. I think what I saw was fear in her translucent eyes.

"You're right," I said, shoving it in a little more. She coughed—snow puked from her mouth and nose. Lilith then giggled.

With one hand I searched my tattered coat for the object I still carried, which probably should have been at one of The

Farms. I held the carved circlet up to her. Her eyes strained to look at it, now waterfalls of blood.

"No, Byron," she said, trying to break the ice without success. "Not that, Dear. We can talk, we—"

"Wrong time to bargain," I said with a forced smile, placing the object over the eight-inch diameter of the spike. "I'm going to count to ten."

She tried to struggle, but her power betrayed her in this compromising position. Extinction would not reach her, but her existence wouldn't obey, either. Like she said, it's going to take a little more . . .

"One-one thousand," I said.

"You don't understand!"

"Two-one thousand."

"If you destroy me, you'll destroy yourself!"

"Three-one thousand."

"I am the Mother of Stargazers, I am the fountainhead. We will all be as if we didn't exist!"

I paused, locking gazes with her, a shadow crossing my face.

"That's it, Sweet Byron. It's always been you and me. You can't do it. Don't you see?"

"You're right," I said sadly.

"You won't do it," she said with joy, even though the place was slowly rising with water. Computers and machines began emitting dangerous sparks.

"I won't do it," I said.

"Good then—"

"There's no point in even counting, bitch."

I let the object slide down the stalactite.

"NO, BYRON!"

Proud of you.

It touched the crown, already glowing in faith-energy.

At first I thought she had been trying to suppress a smile. Then I realized The MoonQueen was trying to scream. The only thing stopping her was the force that she placed on her clenching jaw. Teeth shattered in dusty speckles and her jaw came unhinged. At the same time, the icon, the always-present symbol that Stargazers do not even belong in the spirit world, appeared to melt into her crown.

A brilliant detonation occurred, sending me on my rump, blinding me. A sound, like a million bottles breaking in a garbage can, jolted the area. The last thing I saw was the circlet and crown molding into one scintillating object and dissolving into Lilith in yellow aura. Heat rose. Her contours lost discipline.

And then The MoonQueen screamed.

Light of intense saffron expanded throughout the chamber, liquefying ice and even metal in all directions. Her scream continued, abusing my eardrums, shattering glass for a mile or more.

The energy, once her body, bloated more every second. It expanded, and I knew I didn't have a place here.

Feebly, I flew away, telling her in my mind that she was very right about the elevator. Streams of wicked light struck me, tossing me to the ground a few times. I had to get out. I saw a door several feet away, through a view of rumbling walls and exploding ice sculptures. Water rose over my knees.

I tried to fly again, coming in and out of blackness. The last time I came to myself, I was leaning against the door. I pressed the button. It wouldn't open. Like most doors in Xanadu, it was hermetically sealed as to allow only solid transportation.

"Shit," I mouthed, not turning but knowing that to my back a massive eruption of ancient might and godly extinction was about to take this all away.

I tried to pound the door but found myself sliding down, face pressed against metal. I couldn't do it. I was trapped.

"Open, damn it," I whispered, stroking the button. It wouldn't open. I was trapped . . .

The door slid open, revealing a silhouette brightly painted against the toxic air. I fell into its arms. The wall to our sides was crumbling. The ground changed texture.

"Thought you'd never get here," I said with a weak laugh, just as we zoomed upward, away from the annihilation of her kingdom and, as Balkros's probably wanted, The Council.

As we flew high into the chrome verdant haze of the night, I glanced down tiredly and saw a huge explosion of white and red, both coalescing in each other, as if the whole thing had been nothing but a battle. As the colors joined, they imploded, smashing downward, taking many levels in complete devastation.

Fire and Ice.

Then science took over the spectacle, fuming the top of Xanadu in a feathery garland of dark rust.

I was still here, I thought. She had lied.

"And I thought I'd never find you," Medea told me, beginning her descent.

2

She landed at the top of none other than my favorite bar, Lilac's, darting through the dome completely shattered at each segment, every defense from the radiation more than likely gone. Especially with the demise of The Tower. I doubted even Balkros's new persona could have survived.

Medea broke through many levels until breaking into the storage part of Lilac's. The place had obviously been looted, with several shredded Stargazers adorning the small rooms. Medea was able to find a sizable canister of juice hidden among a few boxes of posters and promotional items. It was type O, my least favorite, but I couldn't complain in my present state.

"We must enter *Moratoria* soon," Medea cooed, gently feeding me. "I don't think the Warm Ones will ever believe I am a Shaman and you the Liberator, so wait here."

As I ate a little more, Medea took time to lock and barricade every door of the place. She told me she skipped the front entrance, a burned, bloody mess, not a nice relaxing area anymore.

She placed a hand on one of the large metal vats, empty for a long time except for a slight tang. Placing me inside it, she lay against me, then sealed us in. We waited for *Sol* to rise again, perhaps mocking the wreck in the wastes and the fall of the daughter of its mortal enemy.

"Is it over, Byron?" Medea asked.

"I don't know," I said, having more energy since I'd eaten but still full of harsh aching. "She is gone, but . . ."

"But what?"

"You know how gods are. How many times have we died, Medea? We live once, but we can surely die several times."

She giggled. "Very philosophical. I want you to take me to gaze at stars soon, Byron. I can feel it in your memory, but I want to see it."

"No problem," I said, but something nagged me. "Medea, what about Balkros? What about the cure for your sickness?"

She didn't say anything, but her chest expanded in mock-sighing.

"Medea, tell me. Please!"

"It's not worth it, Byron," she said levelly.

"Tell me, will you?" I tried to struggle against the drowsiness of the ebbing night.

I could tell she was closing her eyes, I could tell she was biting her lip.

"The fiend said he knew the cure, Byron, but . . ."

"But what?"

"He uploaded it to the other city." She started sobbing.

"New Atlantis? Why? It's miles away."

"To make sure you didn't try anything," Medea said. "Especially when I told him I needed to leave when I felt you in trouble."

"Medea, you shouldn't—"

"Byron." She raised her head from my chest, rivulets of juice dragging down pallid cheeks. "You would have perished. One existence for another, but at least we have a chance once again of both of us making it."

I sighed, closing my eyes at *Moratoria*. "The bastard. Just what I wanted to do . . . visit another Stargazer city."

CHAPTER 23

And I dreamed one more time of one more thing. This was to be my last dream in Xanadu, forever. It was very different from the others. There were no massacres, lost loves, or absent friends. No old gods, either.

It was a strange dream, though. In it, I saw a sky pigmented in majestic light, just like the one Proxos and I had seen after the tornado storm in the wilderness. The only difference was that tufts of greasy clouds roamed part of the celestial portrait. They didn't pilfer any of its beauty, though, appearing as bright and majestic as that night the sky had been rinsed of pollutants.

Adding to the serenity, an endless carpet of rippling black stretched at the bottom of the panorama. I had seen this thing in old pictures, an ocean. It was clean.

What fully caught my attention was the object flying in between water and air, a large, smooth object sheened in metal. I knew it was massive. Its shape . . . it was an egg, an object that came from my Father's generation before the thing called poultry died out after The Holocaust.

For some reason, I knew where it was going, to an island, to a place of life, true life. I wanted to feel joy, but something saddened me about that object. Something made me afraid.

All it did was fly. It just flew, while I dreamed of that wonderful sky.

2

The next evening, we walked out and sat out on the nearest bench for no reason other than to spend a little time. The Warm Ones must have made a visit from their hiding places, probably in the tunnels: More ruin, more vandalism, more felled Stargazers, many dragged out from their resting places and obscenely hung, burned, or mutilated in warning poses around the perimeter. Eights and circles were carved all over the city.

This little revolution couldn't last too much longer. The Citadel's shaven top granted access to the callous radiation, which we could feel nagging us. It would increase, and bring with it dangerous weather. Stargazers had no leadership while Warm Ones probably thought they had some. Status quo. Full circle, except nature had not forgiven both species yet. We couldn't gaze at stars, and they couldn't destroy anything else.

And we both hungered for things that couldn't sate us completely: Juice, memories, death. Call the impostors of the moment, the moment of freedom and life and happiness, what you will. They were all illusions. Full circle.

Against her will, I left Medea for awhile, hopping to one of the demolished stores in another block. On the way, I saw others of my kind, in worse shape than my battered countenance, wandering lost and confused, still hungry. They were exiles now as much as I had been, but soon their instinct would teach them to return to solitary subsistence.

On the way back, holding a carton of cigarettes, I saw one of my old bosses, sitting by a barren fountain, part of his arm slowly growing from some accident.

"It's like a nightmare," Archimedes said, guild clothes singed, acting like he barely recognized me.

"It was," I said, taking a lighter from one of his pockets, knowing he occasionally smoked a pipe. "You just woke up."

I offered him a cigarette, but he simply stared into space and rocked himself on the ledge. I shrugged and returned to Medea.

After smoking a few, we kissed in the vortex of destruction, two lovers on a torrid date that had spanned lifetimes. We were once strangers, enemies, friends, lovers, perfect strangers, lovers, and so much more, but then again, those were all impostors in the play. The reality was us. She and I. Medea and Byron. We had probably been connected long before the Dark Instinct married us in Lilith's domain.

"I hate you," I told her, brushing her hair back, licking her forehead.

"I know," she said, settling her head underneath my chin. "What next, Liberator?"

"What next? We travel to New Atlantis. We will find a cure for The Killer and maybe a cure for loneliness."

"It will be dangerous, Byron."

"I wouldn't have it any other . . ." I said, my voice lost in my sight. A figure appeared in the distance, strolling down one of the tunnels that still had a complete ceiling, wearing a suit that wouldn't be recognized in this place.

"Look who's here," I said, standing up, shoving Medea to the side. "I can't believe it!"

Medea tried to ask something, but I was staggering toward the person, who smiled at me with his usual simplicity.

We stared at each other for a while, smiles growing. He extended a hand.

"Mr. Solsbury," he said, "good to see you. I see you've done well, even though you don't look so well."

Proud of you.

I didn't shake his hand. I hugged him crookedly. He held me back, and we started laughing. I sensed Medea smiling behind me.

"Proxos Commodore!" I leaned back to make sure it was him. "How did you find us?

He shrugged. "I said I would meet you, Mr. Solsbury. It took me a while, since I ran into a few problems."

"But what are you doing here?" I asked after hugging him again.

His smile lessened a little. "I was talking to an old friend of mine."

"A friend?" Medea echoed, but we both knew who he was.

"He told me where you were, thanked me, and urged me to meet you."

"Thanked you?" I questioned. "About the disk? Proxos, what was on that thing?"

He showed me that narrow smile again. "You could say it was one of those things I kept for a rainy night. It's an image I got before The Holocaust of something that would shatter our minds and hearts."

"*Sol*!" I cried, shaking my head. I thought of a conversation I had with a bartender during the most important drink of my existence. "You had an image of it all this time. You wanted Balkros to have it!"

"Not exactly. But I knew the scoundrel always had this dangerous god-complex, me being the closest thing he had to a friend. I gave him a weapon, an excuse to get closer to that, and you folks did the rest. The image probably couldn't hurt any Stargazer, but it sure brought terror or madness against anyone he desired. You could say it was another move of our little chess game, Byron."

I laughed with little humor. "And The Queen has been taken, Proxos, and we're still here for the game."

"Many have been taken, Mr. Solsbury," Proxos said, the narrow smile fading. "It's all part of the strategy."

I shook my head. "I'm sorry about Drisha. It was my fault."

"It's okay." He held my arm gently. "Most have perished who knew me here, except for you, Byron. Looking at things, it was for the better."

"I'm sorry," I repeated.

"Don't be," he said casually. "You came here to do something nobody, including myself, had the will or fortitude to do. Like I said, it was for the better."

Medea put her hand on Proxos's. "Yes, Byron. And we're still here, no matter where here may be."

"You're right," I said, suddenly thinking of that city I'd visited with my father. Proxos would love it, and I wondered if I would ever get back there.

"Well," Proxos said, "I would almost agree with you, Medea. I am pleased to make your acquaintance. I had a feeling you might be with him, since Byron doesn't listen to advice very well. Perhaps that's good. I've heard a lot about you."

"Pleased to meet you, too," she said, "but why do you almost agree?"

"My friend told me we had to leave this city," he said plainly. "It's his playground now. He doesn't want heroes or fools here. He also has a fake *Sol*."

"He can have both of them," I said. "Ready to go to New Atlantis, Prox?"

He flinched. "New Atlantis? More, Byron? I don't think that will be necessary."

"Why not?" I asked, Medea and I looking at each other.

He smiled proudly. "Because I have already destroyed it."

EPILOGUE

That would have been a good ending, but not good enough.

Proxos, for all practical purposes, destroyed New Atlantis. When I left his caverns to go back to Xanadu, he left on his own mission. Apparently, he still had knowledge of hidden missile silos deep in the Rocky Mountains, as he told me they were called. My presence and determination granting him a kernel of valor, he set out to do what he should have done a long time ago. It took him a while, but he reached the empty base once used by Warm Ones to contain other clans using the threat of eradication.

He didn't launch his assault, but set them on a large timer. Maybe he still didn't have the courage to vanquish his own kind that had betrayed him, maybe he needed a chance to change his mind in case I failed miserably. There was one missile there, enough to wipe out any city of any size.

"How much time do we have?" I asked him, as we left Xanadu, the new Mad God's threat not taken lightly.

"About a month," he said. "I'll have to check my logs in the tank."

I didn't have to ask him about the tank, for as we exited through a large hole in the tunnel where trains and cargo once carried nutrients through the veins of our society, I saw it. It was a massive iron thing, a vehicle of war used by Warm Ones centuries ago. "I have a few hidden," Proxos said, "but I don't use them because the fuel is scarce."

"Why didn't you just fly?" Medea asked.

"I didn't know what I would find," he answered, throwing us some suits from a chest. "And this thing can take the brunt of any flamethrower, just in case."

And there we were, rolling into the wilderness, a trio of Heretics in a new world of Heretics. Behind us, our fake home smoldered under a fake light, with its new freedom and new deity. It was no longer Xanadu, The City of Domes, a new metropolis less than two hundred years old that should have been the hub of a bright empire in a dark sky. The only thing that might be similar in its new state was its quiet insanity. Perhaps its desperation.

"I'm sorry about my plan," Proxos commented, driving the weird thing through dust and bony rock. "Especially after seeing your reactions. Did you want to annihilate it personally, Byron?"

Over the next few hours I explained our distress, adding the rest of the story as seasoning. Medea sat silently, looking out the small slit that showed the barren world. She absently toyed with the stuffed head of The Elder named Shibboleth, banished as a Heretic, who Proxos met in the wastes a few weeks ago. Old scores are always around to be settled, and poor Shib didn't even get a chance to go too mad. Lord Commodore vanquished the arch rival who had directly made him into a Heretic.

"Now I'm really sorry," he moaned.

"Don't be," I said. "It only means we have to hurry. Do you think we can make it?"

He nodded. "If we don't waste any time, we should be able to do it, Byron. I could still stop the missile, you know."

"No," I hissed, getting approval from Medea's strong nod. "We made our commitment, and the Stargazer age is over."

"But there are Warm Ones there, Byron," Medea commented, those two words sounding more and more normal on her lips.

"If there are any left that haven't been genetically mutilated," I said. "Then maybe we'll get them out before it's too late. I don't have a concrete plan, so it's a good chance."

"And what about us, Mr. Solsbury?"

What about us, Proxos. Good question.

I've discussed this before, with Proxos, with Drisha. Stargazers own two souls, just as *Luna* and *Sol* are part of the same light, part of the same soul in the cosmos. One is the god-soul, the eternal hunter in a living universe; the other is the soft spirit of potential and annihilation, a small but firm flicker in the void. How this happened is not important, but maybe it can be reversed. My research at the purification fields showed me rituals like these have been attempted in the past, although no results were ever recorded for obvious reasons. Yet, in my dreams, I now understand, I separated myself from myself. Could it not be done again? Perhaps Balkros left that information in some secret file under his name in New Atlantis, another part of his cosmic joke, his first duty as a deity.

Maybe I'm just clutching at my dreams, but haven't I from the beginning? The worst thing is that we'll cease to exist, which is still better than immortality. There are cities in the astral expanse with children playing with balls in parks, and there are dark sides of the moon where skating can be so much fun. Aren't there, Dad?

First, though, we must go on yet another adventure and save my Medea. More lifetimes and dreams might come our way, and all we'll need is a good curse-sputtering and a firm checkmate. I've heard it's the journey, not the destination. That's a consolation, and I'll always remember you in my dreams, *Mon Cheri*.

I'm still thinking about all of this, as I leave Medea, recently entering *Moratoria*, in her stone receptacle. I know Proxos is in the next chamber, also entering a world in which he, too, can separate himself briefly from his curse. Just briefly.

And why is that? I ask myself, walking naked up to the entrance. The answer is the same as from the beginning, when I saw what I wanted to see, what I couldn't see.

Yes, Byron, you puppet, you Liberator, you vampire, and, yes, you impostor, it was always *Sol*, giver of life, granter of night and *Luna*'s evil light. Maybe now all the Stargazers will meet on the other side of *Luna* in respite, maybe they will meet in a calm city on a lazy afternoon and play with their families.

But it was always you, *Sol*.

I can feel your heat already, blistering the horizon, trying to tame the venomous atmosphere, the chemical clouds.

Some have said that it burns us to the bone. Others say it turns one to stone, a witness of time eternal. Some have said it singes away the god-soul forever and warms the heart, which was never truly dead, just frozen.

I don't know why I'm doing this, as my hands grip the rock to gain better footing, as my love sleeps, yes, sleeps calmly, and as my dear friend waits to awaken and set off on yet another mission in which our roles aren't formed.

But what has changed? What differs? *Sol* will rise, the same, lonely in a universe filled with his lonely brethren, overlooking the same themes and plights seen since the beginning.

I just want one glance at you, *Sol*, for you are the true Stargazer. Just one quick glance, and I'll accept my destiny. To stand in the wind and melt with you.

I reach the entrance, shrugging off weariness and instinct, and wait with a new sense of calmness.

I realize I forgot a cigarette. Maybe I should go back. Just one glance. But I would like a cigarette. I turn for a second. *No, I should stay and see. Sol*, why do I do this? Just one glance of something I haven't seen in forever but was always there.

Why?

Because it was always me, Byron.

About the Author

Miguel Conner was born in Lisbon, Portugal, in 1968. He now lives with his wife and two children deep in the heart of Texas.

• A MAN BETRAYED

At Castle Harvell, demented Prince Kylock commits murder to seize the reins of power. Harvell's two young refugees are torn apart by the storms of war: headstrong young Melliandra is captured by brutal slavers and Jack, whose wild power works miracles, falls prey to a smuggler's lying charms.

"A highly successful, popular fantasy epic."

—*Dragon* magazine

(0-446-60351-1) $5.99 USA, $6.99 CAN.

• MASTER AND FOOL

In the fortress of Bren, mad King Kylock and the wizard Baralis spread their sadistic terror across the shattered kingdoms. Meanwhile, the fallen knight Tawl and Jack, the baker's boy, meet in a quest to save widowed Melliandra and her unborn child. Soon sons will turn on fathers and dread secrets will be revealed, as Jack and Kylock clash in a magical apocalypse.

"Jones stamps it all with a distinctive touch."

—*Locus*

(0-446-60414-3) $5.99 USA, $6.99 CAN.

AVAILABLE AT A BOOKSTORE NEAR YOU FROM
WARNER BOOKS